THE
TATAMI
GALAXY

THE
TATAMI
GALAXY

A NOVEL

Tomihiko Morimi

Translated by Emily Balistrieri

 HARPERVIA

An Imprint of HarperCollins*Publishers*

THE TATAMI GALAXY. Copyright © 2008 by Tomihiko Morimi. English Translation Copyright © 2022 by Emily Balistrieri. All rights reserved. Printed in the United States of America. No part of this book may be used or reproduced in any manner whatsoever without written permission except in the case of brief quotations embodied in critical articles and reviews. For information, address HarperCollins Publishers, 195 Broadway, New York, NY 10007.

HarperCollins books may be purchased for educational, business, or sales promotional use. For information, please email the Special Markets Department at SPsales@harpercollins.com.

Originally published as *Yojō-Han Shinwa Taikei* in Japan in 2008 by KADOKAWA Corporation, English-language rights arranged with KADOKAWA Corporation, Tokyo, through Tuttle-Mori Agency, Inc.

FIRST HARPERVIA EDITION PUBLISHED IN 2022

Designed by SBI Book Arts

Library of Congress Cataloging-in-Publication Data is available upon request.

ISBN 978-0-06-315844-3

22 23 24 25 26 LSC 10 9 8 7 6 5 4 3 2 1

Contents

ONE

Tatami and the   1
Obstructor of Romance

TWO

Tatami and the Masochistic   79
Proxy-Proxy War

THREE

Tatami and the Sweet Life   165

FOUR

Around the Tatami Galaxy   249
in Eighty Days

A Note from the Translator   337
Glossary   340

ONE

Tatami and the Obstructor of Romance

et's just say I accomplished absolutely nothing during the two years leading up to the spring of my junior year in college. Every move I made in my quest to become an able participant in society (to associate wholesomely with members of the opposite sex, to devote myself to my studies, to temper my flesh) somehow missed its mark, and I ended up making all sorts of moves, as if on purpose, that need not have been made at all (to isolate myself from the opposite sex, to abandon my studies, to allow my flesh to deteriorate). How did that happen?

We must ask the person responsible. And who is responsible?

It's not as if I was born this way.

Fresh from the womb I was innocence incarnate, every bit as precious as the Shining Prince Genji must have been in his infancy. My smile, without a hint of malice, is said to have filled the mountains and valleys of my birthplace with the radiance of love. And now what has become of me? Whenever I look in the mirror I am swept up in a storm of anger. *How the hell did you end up like this? You've come so far, and this is all you amount to?*

"You're still young," some would say. "It's never too late to change."

Are you fucking kidding me?

They say that the soul of a child at three remains the same even when the man reaches a hundred. So what good can it do for a splendid young man of twenty-one, nearly a quarter century old, to put a lot of sloppy effort into transforming his character? The most he can do in attempting to force the stiffened tower of his personality to bend is to snap it right in half.

I must shoulder the burden of my current self for the rest of my life. I mustn't avert my eyes from that reality.

I can't look away, but it's just so hard to watch.

• • •

It's said that people who become an obstacle to someone on their path to love will be kicked by a horse and die, so as a rule I stay away from the riding grounds on the lonely north edge of campus. If I were to go anywhere near there, the unbroken horses would probably fly into a rage and jump the fence to gang up on me—I'd be trampled into shreds of soiled meat you couldn't even use to make sukiyaki. For the same reason, I am also terrified of Kyoto Prefecture's mounted police.

Why am I so scared of horses? Because even among people I don't know, I am notorious as an Obstructor of Romance. I am a dark Cupid costumed as a god of death who wields not arrows of love, but a battle-ax. Red threads of destiny are strung around like infrared sensors, and I cut every last one in range, severing the invisible bonds between would-be lovers.

Young men and women have shed barrels of bitter tears over these acts of mine.

It's the height of injustice, I know.

When I began college, even I sometimes quivered slightly with the thought that I just might have a rose-colored courtship ahead of me. And only a few months later, though it was clear there was no need to so temper my resolve, I had even decided in my head: *I will* not *behave like a wild animal. In the company of beautiful maidens I will be a purehearted, proper gentleman.* In any case, I should have had the capacity to turn a blind eye to those men and women who forsook reason to recklessly pair off.

Instead, at some point I lost that capacity and turned into the kind of heinous fiend who delights in the sound of red threads being severed. Broken-Heart Alley, where snippets of red thread float in puddles of bitter tears . . . I stepped into this cramped backstreet of despair under the guidance of a detestable character, a man who is both my mortal enemy and sworn comrade.

• • •

Ozu was in the same year as me. Despite being registered in the Department of Electrical and Electronic Engineering, he hated electricity, electronics, and engineering. At the end of freshman year he had received so few credits, and with such low grades, it made you wonder whether there was any point to him being there; but Ozu himself didn't give a damn.

Because he hated vegetables and ate only instant foods, his face was such a creepy color it looked like he'd been living on the far side of the moon. Eight out of ten people who met him walking down the street at night would take him for a yokai goblin. The other two would be shapeshifted yokai themselves. Ozu kicked those who were down and buttered up anyone stronger than him. He was selfish and arrogant, lazy and contrary. He never studied, had not a crumb of pride, and fueled himself on other people's misfortunes. There was not a single praiseworthy bone in his body. If only I had never met him, my soul would surely be less tainted.

On that note, we must say that joining the Ablutions film club in the spring of my freshman year was my first big mistake.

• • •

At the time, I was a fresh-as-a-daisy-man. I remember how exhilarating the vibrant green of the cherry tree leaves was after all the flower petals had fallen.

Any new student walking through campus gets club flyers thrust upon them, and I was weighed down with so many that my capacity for processing information had been far overwhelmed. There were all sorts of flyers, but the four that caught my eye were as follows: the Ablutions film club, a bizarre "Disciples Wanted" notice, the Mellow softball club, and the underground organization Lucky Cat Chinese Food. They all seemed pretty shady, but each one represented a doorway into a new college-student life, and my curiosity was piqued. The fact that I thought a fun future would be waiting on the other side, no matter which door I chose, just goes to show what an incorrigible idiot I was.

After my classes were over, I headed to the clock tower. All kinds of clubs were meeting there to take new students to orientations.

The area around the clock was bustling with freshmen, their cheeks flushed with hope, and welcoming committee members ready to prey on them. It seemed to me that here there were innumerable entryways leading to that elusive prize—a rose-colored campus life—and I walked among them half in a daze.

I found several students waiting with a sign for the film club, Ablutions. They were holding a screening to welcome new students and offered to show me the way. Thinking back on it now, I should not have gone with them. But "Let's all have fun making movies together!" they said, and I was smooth-talked. So, blinded by the prospect of a rose-colored future, I joined the club that very day.

I should have made a hundred friends, but instead I found myself wandering down a path of beasts, making only enemies.

Though I joined the club, I couldn't quite get used to the obnoxiously pally atmosphere. I told myself, *This is a trial to be overcome. It is by boldly mingling with this abnormally cheerful group that I will be guaranteed a rose-colored campus life, a black-haired maiden, and, indeed, the world.* But I was beginning to lose heart.

Driven into a dark corner, I found myself standing next to a creepy fellow with a terribly inauspicious-looking face. At first I thought he was a messenger from hell only I, with my heightened sensitivities, could see.

That was how I met Ozu.

• • •

I'm going to jump ahead two years to the end of May in our junior year.

I was sitting on the floor of my four-and-a-half-mat tatami room, which one couldn't help but love, exchanging scornful looks with Ozu, whom one couldn't help but hate.

My base of operations was a room at Shimogamo Yusuiso in Shimogamo Izumikawacho. From what I heard, it had been standing there since being rebuilt after burning down in the disorder accompanying the last days of the Tokugawa shogunate. If there hadn't been light seeping through the windows, the building would have been taken for abandoned. No wonder I thought I must have wandered into the walled city of Kowloon when I first visited the place on the university co-op's introduction. The three-story wooden structure caused all those who saw it anxiety; it seemed ready to collapse at any moment. Its dilapidation was practically Important Cultural Property level. Certainly no one would miss it if it burned down. In fact, there was no doubt in my mind that this would be a load off for its landlady, who lived just to the east.

That night, Ozu had come over to hang out.

We drank together in our gloom. "Got anything to eat?" he said, so I grilled some fish burgers in my toaster oven, but after one bite he whined, "What about some actual meat? I want beef tongue with salty green onion sauce." He was pissing me off so much that I shoved one of the sizzling patties into his mouth, but then I forgave him when I saw tears silently rolling down his cheeks.

That May, after spending two years single-mindedly wreaking social havoc in the Ablutions film club, we took the initiative to exile ourselves from it. They say a bird doesn't foul its nest when it leaves, but we fouled that nest with all our might, to the point that it was as polluted as the Yellow River.

I kept hanging around with Ozu as usual, but even after we exiled ourselves from Ablutions, he continued to be busy with this and that. Apparently, he was dabbling in a sports club and the activities of some strange organization as well. Even his coming to see me that night was only because he had been to visit someone else living on the second floor of my building. He called that person "Master" and had been coming to Shimogamo Yusuiso since freshman year. So the reason I had such a hard time breaking our fatal bond was not only that we had been driven into the same dark corner within the same club, but also that he frequented my lodgings. Whenever I asked him who this "master" was, he would only smirk this obscene smirk. I figured they must just talk smut.

I was completely cut off from Ablutions, but Ozu with his sharp ears would always have tidbits of news for me as I stewed in my displeasure. We had staked what little honor we had on reform within the club and now had nothing left to stake on anything, but according to Ozu, the protest we risked our very lives on had been in vain, and the club hadn't changed at all.

The alcohol helped fuel the anger surging inside me. I was exiled from my club, just going back and forth between my room and school like some kind of ascetic, and I'd had enough. I could feel a dark passion being called awake, and Ozu was stupidly good at whipping it into a frenzy.

"Hey. That little plan of ours? Let's go for it," he said with a strange wiggle of his creature-like body.

"All right."

"Then we're on. I'll come by tomorrow night ready to go," he said, leaving with a smile on his face.

Somehow I had the feeling I'd been expertly played . . .

I tried to sleep, but the Chinese study-abroad kids on the second floor were having a noisy get-together. I was sort of hungry, so I got out of bed thinking I'd go get some Neko Ramen and wandered out into the night.

• • •

That night I had my first encounter with the god who lived on the second floor of Shimogamo Yusuiso.

Neko Ramen is a ramen stand rumored to make its soup from cats. Regardless of whether that's true or not, the flavor is unparalleled. It'd probably be a pain if I revealed its location here, so I won't write too much. Suffice it to say it's in the neighborhood of Shimogamo Shrine.

As I was sitting there slurping my ramen, wavering between ecstasy and anxiety over the unique taste, a customer came in and sat next to me. I glanced over and noted how strange he was.

He looked perfectly nonchalant in his navy yukata and wore geta clogs like those you might find on a tengu spirit. Something about him reminded me of a mountain hermit. I looked up from my bowl, and as I observed this mystery man, I realized I had seen him a few times around Shimogamo

Yusuiso. I'd seen him from behind, creaking his way up the stairs; I'd seen him from behind, out on the balcony sunbathing while getting his hair cut by a foreign exchange student; I'd seen him from behind, washing some mysterious fruit in the common-use sink. His hair looked like Typhoon No. 8 had just blown through, and the eyes set in his eggplant-shaped head had a carefree look in them. His age was unclear; he might have been older, but he could just as easily have been a college student. I certainly didn't think he was a god.

He seemed to know the owner of the ramen joint, and they grinned while chattering back and forth about this and that. Turning to his bowl, he slurped up the noodles with enough force to make Niagara Falls flow upward. Before I was even done with my noodles, he was downing the last of his soup. A truly godlike feat.

After he finished his ramen, he stared at me rather intently. Eventually, he addressed me in a terribly outmoded fashion. "My good sir, you live at Shimogamo Yusuiso, correct?" When I nodded he broke into a satisfied grin. "I live there, too. Nice to meet you."

"Likewise." When I left the conversation at that, he didn't hesitate to continue staring at my face.

"I see, I see," he nodded. "So you're the one, huh . . . ?" It seemed that things were making sense to him. I was still a little drunk, but his oddly familiar demeanor was creeping me out. Could it be that he was my long-lost big brother? But I hadn't lost my big brother. I never had one to begin with.

When I cleared my bowl and stood up, the guy followed, walking alongside me as if it were the natural thing to do. Then he took out a cigar, lit it, and exhaled a cloud of smoke.

When I increased my pace, he casually caught up without even appearing to rush—exactly the sort of wizardry you'd expect from a mountain hermit.

Just as I was thinking how annoying the whole situation was, he abruptly began to speak.

● ● ●

"They say time flies like an arrow, but the way the seasons repeat one after the other after the other is infuriating. I don't know when heaven and earth began, but it can't have been that long ago. It's absolutely astounding to think that humans have multiplied so much in so short a time. And day after day, everyone is doing their best to make things happen. Human beings are so industrious. I really admire them. I'd be lying if I said they weren't adorable. But no matter how adorable they are, there are so many that I don't have time to shower them with my pity.

"Once autumn rolls around I have to go back to Izumo—and the train is not cheap. It used to be that we'd spend a night in heated debates to make our decisions, scrutinizing each case one by one, but these days we don't have the luxury of taking our time like that. We just chuck all the cases we bring into a wooden box marked 'inspection complete'—it's so boring! No matter how much of our wisdom we pour into matchmaking, the good-for-nothing guys will miss the chances we put right under their noses, and the girls who capitalize on theirs will make their own matches with random other guys, so why should we break our backs over this stuff? It's like trying to empty Lake Biwa with a ladle.

"With the exception of the Month with No Gods, I'm putting

cases together, almost all year round. There are some slackers who just sit with a glass of wine in one hand, picking their noses, and decide by lottery, but I'm a serious guy—I couldn't make matches for these adorable humans in such an irresponsible way! I get involved in spite of myself. I take a good hard look at them and fret as if their fates were my own. I practically rip my hair out trying to come up with suitable encounters for each and every one of them. It's like I'm a marriage counselor! Is that really a job for a god? This is why I chain-smoke, why I'm losing my hair, why I eat too much castella cake—I love castella—why I need Chinese remedies for my digestion, why I don't get enough sleep because my eyes pop open at the crack of dawn, why I've got a stress-induced jaw disorder. My doctor says I should reduce my stress levels, but how can I take it easy when a pile of people's sons' and daughters' destinies rest on my shoulders?

"I've no doubt the other jerks are off taking a twenty-thousand-league sea voyage on a luxury passenger ship like the *Queen Elizabeth 2*, sipping champagne, girls in sexy bunny getups at their elbows, not a care in the world. They laugh at me like, 'He's hopeless. Always so hardheaded.' I see you, you bastards! You're not fit to be called gods! Year after year, why am I the only one who makes sure each red thread of destiny is tied? It's completely understandable that I should wonder how it came to this, wouldn't you say, my good sir?"

• • •

What was this absolute weirdo going on about?

"Who are you, even?" I asked, stopping on the dark street. We were right where Mikage-dori turns east off Shimogamo

Hon-dori. In front of us, Tadasu no Mori was abuzz with nocturnal life, and inside the forest, the long, empty approach to Shimogamo Shrine stretched to the north. Sacred lanterns glowed orange deep within.

"A god, my good sir, I'm a god," he said, as if it were nothing, and then raised an index finger. "I'm known as Kamotaketsunumi no Kami."

"Huh?"

"Kamotaketsunomi mo Kamo—er, Kamotaketsunumi no Kami. Don't make me say it more than once—it's a tongue twister." Then he gestured at the dark approach to Shimogamo Shrine. "You live here and you've never heard of me?"

I'd been to pray at Shimogamo Shrine, but I'd never heard of a god by that name. Kyoto has a lot of shrines with ancient origins, and Shimogamo Shrine is one of the most famous. It's even designated as a World Heritage Site. This guy was rather lacking in persuasive talent if he expected me to believe he was a deity worshipped at a shrine so ancient it was impossible to imagine how far back its history stretched. He was either a mountain hermit or one of those freeloader binbogami. Definitely not Shimogamo deity caliber.

"You don't believe me," he groaned.

I shook my head.

"How lamentable!" he said, not appearing to be lamenting anything one bit. He was sending puffs of pleasant-smelling cigar smoke out on the evening breeze. The buzzing sounds coming from the forest were eerie.

I started walking briskly away, leaving the mystical man and his tobacco behind. Nothing good would come of associating with someone like that.

"Now, now. Just one moment," he called out to me. "I know everything about you. I know your parents' names. I know you were a vaguely acidic-smelling baby because you were always throwing up. I know what your nickname was in elementary school, what happened at that one school festival in middle school, about your blush of a first crush in high school . . . which of course, ended badly. I know how aroused—or should I say 'astonished'—you were when you saw your first 'adult video,' how you had to spend an extra year studying to get into college, and how lazy and shameless you've been since you managed it . . ."

"Lies."

"Nope. I know it all," he nodded with confidence. "For example, I know that you hijacked a screening to show a film exposing the detestable behavior of one Jogasaki and had no choice but to voluntarily withdraw from your film club. And I know what caused you to spend the past two years growing more and more perverse."

"It's Ozu's fault," I blurted without thinking, but he held up a hand to stop me.

"I acknowledge the fact that Ozu's somewhat impure soul has influenced you, but he can't be the only reason."

The nonsense of the past two years flickered across the back of my mind like shadows cast by a revolving lantern. In holy Shimogamo Shrine's forest of all places, the thorny talons of my memories clutched my delicate heart, and I had to suppress an ungentlemanly scream. Kamotaketsunumi no Kami looked on, amused, as I writhed in my private mental agony.

"Mind your own business," I said. "It has nothing to do with you."

But he shook his head. "Take a look at this."

He took a bundle of dirty papers out from inside his yukata and moved closer to the fluorescent light shining on a nearby neighborhood bulletin board. When he motioned to me, I entered the glow as if drawn by some force of attraction.

In his hands was a thick accounting ledger, worm-eaten in spots; it sent up clouds of dust that seemed a hundred years old as he flipped through it. He was licking his finger to turn the pages, so he must have been eating quite a bit of dirt.

"Here it is." He pointed at a place near the end of the ledger. The grimy gray page had a woman's name, my name, and Ozu's written on it. The calligraphy was so terribly dignified it felt almost as if I'd been made a deity myself.

"In the fall, we gods gather in Izumo to match up men and women. You've probably heard of that. This year I have hundreds of cases, and this is one of them. You know what that means, right?"

"No."

"You don't? You're stupider than you look! It means I'm trying to decide who to pair up this girl you know—Akashi—with," the god said. "In other words, it's gonna be either you or Ozu."

Tadasu no Mori clamored and swayed in the night.

● ● ●

The next day I woke up after noon and knelt on my molding futon. Remembering what an idiot I'd been the previous night, I blushed despite being alone.

A god of Shimogamo Shrine had appeared at the Neko Ramen stand. Not only that, but he lived on the second floor of my building. Not only *that*, but he was going to set up a match between me and Akashi. One can only be so delusional. Allowing my loneliness to weaken my willpower to the point where I fantasize so freely is shameless behavior unbecoming of a gentleman.

But actually, meeting that god felt perfectly normal. He didn't perform any miracles; no lightning flashed. There were no foxes, crows, or other divine animal messengers deferentially attending him. He just happened to sit next to me at a ramen stand. A god. It was so unconvincing that it actually ended up pretty convincing; but does that sound unconvincing?

It would be easy enough to ascertain the truth of the matter. I could just go to the second floor and see him. But if he opened the door and said, "And who might you be?" what would I say? Or how pitiful would it be if he opened the door and said, "Ha! Gotcha!"? My life would be one of bleak self-hatred from there on out.

"Once you've made your decision, come and see me. I'm in the far room on the second floor. But I'd like a reply within three days. I'm a busy guy," the peculiar god had said.

Though I was dejected from my days of endless laps between my room and school, it was beneath me to get all flustered over this. I prayed, "Namu-namu, namu-namu," to suppress the wild ideas that threatened to expand like a balloon and float into the May sky.

Oh, but he said—this guy calling himself a god—that he

was going to go all the way to Izumo to do the matchmaking. That couldn't be true.

I fished a dictionary out of my bookcase.

• • •

Plenty of people know that during the tenth month of the old calendar, known as the Month with No Gods, the country's eight million gods leave their respective territories and gather in Izumo. Even I know that.

I'm not going to get into who all these eight million gods are, but eight million is a fifteenth of the current population of Japan. With that many gods, there's bound to be some odd-balls mixed in, just like how even a university that boasts of its brilliant students is bound to have a handful who are quite obviously idiots.

I had to wonder, *What in the world do all these gods talk about once they've gone all the way to Izumo?* How to stop climate change? The globalization of the economy? It's a pretty big deal for all the gods scattered all around the country to go out of their way to gather and debate for a whole month, so you'd think they'd be exchanging heated arguments on some pretty serious topics. There's no way they'd be throwing a hot pot party among friends, having a gay old time telling dirty jokes. That would make them no different from idiot college students.

That day, when I looked it up in the dictionary in my room, my mind was blown.

It said that by the end of the eight million gods' unrestrained disputation, couples are decided. The gods from all over Japan gather under one roof just to tie or untie red threads of destiny. That fishy god at the ramen stand had been telling the truth.

I trembled with rage at the various deities.

Didn't they have anything better to do?

• • •

To clear my head, I applied myself to my studies.

But as I faced my textbooks, it started to feel like it was too little, too late to make up for the two years I had wasted. Being that pitiful is against my aesthetic, so I gracefully gave up on studying. I have pretty high confidence when it comes to this sort of grace. In other words, I'm a gentleman.

And so, I had no choice but to rely on Ozu for the paper I had to turn in. There was a secret organization called the Printing Office through which you could get a paper written for you by placing an order. I'd been relying on this shady org for my every need for so long that it had gotten to the point where I couldn't make it through a crisis without getting their help via Ozu. Both my body and soul were rotting away. This was one major reason I couldn't break our fatal bond.

It was only the end of May, but it was already muggy enough to be summer. I had my window open as far as I could without risking someone being offended by my porn collection, but the air wasn't moving. The various secret ingredients contained in the stagnant air were slowly maturing like the amber whiskey at a Yamazaki distillery; anyone who entered my four-and-a-half-mat tatami room would become altogether intoxicated. Still, when I opened the door to the hall-way, the cat that prowled around Yusuiso came right in and meowed at me, the cute little bugger. It was so cute I wanted to eat it up, and I thought I just might, but of course I couldn't do something so barbaric. A man must be a gentleman even when wearing nothing but his underwear. After cleaning the mucus out of the cat's eyes, I shooed it back into the hall.

Once I'd closed the door, I flopped down on the floor and lay there like a log. I thought I might immerse myself in morally questionable fantasies, but that didn't go very well. I thought I'd plan out my rose-colored future, but that didn't go very well either. I was pissed about this, pissed about that—I had enough piss to fill a swimming pool. Then, when I discovered a cockroach trying to escape to the one piss-free corner of my room, I unleashed the full extent of my rage. The unfortunate thing was crushed to smithereens.

Since I had woken up after noon, it was already starting to get dark. The western sun shining through my window spurred my irritation on. A solitary rogue shogun growing bad-tempered in this orangey pool of light would have wanted to hop on his noble white horse and ride down the endless coast, but I, the Obstructor of Romance, was afraid of horses.

Tormented by mixed and unnecessary feelings, my thoughts turned to the impending meeting with Ozu, and I felt that I should probably stop making my own life so miserable. Did I think that if I kept up this masochistic war on myself that someday the Buddha would lower a spider's thread to me, pull me up, and pat me on the head? I was sure that at the exact moment I started climbing the thread, he'd cut it, and I'd be sent straight back to my four-and-a-half-mat tatami hell for his entertainment.

At five p.m., having arrived at the furthest reaches of masochistic fantasy, I stood motionless in the arctic wasteland of my bad mood. And Ozu came to see me.

"Your face is looking filthy as usual." That's the first thing he said to me.

"Yours too," I retorted in my negativity.

His face really was as grimy as the toilet in the building's shared bathroom. Was the faint smell of ammonia my imagination? Two men just over twenty years old stared at each other in the hot westering sun. Their respective displeasures interacted to form more displeasures, and those little displeasures bore further displeasures in a nightmare chain reaction that reeked to high heaven. I was sick of it.

"You got the stuff?" I asked.

He indicated the plastic bag in his hand. It was overflowing with garishly colored tubes: blue, green, red . . .

"I guess we have no choice, then. Let's go," I said.

• • •

Ozu and I left Shimogamo Yusuiso and its Kowloon ambience permeating the quiet neighborhood behind.

We followed Mikage-dori and cut across the approach to Shimogamo Shrine to come out on Shimogamo Hon-dori. Crossing in front of the Kyoto Family Court building, we ended up in front of the Aoibashi Bridge on the Kamo River. Two men with inauspicious faces (really, enough sulking was enough) looked over the railing, watching the clear water go by, completely wasting the glorious sunset. We crossed our arms and gazed downstream. The vibrant green on both banks was beautiful as it reflected the setting sun. The dimming sky yawned overhead, and from Aoibashi we could see buses and cars going by over the Kamo Ohashi Bridge. Even at that distance we could sense the spineless presence of the students out for the evening on the riverbed. Soon that place would become an absolute hell.

"Are we really gonna do it?" I asked.

"Weren't you the one saying yesterday that they deserved divine punishment?"

"Sure, I consider it divine punishment, but from anyone else's point of view it's just a prank by a couple of idiots."

Ozu snickered. "So you're gonna change your beliefs 'cause you're worried about what they think? That's not the man I entrusted my body and soul to!"

"Shut up."

The only reason he said such repulsive things was to incite me to fight, because it was fun for him. Fueled by other people's misfortune, Ozu liked nothing better than to watch someone get all worked up over idiotic bullshit. It was his raison d'être.

"Okay," I said. "Let's do it."

Though I despised Ozu's stupid personality, I took a step forward with him in order to be true to my beliefs.

We descended to the riverbank from the west end of the Aoibashi Bridge and walked downstream.

The Takano River flowing from the northeast meets the Kamo River flowing from the northwest to continue as one Kamo River. Students call the inverted triangle of land sandwiched between the two rivers the Kamo River Delta. The area is used throughout spring and early summer by all sorts of clubs as a venue for parties to welcome new students.

Eventually we approached the delta. There they were, right

in front of us, laughing and making a general racket sitting on their blue picnic tarps. We grew more cautious and took cover in the darkness under the Demachibashi Bridge. Our surprise attack operation was as bold as the siege of Ichi-no-Tani, but if we were spotted by the enemy camp, all our efforts would be for naught.

I took the fireworks out of the bag and lined them up on the ground. Ozu was watching the other bank with the Carl Zeiss spotting scope I'd lent him.

I lit a cigarette, and the evening breeze scattered the smoke. Parents passing by with their children threw suspicious glances at us as we continued our disturbing activities, but this was no time to fret about the eyes of the average citizen. This was something I had to do to follow through on my beliefs.

"How's it look?" I asked.

"Seems like all the jerks from our year are there, hee-hee-hee. But I don't see Aijima yet. Jogasaki isn't there either."

"They're drinkers! Why would they be late to a party? Have they no common sense?" I groaned. "There's no point in attacking if they're not there."

"Oh, it's Akashi."

Akashi is a sophomore we know. I remembered the ledger that shady god had shown me the previous night.

"Akashi's there?"

"Yeah, see? She's sitting on the embankment over there pouring her own beer. Aloof as always," Ozu said.

"Splendid. But she didn't need to come to this lame party."

"Yeah, it's too bad she'll be mixed up in this."

I turned my thoughts to Akashi's intellectual appearance and graceful carriage.

"Look, look, look!" Ozu suddenly shouted excitedly. "Here comes Aijima!"

I snatched the spotting scope away from Ozu and followed Aijima as he passed by the pine trees on his way down the embankment. The new students waiting on the shore cheered when he arrived.

Aijima was the right-hand man of Jogasaki, who reigned over the Ablutions film club. Aijima had always bullied us. Finding fault with a film someone made is one thing, but he even pulled the stunt of lying about a screening schedule to shut us out on purpose. To borrow editing equipment, we had to practically grovel. I couldn't forgive him. Why was he welcomed with fanfare while we had to resign ourselves to skulking around on the opposite bank? Today we would bring down the iron hammer of justice and settle this old score. I hoped he would flee the rain of fireworks in a panic and regret his past wrongs from the bottom of his heart. I imagined him sniffling tearfully on a sandy shore, poking at a crab.

Breathing roughly through my nose like a starving animal, I grabbed the closest tube of fireworks, but Ozu held me back.

"Hold up," he said. "Jogasaki's not there yet."

"I don't care if he's not there. We can still kill Aijima."

"I get that, but our main target is Jogasaki."

The dispute continued for a few minutes. We might have had impure motives, but Ozu was making sense. Aijima was practically Jogasaki's body double. It would have been stupid to use our full force on just him. I put my half-drawn sword back in its sheath.

But, unforgivably, no matter how long we waited, Jogasaki didn't show up. The evening wind whipped by, and I felt a sadness collecting in the pit of my stomach. On the enemy line, people were starting to get tipsy, and their merry laughter echoed across the delta. Meanwhile, Ozu and I were curled under Demachibashi getting wary looks from joggers and dog walkers.

The clear boundary that had formed over the river between winners and losers threw some oil on the fire of my anger. If it had been a black-haired maiden under the bridge with me, I'd have been willing to endure some huddling in the dark, but it was Ozu. With the party for new club members getting into friendly gear on the opposite bank, why did I have to be cuddling with a guy with a face as sinister as a Taisho-era loan shark? Did I make a mistake somewhere along the way? Was I at fault? I wanted at least to be with someone whose spirit was a bit more kindred (or a black-haired maiden).

"This makes it really obvious who the winners and losers are, huh?" said Ozu.

"Shut up."

"Ahh, it looks like they're having so much fun."

"Whose side are you on, anyway?" I asked.

"Maybe this is a lost cause. I wanna go drink with the freshies."

"So you're ditching me?"

"It's not like we made a promise or anything."

"Weren't you just saying you'd dedicated your body and soul to me?"

"Oh, that was like a million years ago. I forgot," Ozu said.

"You bastard."

"Why are you looking at me like that?"

"Hey, don't hang all over me," I said.

"But I'm *looonely*. And the evening breeze is so cold."

"You're always lonely."

"Eek!"

Eventually, imitating senseless lovers' talk wore thin as well, and that emptiness was what finally depleted our stores of patience. Jogasaki wasn't there yet, but there was nothing we could do about that. We decided to send him a cake full of dead arthropods later and content ourselves with raining on the other members' parade tonight.

Darkness had begun to occupy the riverbank when we crept out carrying our fireworks. Ozu went down to the river to fill the bucket we had brought with water.

• • •

Fireworks are meant to be shot into the sky. They must never be taken into one's hands, pointed at people, and used to bomb a friendly new student welcome party on the opposite riverbank. They are very dangerous. Please do not try this at home.

Even though we had planned for a surprise attack, just suddenly launching into things wasn't my style.

First I shouted across the river to the enemy camp: "Hey, it is I, *mumble mumble*, and I'm about to take revenge! Do take care to shield your eyes!" I scanned the revelers. Many people had turned our way, mouths gaping as if ready to ask, "What the heck?" If they didn't already know what the heck, I would fill them in. I became indignant.

Suddenly the figure of Akashi sitting on the embankment hugging her beer bottle caught my eye. After mouthing the truly apt appraisal "Dumbass" at me, she hastily stood and took shelter beyond the pine trees.

The rest of the bunch had not yet grasped the situation and just sat on their tarps blinking. Once Akashi had evacuated, there was no reason to hold back. I ordered Ozu to fire.

After shooting a decent number of fireworks, the plan was to leave the partiers to their shrieking chaos and make a swift getaway, but it seemed that the guys our age wanted, in their fury, to look cool in front of the younger students, so they began crossing the river with no regard for how cold the water was. We panicked.

"Let's get outta here," I said.

"Wait, wait, this fuse is still burning."

"Hurry up already!"

"There's still a bunch left . . ."

"Leave 'em!"

I went to run up to the bridge, but there were people streaming down the embankment. It looked like they meant to make us pay. I recognized the savage voice that screamed, "You bastards!"

"Ugh, now Jogasaki shows up?" Ozu shouted.

"What timing."

Ozu shrieked and did a 180, slipping past me to run the opposite way. He headed for Kamo Ohashi at an impressive pace, yelling, "Sorry! I'm sorry!" as he went without a shred of anything even resembling pride.

Jogasaki nearly caught me by the collar, but I brushed him aside, lithe as a panther, and ran after Ozu toward Kamo Ohashi.

"When are you guys gonna give up these stupid pranks?!"

Jogasaki stood on the bank scolding us as we ran off. *How dare you lecture me*, I thought. *Maybe take a good, hard look at yourself before going off on other people!* My anger was so righteous I nearly turned around, but we were outnumbered; even if we were right, it was clear we'd be defeated by the tyranny of the majority. I had no intention of submitting to such a disgrace. In other words, we were not running away, but making a strategic retreat.

Ozu had already made it to Kamo Ohashi and was rapidly moving out of view. When he needs to make a getaway, he's off like a damned shot. Just as I thought, *Okay, I need to get over there, too,* a hot mass hit my back. I groaned.

A cheer went up behind me.

Apparently, they had retaliated by shooting me with one of the fireworks as I fled. All the various things I had done over the past two years went flickering across the back of my mind like shadows cast by a revolving lantern.

• • •

My two years since entering college had been a series of futile battles. Though I could state with confidence that my fight had been admirable enough to bring no shame to the title of Obstructor of Romance, I couldn't hold back my tears. My path had been a thorny one that no one had praised, and why would they?

At the beginning of school, my brain had been rather rose-colored, but it lost those warm hues, and its transition to the blue and purple end of the spectrum is not something I will talk much about. There's not much to say on the topic, anyhow, and even if I said things so devoid of all merit, what's the point of seeking empty sympathy from my readers?

The summer of my first year, when the extremely sharp blade of reality flashed, my brief, silly, rose-colored dream vanished along with the campus dew.

After that, I faced reality with a cold gaze and resolved to bring the iron hammer down on people intoxicated by their frivolous dreams. To put it bluntly, I got in the way of people on their path to love.

If there was a lovesick maiden in the east, I told her, "Ditch that creep." If there was a delusional man in the west, I told him, "Don't waste your time." If fireworks of passion were about to explode in the south, I immediately doused them in water, and in the north, I constantly preached that romance was unnecessary. Thanks to all that, I was labeled "that guy who can't read the room." But that's a misunderstanding. I read the room more closely than anyone else and proceeded to purposely obliterate the atmosphere.

There was someone who was amused by my battles and egged me on, a shady figure who enjoyed sparking arguments in our club. And that person was Ozu. Utilizing his independent information network, there wasn't a lewd rumor he hadn't heard, and while I was pouring out the oil, he spread both truth and lies, skillfully setting fires as if it were his craft. He created his preferred ambience—discordant shrieks echoing somewhere in the club as if from a bloody battlefield. You could truly call him evil incarnate. A disgrace to *Homo sapiens*. I don't want to be that kind of person.

The Ablutions film club didn't have a long history, but despite that it had about thirty regular members across all years—which made our enemies number that many more. There were even some people who left the club on account of our antics. I was nearly drowned once in Lake Biwa when someone who quit ambushed me. One time, unable to return to my apartment, I lay low in Kitashirakawa, in the room of this guy I knew who was out of town. Once I said too much to a classmate directly, and she burst into tears on Konoe-dori.

But I didn't lose. I couldn't lose.

And it goes without saying that if I would've given up back then, me and everyone else could have been happy. No need for Ozu to be happy, though.

• • •

It was the film club's organization that irritated me, first of all.

Ablutions had been established with a detestable structure, consisting of Jogasaki's dictatorship, with everyone else harmoniously creating films under his guidance. At first, I worked beneath him since I had no choice, but my discontent for the regime grew. Still, simply leaving would be admitting defeat, which offended my sensibilities. Thus, in order to launch a blatant rebellion that Jogasaki could see, I began making my own movies. Naturally, not a single person sympathized with me, so by necessity, it was Ozu and I filming them.

The first was a film brimming with violence about two men who inherited a prank battle with roots in the pre–Pacific War period as they obliterated each other's pride with all the wit and strength they could muster. Between Ozu's bizarre performance, his expression as unchanging as that of a Noh mask, and my overly energetic theatrics, plus all the merciless pranks, it was an indescribably revolting piece. The finale, in which Ozu, his entire body dyed pink, and I, with half my head shaved, clashed on Kamo Ohashi, was probably worth a watch. But of course it was ignored. The only one who laughed at the film festival was Akashi.

Our goal with our second film was to employ the underpinning of Shakespeare's *King Lear* to depict a man's emotions wavering between three women, but unable to conceal the fundamental issue of having zero female cast members, the whole thing became somewhat incomprehensible and lost all connection to *King Lear*. Not only that, but the wavering man's emotions were portrayed with such care that it garnered a shower of curses from the women in the club and was forcibly given the distinguished title "Best Hentai." The only one who laughed was Akashi.

Our third film was a survival story about a man trapped in a never-ending maze of four-and-a-half-mat tatami rooms and his journey to escape, but that ended with us being told "I've seen this scenario somewhere before" and "It's not even a survival story." The only one who gave us a slightly better comment was Akashi.

The more films I made with Ozu, the more the other members encircled us from a distance, as they might a campfire, and the frostier Jogasaki's icy gaze became. In the end, he began ignoring us as if we were pebbles by the wayside.

The strange thing was that the harder I worked, the more his charisma seemed to grow. Thinking back on it now, it's clear we were used to lift him up, like the fulcrum for his lever, but saying that now won't accomplish anything.

Actually, I just wasn't resourceful enough with my way of life.

I was so very upstanding.

• • •

Following our successful strategic retreat from the Kamo River, we went out to celebrate our victory.

Buffeted by the chilly wind as I pedaled my bicycle, I felt somehow ill at ease. Leaving our bicycles, the two of us sulkily strolled Kawaramachi. The neighborhood's lights sparkled, illuminating the navy-blue sky. Ozu suddenly turned off at the Sanjo Ohashi Bridge to go into the old-fashioned scrub brush shop at its west end. I waited in the dark under the eaves.

He eventually came out looking frustrated.

"What? Did you buy a brush?"

"No. I need to give Master Higuchi tribute, but he says he wants this elusive luxury scrub brush that can remove any grime."

"Does that even exist?"

"There are rumors, anyhow . . . The shopkeeper laughed at me! I'll just have to give him something else."

"You sure are burning out your brain on some idiotic nonsense."

"Master wants so many different things; it's a lot of work. Mame mochi from Demachi Futaba or chirimen-zansho are doable, but then he asks for an antique globe, a banner from the used book fair, seahorses, and giant squid. And if you bring him something that displeases him, you get expelled. Always gotta be on your toes."

That's what Ozu said, but he seemed strangely amused.

After that we sauntered in the direction of Kiyamachi.

Our retreat had definitely been strategic, so the self-doubt that arose—*Are you sure that wasn't a defeat?*—was unpleasant. The look on Ozu's face said, "As long as it's fun, anything goes," but I couldn't be so carefree. The surprise attack operation on the Kamo River Delta this eve was to show the target of our enmity, our peers and seniors in the club, that we existed, but when I recalled the battle with a clear head, it seemed almost like they had been enjoying it. Our fight was not some entertainment for their drinking party. No matter how much it might have appeared like entertainment for their drinking party, our pride in the matter towered higher than Mount Hiei.

"Khee-hee-hee," Ozu suddenly laughed as we were walking. "Jogasaki acts all big in front of the younger club members, but he's dying on the inside."

"Oh, yeah?"

Ozu put on a smug face. "He's staying on to get his doctorate, but since he's spent all his time filming movies instead of studying, he can't get a single experiment to go well. His parents say they're going to start sending him less money, but he got in a fight with his boss at his part-time job, so he quit. Last month he broke up with the girl he stole from Aijima. He doesn't have a leg to stand on when it comes to lecturing anybody."

"How do you even know all this?"

In the light of the streetlamps, Ozu smirked like Nurari-hyon, that obnoxious yokai. "I can't have you pooh-poohing my intel-gathering abilities. I know more about you than even your girlfriend does."

"I don't have a girlfriend."

"Well, if you had one, I mean." Ozu seemed to be pondering something. "But really, Aijima is weirder than Jogasaki."

"I wonder."

A nasty smile appeared on Ozu's face. "That's because you don't know his other side."

"Tell me."

"Nope, nope. It's way too horrifying. I can't possibly."

The Takase River flowed by, as shallow as the indie movies Jogasaki churned out as if possessed. As I gazed at the surface reflecting the sparkling city lights back at us, I got pissed again.

The utter smallness of Jogasaki's swagger as he gathered such concentrated respect in that courtyard-sized world of Ablutions. At this very moment, he was the focus of the new students'—especially the girls'—respect; he had forgotten the reality he should have been fixated on, spellbound as a cat given catnip. Brandishing his empty film theory, he pretended to be every bit a gentleman, but all he really cared about was breasts. They were all he saw. *It'd be swell if his stubborn breast habit ended up ruining his life.*

"Hey, your eyes are glazed over!"

Hearing Ozu's comment, I finally unfurrowed my brow.

Just then, a girl who nearly passed us by smiled at me instead. A woman with gallant, valiant eyebrows. I accepted her gaze calmly and returned her smile with an air appropriate for a model modern gentleman. She approached, and I thought she was going to address me, but shocking as it may be, she turned to Ozu.

"Oh, hey, evening," she said, and so on, adding in a slightly alluring voice, "What are you up to around here?"

"Just running some errands," said Ozu.

I gave them space. I had no intention of eavesdropping—especially not if the vibes were vaguely amorous. As they were standing amid the hustle and bustle, I couldn't hear what they were saying, but as I watched from my distance, I saw the girl point a finger and stick it into Ozu's mouth. Well, they seemed quite close, but I wasn't jealous.

Rubbernecking disagreed with my nature, so I cast my gaze on the shops lining Kiyamachi-dori.

• • •

Among the bars and sex shops crouched a dark house.

Under its eaves, an old woman sat before a wooden table covered with a white cloth—a fortune-teller. A sheet of paper hanging from the table was crammed full of kanji whose meaning I couldn't fathom. Something like a little lantern glowed orange, bringing the woman's face into view. There was something strangely intimidating about her. She was a yokai licking her lips at the souls of the people passing by. *Get a single fortune read and forevermore the shady old woman will haunt you day and night, nothing you try to do will go well, the one you're waiting for won't come, your lost items will never turn up, you'll fail the classes that should have been easy credits, your graduation thesis will spontaneously combust just before you hand it in, you'll fall into Lake Biwa Canal, you'll be solicited on the street by one of those people on Shijo-dori*—I was resolutely imagining all of this terrible luck while staring at

35

her, so eventually she sensed my presence. From the depths of the darkness, she flashed her eyes at me. The unearthly atmosphere she emitted ensnared me. That atmosphere was persuasive. I considered it logically: there was no way someone giving off supernatural vibes this potent for free would tell a fortune that missed the mark.

I've been alive in this world for nearly a quarter century, but I can count on my fingers the number of times I listened so humbly to another person's opinion. Maybe that was how I ended up purposely taking this thorny path there was no need to walk down at all? If I had abandoned my own judgment sooner, my life as a college student would have turned out very differently. I wouldn't have joined the warped film club, Ablutions, I wouldn't have met Ozu with his labyrinthine character, and I probably wouldn't have been branded the Obstructor of Romance, either. I would have been blessed with good friends and upperclassmen associates, employing my overflowing talents in full to excel in both the literary and military arts, the result of which would have been a beautiful black-haired maiden at my side and, before me, a shining future of pure gold; if things went well, perhaps even that elusive, supreme treasure—a rose-colored, meaningful campus life—would have been within my grasp. For a person of my caliber, such a stroke of luck wouldn't be even a little unusual.

Right.

It's not too late. With all possible haste, seek an objective opinion and escape into one of the other lives you could have!

I stepped forward as if drawn by the old woman's otherworldly aura.

"Well, my boy, what would you like to know?"

She spoke in a mumble as if her mouth was full of cotton, which really made me feel like I was speaking with a wise elder.

"Hmm. Good question."

When I remained lost for words, the old woman smiled. "From the look on your face right now, I gather you're terribly irritated. Dissatisfied. It seems that you aren't making full use of your talents. Your current environment doesn't appear to be a good fit for you."

"Yes, that's right. That's exactly it."

"Let's have a look."

The old woman took my hands and pored over them, nodding to herself.

"Mm. You seem to be extremely hard-working and talented."

I was already impressed by her keen insights. Just as in the proverb "a clever hawk hides its talons," I had modestly kept my good sense and talents hidden so no one would find them, but I did such a good job that I hadn't been able to locate them myself for the past few years; for her to spot them within five minutes of our meeting meant she couldn't be any ordinary fortune-teller.

"It's essential that you not let chance pass you by. What I mean is a good opportunity. Do you understand? But chance is rather hard to seize: sometimes something that doesn't look like a chance at all is one, while other times what you were sure was your chance turns out, in retrospect, to not have been it at all. But you must perceive your chance and act on it. It looks like you'll have a long life, so I'm sure you'll be able to seize one at some point."

Profound words befitting her otherworldly aura.

"I can't wait that long. I want to seize my chance now. Could you explain in a bit more detail?"

When I pressed her, the old woman's wrinkles warped slightly. I wondered if her right cheek was itchy, but apparently this was a smile.

"It's difficult to speak in particulars. Even if I tell you now, your fate might change, and then it won't be your chance anymore. Wouldn't I feel bad about that? Fate can change from second to second, you know."

"But what you said is so vague I have no idea what to do."

When I cocked my head, the old woman said "Hmm-hmm!" with a sniff. "Very well. I'll refrain from talking about the too distant future, but I'll tell you something very near."

I opened my ears as big as Dumbo's.

"*Colosseo*," she whispered suddenly.

"Colosseo? What's that?"

"Colosseo is the sign of your chance. When your chance appears, there colosseo will be," she said.

"You're not telling me to go to Rome, are you?" I asked, but the old woman only grinned.

"When your chance comes, don't miss it. When it comes, you can't go on idly doing the same things you've always done. Be bold, and try seizing your chance by doing something completely different. If you do that, your dissatisfaction will disappear, and you'll be able to walk down a new path—though there may lie a different dissatisfaction. I'm sure you understand."

I didn't understand one bit, but I nodded anyway.

"Even if you miss this chance, you needn't worry. You're a fine person, so I'm sure you'll be able to seize one someday. That I know for sure. There's no rush."

With that, she ended the reading.

"Thank you."

I bobbed my head and paid her fee. When I stood and turned to go, Ozu was standing behind me.

"Playing little lost lamb, are you?" he said.

• • •

That day, it had been Ozu's idea to wander around town.

I'm not fond of the clamor of night life, so I almost never go out. But apparently Ozu is different. This is him we're talking about, though, so he probably prowled around with a belly full of no-good intentions hoping for some obscene incident to occur.

He kept saying, "I want beef tongue with salty green onion sauce," so we decided to supplement our regularly inadequate nutrition on the second floor of a yakiniku joint facing Kiyamachi-dori.

In between meats, I ordered some vegetables, and as I was happily chomping on mushrooms, Ozu looked as if he had stumbled on a hidden scene of humans noshing on horseshit.

"It's wild that you eat such creepy-looking stuff. That's fungus, you know. It's a brown lump of fungus. I can't believe it. What're those pleat-y white things under the cap? What're those for?"

I got pissed because he was eating only the beef tongue and

none of the vegetables, and I recall wrenching his mouth open and cramming one of those spicy onion things in his mouth, half-grilled. Ozu is utterly committed to his unbalanced diet; I've never seen him eat a proper meal.

"Who was that girl earlier?" I asked, and Ozu looked at me blankly. "You were talking to her by where the fortune-teller was."

"That was Hanuki-san," he said, and ate another slice of beef tongue. "We're good friends; I got to know her through Master Higuchi. She was on her way home from English class and invited me out for drinks."

"You shameless jerk. Look at you being all popular—it's out of character."

"Oh, yes, I'm so popular I hardly get a break. But I politely turned her down."

"Why?" I asked.

"I mean, when she gets drunk she goes around licking people's faces."

"Even your filthy mug?"

"Yes, she licks my adorable little face. It must be how she expresses affection."

"Anyone who licks your face would contract an incurable disease. She must be fearless."

As we carried on like idiots, the meat sizzled.

"What did the fortune-teller say to you?" He grinned, ready to rehash that convo.

I had gotten advice on a topic of grave importance—how I should live my life going forward—but Ozu jumped to the vulgar conclusion, "I'm sure it was about romance. What a waste." He added, "Eww, so revolting," followed by, "Pervert,

pervert, pervert," repeated like a broken alarm clock, disturbing my solemn contemplations. Swept up in my anger, I stuffed an underdone shiitake in his mouth, and it was quiet for a time.

She had said "colosseo," but I had no connection to Rome. Or the Colosseum. I attempted to recall my daily life in detail but could think of nothing that related. So maybe it was something that would have to do with my life in the future. What in the world would that be? If I didn't start thinking of a way to capitalize on it now, I would miss my chance again. I was anxious.

It was hopping at the yakiniku place, and I saw people who looked so young they had probably been high schoolers until just the other day. Someone must have been holding a welcome party for new students. I didn't want to remember, but I had once been a new student, myself. That period during which I was filled to overflowing with hope for a future that would make me both happy and bashful may have lasted only a moment, but I had it.

"You're probably wishing you had spent your time as a student better, huh?" Ozu abruptly struck to the heart of the matter.

I snorted and said not a word.

"Couldn't happen," Ozu said, eating more beef tongue.

"What?"

"No matter what path you chose, you would have ended up here."

"You really think that? I sure don't."

"Nope. You just have that kind of face."

"What kind of face?"

"Hmm, a face that is rightly described as belonging to someone born under the star that makes a person incapable of leading a meaningful student life."

"You're one to talk, with your Nurarihyon face."

Ozu grinned. It made him look even more like a yokai.

"I take a positive attitude toward the fact that I was born under the star that makes a person incapable of leading a meaningful student life. I'm enjoying my meaningless student life with every fiber of my being, so there's no reason I should be getting an earful."

I sighed. "It's because of your lifestyle that I ended up like this!"

"But don't we have fun wasting our days on pointless bullshit? What are you complaining about?"

"Everything! The cause of these disagreeable circumstances I'm in is *you*!"

"Anyone would be ashamed to say such a thing, but here you are declaring it for the world to hear," Ozu replied.

"If I hadn't met you, I would have lived more purposefully. I would have applied myself to my studies, dated a black-haired maiden, and relished every moment of my untarnished student life. That's right. I'm sure of it."

"Were those shiitake actually shrooms?"

"It hit me today how utterly I've wasted my time here!"

"Not that it's any consolation, but I think you would have met me no matter what. I just know it. No matter what happened, I would have done everything in my power to corrupt you. You can struggle against fate all you want, but it's futile." He held up a pinky finger. "We're connected by the black thread of fate."

The horrific image of two men, bound like boneless hams by

a dark thread, sinking to dark watery depths, came to mind, and I shuddered. Ozu watched me as he continued to cheerfully eat only the meat. *This rotten, worthless yokai asshole.*

• • •

Our strategic retreat from the Kamo River Delta, the mysterious pronouncement of the fortune-teller, Ozu sitting there before me, and the rest of it all got to be a bit much, and I started drinking faster.

"Akashi's still in Ablutions, huh . . ." I groaned, but Ozu shook his head.

"Nah, just last week I heard something about her quitting. Apparently Jogasaki tried to stop her, but . . ."

"Huh. So she quit right after we did?"

"I think tonight she showed up at the party as a former member. So dutiful," Ozu said.

"Jeez, how do you know all this?"

"I mean, we were out drinking the other day. As engineering department pals."

"Always one step ahead of me, aren't ya . . . ?"

The image of Akashi as she had appeared sitting next to a pine tree drinking her beer, aloof and removed from the group at the Kamo River Delta below the embankment, entered my mind.

"What do you think about Akashi?" asked Ozu.

"What do you mean, what do I think?"

"So, until now, I've been the only one unfortunate enough to understand the person of such extraordinary idiocy and unparalleled hideousness who is you, but . . ."

"What the hell are you trying to say?" I asked.

"She can, too. This is your chance. If you don't seize this chance, there will be nothing left for you." Ozu stared at me with a smile. I waved him off.

"Listen, you. I hate women who can understand people like me. I'm more into black-haired maidens who are soft, delicate, and sensitive, with heads full of beautiful, dreamlike things."

"Not that incomprehensible ego again."

"Shut up—leave me alone."

"You're not still hung up on being dumped by Kohinata as a first-year, are you?" Ozu asked.

"Don't you dare say that name."

"Ah, so that's a yes, then. You're so stubborn."

"If you keep talking, I'm going to throw you on the grill," I said. "I have no interest in discussing my love life with you."

Ozu abruptly leaned back in his seat and snorted.

"Then consider your chance mine. I'll be happy in your place."

"You're too twisted—it'll never work out. Akashi has an eye for people. Plus, don't you already have a girlfriend? I know you've been getting freaky and hiding it from me."

"Neh-heh."

"What are you laughing about?" I asked.

"Not telling."

• • •

As we were having that irritating exchange, what unexpectedly came to mind was that dreamlike encounter with Kamota-ketsunumi no Kami at Neko Ramen. Though the meeting had been faintly mystical, it had been shady above all, and during it, the man who dared call himself a god suggested that he was weighing me against Ozu.

Right, right. It was so shady I had completely forgotten about it.

When I thought about it calmly with my drunken brain, wasn't it possible to say that the mysterious fellow had predicted this very situation? No, something so idiotic couldn't possibly be true. That *I* would be so lonely I would fall captive to a convenient delusion and hope to be lucky enough to get intimate with the black-haired maiden Akashi? Unpardonable. But it was strange. That god had proved he knew what kind of experiences I had had, and not only that, but he hinted at my thorny, embarrassing past, and he also anticipated this situation correctly. There was no way to explain it. Was that god the real thing? Was he actually going to Izumo each fall to tie and untie red threads of destiny?

As I was pondering those things, the scenery started to waver, and just as I began to think I was a bit wasted, I realized that Ozu was gone. He said he was going to the bathroom, but then he never came back.

At first I thought nothing of it, leisurely amusing myself by inflating and deflating my fantasies like a balloon, but when he didn't come back after fifteen minutes, I figured he must have left me drunk and slipped away, which swept me up in a fury so intense my hair stood on end. Gracefully exiting partway through dinner like a spring breeze and sticking the other person with the bill was something he did well and often.

But just as I was getting desperate and mumbling, "Shit, not again," he came back.

"Huh?"

As I faced the person across the table in relief, I realized it wasn't Ozu.

"All right, eat up. If you want to eat any more, please make it quick," Akashi said matter-of-factly as she began to grill the rest of the meat.

• • •

Akashi was a year behind me and belonged to the engineering department. As someone who didn't mince words, she seemed to be given a wide berth by her peers. Looking at this girl, who didn't balk at challenging Jogasaki when the situation called for it, I was left with a positive impression. Her tongue was no less scathing than Jogasaki's, and he was afraid that his charisma might be injured, so though he had an interest in her cool, intellectual face and her breasts, talking to her had become difficult.

The summer of her first year, they were on Mount Yoshida no doubt filming something according to Jogasaki's incomprehensible vision, as usual. During a break while eating lunch, the new students were chatting about this and that without a care in the world. One of the kids in Akashi's year asked her, like a dope, "Akashi, what do you do in your free time on the weekends?"

Akashi replied without even looking at him.

"Why should I tell you?"

No one asked Akashi about her weekend plans after that.

I heard the story after the fact from Ozu, and sent her a passionate mental cheer: *Akashi, you keep running right down your own path!*

I don't know why a girl with such a rational mind would belong to a weird club like Ablutions, but she was good at planning, could handle any sorts of arrangements that needed to be made, and was smart enough to learn the operation of any sort of equipment in a flash, so though people kept their distance, they also respected her. On that point, the difference between her versus Ozu and me, whom people also kept their distance from yet despised, was like night and day.

This girl, tough like a medieval European castle town though she was, had one weakness.

The previous autumn, I had been told, "We're short people, so come help out," and reluctantly participated in a shoot, putting in middling efforts. As usual, we were filming on Mount Yoshida.

Climbing a tree to set up some audio equipment, face as hard-boiled as a wartime censor, Akashi suddenly screamed, "Gyoaehhh!" like you'd see in a manga, and fell. I swooped in to catch her with a precise motion. That is, I didn't manage to get out of the way in time, and she landed on me. With her hair a mess, she clung to me, frantically waving her right hand around.

As she had been climbing the tree, she took firm hold of what she thought was a branch, but something felt squishy. When she looked, she saw she was clenching a huge moth.

She was more frightened of moths than anything.

"It was so squishy, it was so squishy . . ."

She said it over and over as she trembled, her face as pale as if she had seen a ghost, and there was something about it impossible to capture with words—the charm of that moment when someone who usually has such a solid outer wall exposes a vulnerable part. I, the Obstructor of Romance, very nearly fell in love. The burning of my earthly desires that should have flared out after the summer of my first year nearly roared once more, but I gritted my teeth and consoled her like a gentleman as she repeated "It was so squishy," as if delirious: "All right, calm down."

I don't think she sympathized with the meaningless battle Ozu and I were engaged in. At least, when we were screwing around in club meetings, she was only ever a bystander with a chilly gaze; that said, she never made an issue out of us, either.

When she saw the films I made with Ozu, these were her impressions: "You made another dumb movie, huh?"

She said this three times.

No—including our last film, it was four times. But the one we made this spring was the only one she didn't care for. She added, "It makes me question your character."

• • •

"Akashi, what are you doing here? Weren't you just on the Kamo River Delta? Did your carnal desires lead you here?"

When I asked her that in an unsteady tone, she furrowed her eyebrows and, lowering her voice, put a finger to her lips. "You really should use your brain more. Did you forget that our club comes here all the time?"

"Nah, I know that. I've been here plenty of times."

"After the party on the delta, Jogasaki suddenly said he wanted to eat some meat for some reason and made sure to round up all the new kids before bringing everyone here. They're all over there."

She pointed toward the exit. I stretched out of my seat to try to see over the partition, but she put a stop to that with a "They'll see you!" and I shrank back.

"Why would they come for yakiniku after the party? Those beasts and their carnal desires. Have they no pride in their agricultural roots?" I moaned, but she ignored me.

"If they find you, it'll be a huge pain in the ass."

"If it's a fight they want, I accept . . . if that's what they want. But I'm confident I'm incapable of winning."

"A fight would be something, at least. Probably he'll just mock the shit out of you, and that'll be it. The newbies are as youthful as a bunch of cherries, and you'll be utterly disgraced in front of them. Come on, hurry up and finish your meat, please."

She thrust the meat she had grilled toward me. And though she was telling me to eat, she was chowing down, herself, as well. As I stared at her in astonishment, she admitted, with some embarrassment, "It's been a long time since I had any meat, so don't mind me." For how embarrassed she was, she sure ate a lot. I was already full, so I picked at a bit and then said, "I'm good. You can have it. I'm gonna go home. What happened to Ozu? Did you see him?"

"Ozu has already escaped via the back exit. I'd expect no less from someone called Ozu the Runner."

Swift as the wind. Just like the army of Takeda of Kai.

"I already paid your bill. If you leave out the front, Jogasaki and the others will spot you, so please leave through the back. I already set it up with the staff, so they'll let you out that way. I'm a regular, so . . ."

Amazed by her frighteningly thorough plan, I obeyed without complaint. I gave her the money for the food.

"I'll be sure to repay this debt someday."

"Never mind the debt, just keep your promise." She wrinkled her brow and glared at me.

"What promise was that?"

When I cocked my head, she waved me off. "It doesn't matter. Just get out of here, please. I need to get back to them soon."

I downed the rest of my oolong tea and bobbed my head to excuse myself. Planting my feet extremely firmly on the ground that seemed liable to roll due to my drunkenness, I stood, taking cover behind the partition, and proceeded down the dim hallway to the rear.

A woman wearing a white apron was standing next to the door marked "Employees Only," and she opened it for me as I approached. When I thanked her politely, she said, "You've got a lot of problems for someone so young," in a sympathetic voice. I wondered for a moment how Akashi had explained things to her.

When I went outside, I found myself in a dark, narrow alley.

Then I walked out into the Kiyamachi neighborhood. I looked for Ozu but didn't find him anywhere.

• • •

I'm going to write about the final film we made.

Spring had come again, and my annoyance had reached new heights. Jogasaki stubbornly remained in charge, showing not even the slightest intent to retire. He sucked on his power in this fishbowl society with the energy of a baby sucking a pacifier, his eyes constantly straying to the fresh breasts of the newbies. And the lowerclassmen were charmed by his puny charisma, seemingly intent on wasting their student days that should have been spent so meaningfully. Now was the time for someone to throw a bucket of cold water over their heads. And I was determined to step up and take that unprofitable role.

In preparation for the new-member recruitment screenings we held in April and May, I created two films. One was of Ozu sitting alone in a drab four-and-a-half-mat tatami room reciting the Nasu no Yoichi scene from *Tale of the Heike* in a sonorant voice. All of the upperclassmen, Jogasaki among them, were against showing the film. And I thought that was only natural.

"I don't mind if you film whatever stupid shit you like," Jogasaki declared in the darkness. "Just don't mess up the recruitment screenings."

But I pushed back with a speech as dignified as Winston Churchill might have given and made them approve our screening. Maybe the soul of my appeal, that this would be my last film, got through to them.

Actually, though, I prepared one other, completely different film.

It was a puppet show based on the story of Momotaro, but for some reason the old couple who find the baby born from a peach name him Masaki instead of Momotaro. From there begin the nauseating exploits of Masaki. He founds the film club Onigashima, tricks the lowerclassmen with poisoned kibi dango to secure power over their terrarium society, prattles on about his idiotic philosophies of life and love, gazes in fascination at the breasts of the maidens brought to him by his lackeys (dog, monkey, and pheasant), exercises his terrifying perverted nature behind the shield of his handsome features, and lets his hair down at extravagant banquets, finally establishing the Masaki Empire and reigning over it. But before long, two allies of justice appear. After dyeing Masaki's entire body pink, they wrap him in a bamboo mat and throw him into the Kamo River, thereby bringing peace to the world.

On the surface, it seemed to be one of those many riffs on Momotaro injected with black humor, and I did my utmost to entertain the viewers. But Masaki is Jogasaki's given name, and I named all the other characters after real people, too. This was a Jogasaki exposé that borrowed Momotaro as the vehicle.

For the inside scoop about Jogasaki, I relied entirely on Ozu's intel. Ozu was so informed about Jogasaki that he knew things—the depths of the depths—that my pride as a member of *Homo sapiens* won't let me reveal. "I have some connections with an intelligence agency" was all he said, but that was a mystery. Once again I was struck by what a wicked human being Ozu was and vowed that I would cut ties with him as soon as I could.

On the day of the screening, I swapped the original film I had made of Ozu reading *Tale of the Heike* with this Jogasaki version of the story of Momotaro and rolled it.

Then, under cover of darkness, I fled the theater.

● ● ●

After escaping the Kiyamachi yakiniku joint, I cycled north along Kawabata-dori.

The Kamo River was running high, and on the opposite

bank, the city lights sparkled; it was like a scene from a dream. Between the Sanjo Ohashi and Oikebashi Bridges, there was the usual coed crowd known for obeying the Kamo River Law of Equidistant Seating, but it didn't bother me—no, there was no reason to care; or rather, I didn't have the wherewithal to care. As I rode on, soon both the lights of the bustling streets and the Kamo River Law of Equidistant Seating grew distant.

At this time, there were still people on the Kamo River Delta, and the atmosphere was buzzing. The flippant college kids milling about must have been up to no good. To the north, I could see Aoi Park's densely growing forest. I headed from the delta to Shimogamo Shrine, feeling the crisp night air on my cheeks as I rode.

The approach to Shimogamo Shrine was dark.

I left my bicycle near the beginning of that road and walked through Tadasu no Mori in the darkness. A short way in there was a little bridge, and I remembered sitting on the railing drinking ramune.

It was a memory from a year ago at the Shimogamo Shrine used book fair.

The riding grounds stretching north to south alongside the approach to the shrine were crammed full of sellers' tents, and tons of people were strolling around on the hunt for books. It was only a short walk from Shimogamo Yusuiso, so I attended practically every day. That spirited atmosphere almost felt like a dream; the dark riding grounds were usually so empty and creepy.

It was at that used book fair that I met Akashi.

After basking in the charms of summer to my heart's content, drinking a ramune in the sunlight filtered through the treetops, I strolled among the bookseller stalls on either side, browsing as I went. No matter where I looked, I saw wooden shelves crammed with books; it made me a little dizzy. On the cloth-covered benches set up in rows, people who must have gotten book fair sick like me hung their heads. I had sat down, too, dazed. It was August, which meant it was muggy and hot, so I wiped the sweat off my forehead with a handkerchief.

Straight ahead was the used bookshop Gabi Shobo's stall. And it was Akashi sitting in the folding chair at the entrance. *She's in my club at school, isn't she?* I realized. She appeared to be working part-time at this shop. Akashi had only just joined Ablutions, but this clever hawk didn't hide her talons; her talent and standoffish manner were apparent to all.

I rose from the bench, and when I made eye contact with her while looking through Gabi Shobo's stacks, she bowed her head slightly. I bought *Twenty Thousand Leagues Under the Sea* by Jules Verne. I was walking away afterward when she got up and came after me.

"Here, you can use this," she said, handing me a paper fan with the words "Summer Book Fair" printed on it.

I remembered fanning my sweaty face as I left Tadasu no Mori carrying *Twenty Thousand Leagues Under the Sea*.

• • •

The next day . . .

I woke up late and decided to go to a café next to Demachi-yanagi Station for dinner.

As I passed by the Kamo River Delta, I could see the kanji

for "big" on the mountain in the distance, illuminated clearly by the evening sun. *I bet you can see the bonfire really well from here.* I nearly began imagining what it would be like to stand there with Akashi and watch the shape of the okuribi burn, but daydreaming out in the evening breeze wouldn't satisfy me, anyhow, so I found a good stopping point and cut it out.

Having given up, I returned to my four-and-a-half-mat tatami room and read *Twenty Thousand Leagues Under the Sea.* But even if I tried to let my imagination take flight into this world of classic adventure, it was only my delusions that lifted off. I had the fantastical idea that the fortune-teller, Kamotaketsunumi no Kami, and whatnot were connected. I tried quietly saying the word the fortune-teller told me: "colosseo." Seize your chance, she said. *But how am I supposed to know what my chance is?*

Once the sun had gone down, Ozu came to visit.

"Thanks for last night," he said.

"You're as fast as ever when it comes to beating a retreat."

"You're as sulky as ever," he said. "You have no S.O., and you exiled yourself from your club, but it's not like you're a serious student—what the hell are you thinking?"

"You better watch your mouth or I'll smack you dead."

"Smack me, sure, but dead? Why would you do such a horrible thing?" Ozu grinned. "Here, you can have this, so please improve your mood."

"What is it?" I asked.

"Castella. I got a bunch from Master Higuchi, so I'm sharing."

"Huh—it's not every day I get a gift from you."

"Well, it's because cutting up a huge castella and eating it alone is the far reaches of solitude. I want you to get a good taste of loneliness," Ozu said.

"Oh, that's what you're up to? Sure, I'll taste it. I'll keep tasting it till I'm damned well sick of it."

Then Ozu spoke about his master—something he almost never did.

"Oh, so, back when my master wanted a seahorse, I found an aquarium on the street and took it to him. When I tried filling it up, it sprang a furious leak, and the water came rushing out, causing a whole scene. The master's whole room was soaked."

"Wait, what number is your master's room?"

"It's the one directly above this."

I flew into a rage.

Previously, while I was away, there had been a flood on the second floor. When I got home, the water had dripped down to make all of my precious documents—both obscene and not—soggy. But that wasn't the only damage I suffered. All my precious data—both obscene and not—was lost from my waterlogged computer, vanished into the electron sea. It goes without saying that this incident hastened the decay of my academic life. I thought I would complain, but getting involved with this unknown upstairs resident seemed like a pain, so I had left the matter unresolved.

"That was your doing?"

"So your library of obscenities got a little wet—that's not such a big loss, is it?" Ozu said impudently.

"Just get out already. I have shit to do."

"That I shall. We're doing a Blackout Hot Pot party at Master Higuchi's tonight."

Kicking Ozu and his smirk into the hallway, I finally achieved some calm.

• • •

And the night deepened.

Listening to the coffee burble, I stared at the castella Ozu had brought me. He had said that I should taste loneliness at the far reaches of solitude, but I had no intention of rolling over. I had resolved to quietly clear my mind and eat the cake with perfect calm.

The sweet, familiar smell seemed to send me back to my childhood.

As I chowed down, I felt that it was actually quite depressing to eat this much castella on one's own—wrong as a human being—and it would be better to enjoy it more gracefully with someone pleasant, sipping some tea or something, someone like—I was surprised to find myself thinking—Akashi; absolutely not Ozu, but Akashi. The retreat from the Kamo River Delta, that god's meddling, the mysterious pronouncement from the fortune-teller, the events at the yakiniku place—all those unexpected occurrences together made my heart weak, and my reason crumbled like a sugar cube.

I wasn't even in the grips of a fiery crush; to seek the companionship of a total stranger out of momentary loneliness was against my principles. Wasn't it precisely my scorning the uncouth students who ravenously pursued others when they could no longer endure their solitude that had distinguished—in a way that was infinitely close to disgracing—me as the Obstructor of Romance? Hadn't I indulged in a futile conflict and claimed a victory that was infinitely close to defeat?

Then consider your chance mine. I'll be happy in your place.

That's what Ozu had said at the yakiniku restaurant.

While it wasn't as if I believed the stuff that shady god had said, and I didn't think Akashi was such a poor judge of people that she would be tricked by the likes of a perverted picky eater of a yokai like Ozu, I did feel like she was the kind of person who was broad-minded enough to be amused by even a yokai if she had some connection to him. He was in the engineering department, like her. And they had both quit the same club. If, while I was twiddling my thumbs, the unthinkably strange outcome of Ozu and Akashi becoming intimate occurred, that would be very grave indeed. This wasn't merely an issue of my personal loneliness. Akashi's future was at stake.

Overhead, a big moth that had slipped into my room at some point was fluttering noisily around the new fluorescent light.

Soon I heard a woman and a man talking.

When I strained my ears to listen, the voices seemed to be coming from the room next door. It didn't sound unlike sweet nothings. Stifled laughter. I went out into the hall to check, but there was no light coming from the little window above the door. Yet when I pressed my ear to the wall, syrupy whispers.

The person next door was a study-abroad kid from China. These two had come from the continent across the sea and met in this foreign land; surely they struggled with some aspects of living in a different country. It's only human nature for two people in that situation to grow close, so it's not my place to talk. I know that. I know that, and yet I couldn't overlook it. In a room with the lights dimmed, precious murmurs were being exchanged in Chinese, so it wasn't even possible to dispel my melancholy by listening in. I so regretted not taking Mandarin as my second language that I stress-ate more castella.

I will not lose.

I refuse to lose to loneliness.

In order to distract myself, I asserted my determination to no one in particular by chomping into the whole castella, but after biting like a wild animal into its boxy shape from every possible angle, I finally returned to myself. Holding back the juices that threatened to spring from my tear ducts, the emptiness was so profound that I gently set the cake down. I took a good look at it. The mess of mercilessly half-eaten castella didn't even look like castella anymore—it looked just like that ancient Roman building. . . .

"Colosseo."

I said it quietly.

What a roundabout fortune that old lady told.

• • •

I remembered meeting Akashi before quitting the club.

The spring welcome screening was taking place in a lecture hall at the university. As soon as I rolled Momotaro, I slipped out under cover of darkness, and walked to the club room situated in one corner of the campus. No matter how much of a moron Jogasaki was, I was sure he would catch on after a few minutes. It was clear that once that happened, his lackeys would string me up, so I had left the screening to clear my personal articles out of the club room.

The golden light of evening made the campus's fresh green sparkle, and for some reason I recall how the leaves glimmered like candy. I had stayed in this club for two years without really knowing why, but apparently leaving still made me sentimental.

Ozu had arrived ahead of me and was already looking for his stuff and filling his backpack. He was like a yokai rummaging through human bones. I admired him for being so thoroughly spooky and quick to escape.

"You're so fast," I groaned.

"I hate any kind of trouble. I don't want to deal with any loose ends, so I'll just disappear as quickly as possible. Of course, I've already clipped my loose ends . . ."

"Yeah." I packed my personal items into a bag I brought for that purpose, and after looking through the collections of manga and novels I had been keeping there, I decided to leave them all. You could consider it a donation. "You don't have to quit with me, you know."

"I'm shocked you can even say that after what you made me do. What kind of idiot would I be if I stayed alone?" Ozu replied crankily. "Also, unlike you, I'm living a multifaceted student life. I have any number of other places where I belong."

"I've been wondering about that for a while. What else are you up to?"

"I'm a member of a secret society, I have to take care of my master, I was in a religious club . . . and my love life keeps me busy."

"Wait, I thought you didn't have a girlfriend," I said.

"Meh-heh."

"What's that lecherous grin for?"

"Not telling."

As we were searching around the club room, Ozu suddenly said, "Ah, someone's coming." Before I could even say, "Wait!" he had shouldered his backpack and flown out of the room—truly a master of speedy exits. Just as I had grabbed my bag to go after him, Akashi walked in.

"Oh, Akashi." When I stopped to acknowledge her, she took a swig of a bottle of cola and furrowed her eyebrows to glare at me.

"You made another dumb movie, huh?" she said. "I watched part of it."

"They didn't stop it?"

"The audience is into it, so they can't stop it even if they want to. But Aijima and a few of those guys are looking for you. I'm sure they'll be here soon. If you don't want to be obliterated, you should probably run for it."

"Hmm. If the audience is laughing, that seems good."

She shook her head. "This one isn't as good as your others. It makes me question your character."

"Well, whatever. The point was to make it and run, anyhow."

Her eyes rested on the bag I was carrying.

"Are you quitting?"

"Duh."

"Right, I guess after making a film like that . . . With this, your last shred of respectability has been blown away," she said.

I emitted a laugh that was empty, even for me. "That was the idea."

"You're such an idiot."

"Yes, I am."

"You were originally planning on showing a film where Ozu reads *Tale of the Heike*, right? I wanted to see that."

"If you want to watch it, I'll give it to you," I said.

"Really? Make it a promise."

"Okay. Then next time I see you. Still, I'm not sure if it has any merit."

"It's a promise," she insisted.

"I'm leaving my manga, so I hope you'll read it."

For two years, I had engaged in a fruitless battle and fruitlessly polished my character in that space I was leaving. I thought if my final work could rain on Jogasaki's charisma parade, that would be great—although, to be honest, part of me felt it was impossible and had already given up.

When I stopped at the door and turned around, Akashi was sitting down about to read some of the manga I left behind.

"Farewell, then, Akashi. Don't be tricked by the Jogasaki magic."

She looked up with a frown. "Do I look like that much of a dimwit to you?"

Just then I saw Aijima and a bunch of his rather robustly built lackeys rushing toward the club room. I took off without replying to her.

• • •

Hanging my sleepy head after spending the night with reason and loneliness—truly a pair of formidable rivals—grappling in a death match, I headed to school. I spent the whole day fretting about this and that, so I hardly remember anything.

I'm the type of man who, after analyzing in such detail that there is nothing left to analyze, calmly takes the safest measure. I analyze even at the risk of it being too late to take the safest option. I analyzed multiple patterns of how Akashi's life, Ozu's life, and my life could go, comparing, weighing, and mulling over all the outcomes. I also considered who should be happy and who should not, but I reached a conclusion with surprising speed. I also considered whether I could—after all this time obstructing people on their path to love, destined to be kicked to death by a horse—change my ways. This was a rather more difficult question.

• • •

About the time indigo twilight began to blanket the area, I came home from school. Taking a breather in my room, I mulled my options for the last time.

Finally making up my mind, I proceeded to the room where I was to meet the god.

Although I had been living at Yusuiso for two years, it was my first time going up to the second floor. Many things had been left in the second-floor hallway, and it was even grimier than the first floor. It was as chaotic as a city street, and the farther down you walked, the darker it got—it seemed like it might very well connect up with a back alley in Kiyamachi. I went all the way to the end. The room number was 210. Outside the door were a chair with armrests and an ottoman, a dusty aquarium, a faded Keroyon figurine, a banner from the used book fair, and other items in a jumble. There was no room to step. I felt that the place lacked the formality one would expect of a god's residence. I considered fleeing the messy second floor and returning to the peaceful first floor to quietly live out the rest of my days. These were some idiotic hopes to have, even for me, and I plunged into a pit of self-loathing. There was no name on the door plaque.

At any rate, I decided that if it was a joke, that was fine—I would laugh and get it over with. Thus, I manned up and knocked.

"Fuwahyai!" With a dopey cry, the god popped his head out. "Oh, it's you. So what did you decide?"

He asked so simply, as if he were inquiring about my weekend plans.

"It can't be Ozu. Please pair me with Akashi."

The god smiled. "Very good. Take a seat right there and wait one second."

With that, he slipped back into his room. Some rummaging noises came from inside. I couldn't get myself to sit on the dust-shrouded chair, so I just stood there in the hallway.

After a moment, the god appeared and said, "All right, let's go. Follow me, my good sir."

● ● ●

Where were we going? It couldn't be that we had to go make a sacrifice at Shimogamo Shrine or something, right? Anxiously trembling, I followed him, but he didn't go to Shimogamo Shrine. He passed Shimogamo Saryo, casting its light out into the dusk, and continued striding briskly south. As I was racking my brains, we reached Demachiyanagi Station. Then he followed the river to Imadegawa-dori and stopped to stand at the eastern end of Kamo Ohashi, where he looked at his wristwatch.

"What are we doing?" I asked, but he laid a finger against his lips and said nothing.

The area was submerged in indigo twilight by this time. The Kamo River Delta was occupied by lively college kids. The river was running high from the rain that had lasted until just the other day, and it rushed noisily past; in the lights reflecting here and there, the surface of the water looked like a sheet of metallic paper being waved like a stage prop. Imadegawa-dori was busy, and the bridge was packed with brilliant head- and taillights. The orange lights affixed at intervals along the bridge's thick railing shone with a hazy, mystical air in the darkness. Kamo Ohashi felt larger than usual on this night.

As I was standing there absentmindedly, the god clapped me on the back.

"All right. Time to cross the bridge."

"Why?"

"My good sir. Akashi will come from the opposite direction. Say something to her—invite her to a café or something. I chose this romantic setting precisely for that purpose."

"I can't. I refuse."

"Don't be a brat. Go on, get out there and do it."

"Isn't this a bit strange? You said you're going to Izumo this autumn to do the matchmaking, right? We're not a pair yet, so anything I did now would be pointless."

"So you're the type to cut up some weird logic, eh? Even if I make the match, you still need to set up your move. Now go."

With a shove from the god, I was on my way across the bridge to the west side. How irritating. *There should be a limit to how much you're allowed to tease someone*, I was thinking, when a voice from behind me shouted, "*Heyyy!* There's going to be a strange fellow walking ahead of Akashi, but don't pay him any mind!"

I continued walking and had passed by a few people when I saw a face I recognized coming toward me. An ominous set of features appeared in the glow of the railing's lamplight. A yokai you couldn't forget even if you wanted to, that Nurarihyon. *Why is he here?* When I narrowed my eyes at him in a glare, Ozu smiled at me. Then with a bizarre little hop, he socked me in the stomach. "Urgh!" With no regard for me groaning in pain, he continued toward the east end of the bridge.

Where I was stopped, holding my stomach, was about the middle of the bridge, and the Kamo River was flowing by directly below. Glancing south, farther down the dark river's course, I saw the distant Shijo neighborhood's lights gleaming like jewels.

That was when Akashi came along.

I was about to call out to her, perfectly unruffled, when I suddenly became flustered.

I was her trustworthy older friend and had no trouble talking to her on any normal day. But the moment I decided to clear my name of the title Obstructor of Romance and cool-headedly move forward with this matchmaking scheme, my body tensed up as stiff as if I'd been reinforced with an iron rod, and my mouth was as parched as the surface of Mars. My eyes refused to focus, and my vision swirled; I forgot how to breathe, inhaling as weakly as someone at death's door. That is, I looked shadier than I ever had in my entire life, and if it meant I could evade Akashi's suspicious gaze, I felt I could hurl myself into the roaring current of the Kamo River and escape Kyoto with no regrets.

"Evening," Akashi said with a guarded look. "Were you able to make your getaway the other day?"

"Yes, thanks to you."

"Are you on a walk?"

"Uh-huh."

With that, my brain of many wrinkles ceased all operations. Silence is golden.

"'Kay then," she said as she moved to pass by me.

It was unavoidable. Having devoted myself all this time to obstructing people on their path to love, I had never learned the first thing about how to race down such a path. And I was so damned proud, my path to love was practically buried in a thicket of self-esteem, so how was I supposed to race down it without any shame? I at least needed some practice. *This is far enough for today. I've done all I could. Nice work, buddy, really.*

Just as Akashi and I were about to go our separate ways, we suddenly noticed a creepy monster perched forbiddingly on the railing next to us, and we leapt out of the way. Standing on the railing was Ozu. I had no idea what he was thinking, but the lamplight illuminated his face from below, giving him a spooky air. We stood next to each other looking up at him.

"What are you doing up there?" I asked, and he made a face as if he were ready to bite my head off.

"You're not thinking, 'This is far enough for today,' are you? I have no words for how disgusted I am with you. Quit disobeying the god and sprint down your path to love!"

Suddenly I remembered what was going on and glanced toward the east end of the bridge. Kamotaketsunumi no Kami was standing there with his arms crossed observing our exchange with great interest.

"So you were the mastermind behind this whole scheme, Ozu?" Everything finally made sense. "I see. You got me, you asshole."

"What? What's going on?" Akashi whispered.

"Didn't you promise the god of Shimogamo Shrine?" said Ozu. "This is your chance—now, seize it! Look, can't you see? Akashi is standing right there."

"Yeah, thanks a lot."

"If you don't take the plunge right now, I'm jumping."

Ozu blurted some nonsense and turned his back to us. He spread his arms wide as if he was going to jump at any moment.

"Hold on. What does my path to love have to do with you jumping off the railing?" I asked.

"I'm not sure either," replied Ozu.

"Ozu, the river's running high. It's dangerous. You could drown." Akashi began reasoning with him as well.

As we were having this meaningless exchange, a shriek shot up from the Kamo River Delta, north of the bridge. The partying kids had begun running around in a panic.

"What's that?" Ozu said, bending over slightly with a puzzled look on his face. Without thinking, I pressed up against the railing to look: something like a black fog eerily spread out from Aoi Park to the Kamo River Delta, swiftly coating the delta's bank below. And within that black fog was a muddle of young people. They were half mad, flailing their arms and ripping out their hair. The black fog glided along the river and seemed to be heading straight for us.

The clamoring on the Kamo River Delta grew even louder.

Black fog poured continuously from out of the pine grove. This was nothing to sniff at. With a trembling, fluttering, rustling, and flapping, the wriggling black fog was spreading out like a carpet below us when it began to rise up from the river's surface before suddenly exploding over the railing and rushing onto Kamo Ohashi.

"Gyoaehhhh!" Akashi emitted a shriek straight out of a manga.

It was a swarm of moths.

• • •

A news item appeared in the next day's *Kyoto Shimbun*, but no one knew exactly why the extraordinary number of moths had appeared. Retracing their flight path, they seemed to have come from Tadasu no Mori—that is, Shimogamo Shrine—but this wasn't clear. Even if every moth that lived in Tadasu no Mori had decided to migrate all at once, there wasn't a good reason for it. Apart from the official explanation, there were rumors that the moths had come, not from Shimogamo Shrine, but the neighborhood next to it, Shimogamo Izumikawacho; but that only made the story even stranger. Apparently, it was the area right around my apartment that had been flooded with moths and thrown into an uproar.

When I returned to my room that night, there were dead moths strewn throughout the hallway. My door was half open, as I had forgotten to lock it, so there were moth corpses all over my room, too. I gave them a respectful burial.

• • •

Pushing my way through the swarm of moths as they flapped into my face, sprinkling their scales around, sometimes trying to force their way into my mouth, I moved to Akashi and protected her like a total gentleman. I used to be a city slicker, so I had been above living alongside insects, but after residing in my lodgings for two years, I'd had numerous opportunities to become familiar with all manner of arthropods, so bugs didn't bother me anymore.

That huge swarm of moths, though, was beyond the realm of common sense. The awful sound of their beating wings cut us off from the outside world; it was less like moths and more like little winged yokai passing over the bridge. I couldn't see much of anything. Through the slits of my barely open eyes, I could make out a riot of moths fluttering around the orangey glow of the lamps on the railing and Akashi's shiny black hair.

Once the swarm had finally gone, a few stragglers had been left fluttering here and there. Akashi stood up with a deathly pale face and screamed, "Are there any on me?! Are there any on me?!" as she frantically brushed off every part of her body before running toward the western end of the bridge at a tremendous speed to flee the moths twitching on the ground. It was in front of a café casting a soft glow into the twilight that she eventually crumpled.

The swarm of moths became a black carpet again and went down the river to Shijo.

I noticed the yukata-clad god was standing next to me looking over the railing. His eggplant-shaped face was all scrunched up, and it was hard to tell whether he was laughing or crying.

"I think Ozu really did fall in," he said.

• • •

The god and I ran down to the bank from the western end of the bridge. Before our eyes, from left to right, roared the Kamo River. Since the river was running high, areas that were usually underbrush were submerged, so it was wider than usual.

We entered the water from there and approached the area beneath the bridge. Something wriggled in the shadows by the foot of the bridge. Ozu was clinging to it like a piece of litter, apparently unable to move. The water wasn't deep, but the current was fast, and despite his divinity, the god got his feet swept out from under him and was nearly washed away.

It took a lot of effort, but we finally reached the Ozu-like thing.

"You idiot!" I screamed, getting doused in the spray of the river, and Ozu wheezed with half-crying laughter.

"Look what I found." He proudly thrust out his hand, which was clenched around a spongy little bear plushie. "It was floating here." He was groaning in pain. "Foolish me, it's not free to take all that grist to the mill."

"Okay, just shut up," said the god.

"Yes, Master. For some reason my right leg is in terrible pain," Ozu confessed.

"You're Ozu's master?" I asked.

"That I am." He smiled broadly.

With the help of the god who was also Ozu's master, I lifted Ozu up. "Ow, ow, ow—be more gentle, please!" Ozu made extravagant demands as we carried him to dry land. Akashi had come down to the riverbed after us. The shock of being buffeted by the swarm of moths had left her pale, but she had called an ambulance without missing a beat. After calling the emergency number, she sat on a bench with her hands over her pale cheeks. We rolled Ozu like a log and shivered as our clothes dried.

"It hurts, it hurts. It really hurts. Do something!" he moaned. "Nnngh!"

"Quit your whining. It's your fault for climbing up on the railing," I said. "The ambulance will be here soon, so just deal till then."

"You're quite a promising disciple, Ozu," said Ozu's master.

"Thank you, Master."

"But doing anything for your friends doesn't mean breaking bones. You're an incorrigible idiot."

Ozu cried softly.

It took about five minutes for the ambulance to arrive at the end of Kamo Ohashi.

Ozu's master ran up the bank and came down with the medical techs. The techs wrapped Ozu in a blanket and loaded him onto a stretcher with skills pros could be proud of. It would have been hilarious if they had just thrown him into the river like that, but emergency workers are admirable individuals who sympathize with all injured people equally. Ozu was packed into the ambulance with a gravity disproportionate to his nasty ways.

"I'll go with Ozu," said his master, and he leisurely boarded the ambulance.

A moment later, it had driven away.

• • •

The only ones left were Akashi on the bench, holding her pale face, and me, sopping wet. I had the bear plushie Ozu had been clenching as he clung to the foot of the bridge. When I squeezed it, it made a helpless face as water dribbled out. *I've never seen a bear dripping with so much ennui,* I thought.

"Are you okay?" I asked Akashi.

"I really can't handle moths," she groaned, still seated on the bench.

"Why don't we get some coffee to calm down?" I suggested.

It's not as if I was thinking anything so rude as stooping to using her weakness against moths to my advantage. Seeing her so pale, I was offering out of concern.

I walked to the nearest vending machine and bought two hot coffees, which we drank together. She gradually relaxed. Kneading the little bear plushie over and over, she cocked her head a number of times.

"This is a mochiguma," she said.

"A mochiguma?"

She said she had a few of the same type that she loved. Their squishiness was of such a rare quality that she named them "mochi bears" and collected five to create the Fluffy Mochigu-men Rangers. Thus, poking their squishy bottoms became her daily healing practice, but the previous year she had attached one to her backpack and lost it at the Shimogamo Shrine used book fair. Ever since then, she had no way of knowing where the poor bear had gone.

"So this is the one?" I asked.

"It's awfully strange. What's a mochiguma doing here?"

"It must have floated down the river." That was my guess. "It's just something Ozu found, so it's fine for you to take it."

For a moment, she looked doubtful, but then her expression changed; her face seemed to say, *At any rate, I'm glad the Mochigumen are back together*, and she straightened up. It looked like she had recovered from the shock of being attacked by the swarm of moths.

"Today Ozu invited me out to that café. Then he told me to cross Kamo Ohashi . . . I wonder what that was about."

"Hmm, I dunno."

"But he's such a goofy guy. Once I saw him run diagonally across the Hyakumanben intersection waving a big Ferrari flag."

"Don't pay attention to him. You might catch the stupid."

She nodded, hmm-ing to herself. "It's too late for you, huh? As far as I can tell, you've caught it pretty bad."

I sat there in disappointment until—"Oh, I just remembered."

"What?" she asked.

"I promised I would give you that thing." I mentioned the film I had made just before exiling myself from our club. That film of Ozu reading *Tale of the Heike* was impenetrable even for me.

"Oh, that!" she said happily.

We agreed to meet and talk the next week, when I would give her the aforementioned film. We chose Madoi, the restaurant on the southwest corner of the Hyakumanben intersection, for a place to talk, and had dinner together merely because it happened to be convenient.

Opinions were split about the film's production quality, and I myself was more on the negative side, but Akashi, at least, was satisfied.

• • •

How my relationship with Akashi developed after that is a deviation from the point of this manuscript. Therefore, I shall refrain from writing the charming, bashfully giddy details. You probably don't want to pour your time down the drain reading such detestable drivel, anyhow.

There's nothing so worthless to speak of as a love mature.

• • •

It's not fair for you to assume that I'd naively approve of my past just because there have been some new developments in my student life lately. I'm not the kind of man who would so readily affirm his past mistakes. Certainly I considered giving myself a big, loving embrace, but regardless of how it would go with a black-haired maiden of a tender age, who would have any interest in hugging a mess of a twenty-something guy? Driven by that inescapable anger, I firmly refused to give my past self salvation.

I can't shake the feeling that I never should have signed up for the Ablutions film club at the foot of that fateful clock tower. I think about what could have happened if I had chosen something else. If I had answered that bizarre ad for a disciple, or chosen the Mellow softball club, or if I had joined that underground organization Lucky Cat Chinese Food, I would have had a very different couple of years. At least, it's clear that I wouldn't be as warped as I am now. I might have attained that elusive treasure, a rose-colored campus life. No matter how I try to avert my eyes, I can't deny the fact that the past two years have been utterly wasted on a pile of mistakes.

More than anything, the stain of having met Ozu is sure to linger for the rest of my days.

• • •

Ozu stayed in the hospital next to the school for a little while.

I have to say, it felt pretty great to see him strapped into a crisp white bed. He always had such a horrible complexion that he looked like a patient with an untreatable illness, but it was just a broken bone. I suppose it's lucky that he got away with just a broken bone. He grumbled that he wasn't able perpetrate any of the misdeeds he preferred over three square meals a day, but I just thought, *That's what you get.* When his grumbles got to be too much, I crammed the castella I brought him into his mouth to shut him up. Still, though, he showed what could only be called an incredible eccentricity in coming up with this idiotic plan, roping in his master, and even falling off Kamo Ohashi for no reason and breaking his leg, all just to get Akashi and me together. His way of enjoying life made absolutely no sense to me. Nor did it need to.

"So now you've learned your lesson and can quit meddling

in other people's business, right?" I said with my mouth full of castella, but Ozu shook his head.

"No thank you. I mean, what else do I have to do?"

This guy is rotten straight to the core.

"What was so fun about toying with me in my innocence?" I grilled him.

• • •

Ozu put on his usual yokai grin and laughed his head off.

"It's my love language."

"Gross—you can spare me," I replied.

TWO

Tatami and the Masochistic Proxy-Proxy War

Let's just say I accomplished absolutely nothing during the two years leading up to the spring of my junior year in college. Every move I made in my quest to become an able participant in society (to associate wholesomely with members of the opposite sex, to devote myself to my studies, to temper my flesh) somehow missed its mark, and I ended up making all sorts of moves, as if on purpose, that need not have been made at all (to isolate myself from the opposite sex, to abandon my studies, to allow my flesh to deteriorate). How did that happen?

We must ask the person responsible. And who is responsible?

It's not as if I was born this way.

Fresh from the womb I was innocence incarnate, every bit as precious as the Shining Prince Genji must have been in his infancy. My smile, without a hint of malice, is said to have filled the mountains and valleys of my birthplace with the radiance of love. And now what has become of me? Whenever I look in the mirror I am swept up in a storm of anger. *How the hell did you end up like this? You've come so far, and this is all you amount to?*

"You're still young," some would say. "It's never too late to change."

Are you fucking kidding me?

They say that the soul of a child at three remains the same even when the man reaches a hundred. So what good can it do for a splendid young man of twenty-one, nearly a quarter century old, to put a lot of sloppy effort into transforming his character? The most he can do in attempting to force the stiffened tower of his personality to bend is to snap it right in half.

I must shoulder the burden of my current self for the rest of my life. I mustn't avert my eyes from that reality.

I can't look away, but it's just so hard to watch.

• • •

The main character in this memoir is me. The second leading role is Master Higuchi. Sandwiched between these two noble men is a supporting character with a stunted soul: Ozu.

First, regarding myself, apart from that fact that I was a proud third-year student, there is not much to say. But for your convenience, readers, I'll explain what kind of man I am.

Say you're in Kyoto, strolling west from the Kawaramachi Sanjo district through an arcade. It's a spring weekend, so there are many people out and about. As you're walking along, gazing at the souvenir shops, the Lipton teahouse, and so on, a black-haired maiden coming this way catches your eye. It's almost as if the space around her—and only her—sparkles. Her beautiful, melancholy eyes look up at the man walking next to her. He must be a bit over twenty; clear eyes; neat, dark eyebrows; a pleasant smile gracing his cheeks. No matter what direction or how acrobatic an angle you observe him from, his visage is flawless and intelligent—it would never be taken as the face of an idiot. He's about five foot eleven with a sturdy frame, but he certainly doesn't give off any blatant wild-animal energy. Though he appears to be in a relaxed mood as he walks, there is power in his gait. In everything he does, there is dignity and a comfortable amount of tension. This is a man completely in control of himself.

I'll come out and say that I'd like you to think of that man as me.

This is merely for your convenience, as I would never dream of embellishing reality, nor do I want to be squealed about by high school girls, nor do I want to be class representative and receive my diploma directly from the hand of the president of the school—I have no such disingenuous aspirations. So readers, I kindly ask that you take this aptly depicted man, burn that image into your brain as me, and maintain it throughout.

True, there is no black-haired maiden next to me. There may be other discrepancies as well. But those are trivial matters. It's the heart that counts.

• • •

Next, I'll write about Master Higuchi.

I lived in room 110 of the Kowloon-like apartment building Shimogamo Yusuiso in Shimogamo Izumikawacho, while his residence was directly above, in room 210.

For the two years until our abrupt parting at the end of May of my third year, I was his disciple. As a result of ignoring my studies in favor of this training, I'm sure I learned only things that are useless, cultivated only those qualities a person should not cultivate, and failed to cultivate those that should have been cultivated until they were no longer visible at all.

Rumor had it that Master Higuchi was in his eighth year. Just as a long-lived animal acquires a mystical air, so too does a student who spends many years at university.

He always had a carefree grin on his eggplant-shaped face, and there was something noble about him you couldn't quite put your finger on. But his chin was forever scruffy. He always wore a navy yukata, and in winter, he threw an old jacket over it. He'd show up to a chic café looking like that and leisurely sip a cappuccino. He didn't even own a fan, but he knew probably hundreds of places one could cool off for free on hot summer days. His hair was nothing short of improbable in its unruliness and always looked like a typhoon had made landfall only on his head. He often puffed cigars. Sometimes he seemed to remember he was a student and show up to classes, but no matter how many credits he had acquired at this point, it was surely too late. Despite not knowing a word of Mandarin, he got along well with the Chinese study-abroad kids who lived in our building. Once I saw one of the girls giving him a haircut. He had started reading the copy of Jules Verne's *Twenty Thousand Leagues Under the Sea* that I lent him, but he was taking his time, as it had been almost a year and he hadn't returned it. The globe he had taken from me was on display in his room, and he had stuck cute little pins in it. I later learned that they charted the position of the submarine, *Nautilus*.

He didn't take any sort of action but boldly specialized in

simply living his life. That was either a gentlemanly manner maintained by formidable self-control or the height of idiocy.

• • •

Lastly, I'll write about Ozu.

He was in the same year as me. Despite being registered in the Department of Electrical and Electronic Engineering, he hated electricity, electronics, and engineering. At the end of freshman year he had received so few credits, and with such low grades, that it made you wonder whether there was any point to him being there, but Ozu himself didn't give a damn.

Because he hated vegetables and ate only instant foods, his face was such a creepy color it looked like he'd been living on the far side of the moon. Eight out of ten people who met him walking down the street at night would take him for a yokai goblin. The other two would be shapeshifted yokai themselves. Ozu kicked those who were down and buttered up anyone stronger than him. He was selfish and arrogant, lazy and contrary. He never studied, had not a crumb of pride, and fueled himself on other people's misfortunes. There was not a single praiseworthy bone in his body. If only I had never met him, my soul would surely be less tainted.

On that note, we must say that becoming a disciple of Master Higuchi in the spring of my freshman year was my first big mistake.

• • •

At the time, I was a fresh-as-a-daisy-man. I remember how exhilarating the vibrant green of the cherry tree leaves was after all the flower petals had fallen.

Any new student walking through campus gets club flyers thrust upon them, and I was weighed down with so many that my capacity for processing information had been far overwhelmed. There were all sorts of flyers, but the four that caught my eye were as follows: the Ablutions film club, a bizarre "Disciples Wanted" notice, the Mellow softball club, and the underground organization Lucky Cat Chinese Food. They all seemed pretty shady, but each one represented a doorway into a new college-student life, and my curiosity was piqued. The fact that I thought a fun future would be waiting on the other side, no matter which door I chose, just goes to show what an incorrigible idiot I was.

After my classes were over I headed to the clock tower. All kinds of clubs were meeting there to take new students to orientations.

The area around the clock was bustling with freshmen, cheeks flushed with hope, and welcoming committee members ready to prey on them. It seemed to me that here there were innumerable entryways leading to that elusive prize—a rose-colored campus life—and I walked among them half in a daze.

First, I found several students waiting with a sign for the film club, Ablutions. They were holding a screening to welcome new students and offered to show me the way. For whatever reason, I couldn't make up my mind to approach them, and I ended up going around to the other side of the clock tower. As I walked, I read one of the flyers I had taken more closely.

First, in a bigger font than the rest, it said, "Disciples Wanted."

> With his all-seeing eyes, he can pick the maiden on
> his mind out of the crowd; with his all-hearing ears,
> he doesn't miss even the sound of cherry blossoms
> fluttering into the canal. Appearing all over town
> and disappearing without a trace, he comes and
> goes freely between the earth and skies. Surely there
> is no one in this land of the gods unfamiliar with
> his name, no one who doesn't fear him, no one
> who would defy him. Yes, he is Seitaro Higuchi.
> Come, youth of mystical potential. Meet on April
> 30 beneath the clock tower. No phone number
> available.

There are many suspicious flyers in the world, but surely none as suspicious as this. Nevertheless, I thought that maybe it wouldn't be a bad idea to jump headfirst into this mysterious world, put in the effort, and make some moves toward the glorious future I deserved. There's nothing wrong with a desire for self-improvement, but if you err in choosing your direction, you're in trouble.

As I was poring over the flyer, a voice called out to me: "My good sir." I turned around to see a suspicious character standing behind me. Though this was a college campus, he wore a navy yukata and was puffing on a cigar, and his chin was flecked with scruff. It wasn't clear whether he was a student or not. On one hand, he was putting his innate shadiness on full display, but there was also something noble about him, and his smiling face was actually charming.

This was Master Higuchi.

"Did you read the flyer? I'm recruiting disciples."

"Disciples for what?"

"Well, we don't have to jump right into specifics, do we? This is your senior disciple." Standing next to Master Higuchi was a creepy fellow with a terribly inauspicious-looking face. At first I thought he was a messenger from hell only I, with my heightened sensitivities, could see.

"My name's Ozu. Nice to meet you," he said.

"He is your senior, but only by about fifteen minutes," Higuchi quipped with a dry laugh.

After that we were taken to a drinking establishment at the Hyakumanben intersection, and it was the one and only time our master ever treated me to anything. I wasn't used to drinking alcohol, so I loosened up considerably, and when I learned that Master Higuchi lived in the same building as me, we really hit it off. From there we tumbled into Master Higuchi's four-and-a-half-mat tatami room, and for the rest of the night, Ozu, our master, and I engaged in heated, meaningless debate.

Ozu, who at first was about as talkative as a god of death standing at your bedside, began giving an impassioned lecture about breasts. A deep debate about whether the breasts we see actually exist or not ensued, and after quantum mechanics entered the discussion, Master Higuchi made the profound observation that "it doesn't matter whether they exist or not—it's whether you believe in them or not," which was about the time I lost consciousness.

This is how I became Master Higuchi's disciple and how I met Ozu.

What sort of a disciple was I, you ask? It goes without saying that even after two years that never became clear.

. . .

If you think that associating with such a tough customer as Master Higuchi requires patience, humility, manners—some sort of high-level finessing like that—you're fantastically mistaken. You can face him ostentatiously equipped with such finery, but the interactions will be lamentably devoid of benefits for either side. In order to associate with Master Higuchi, the one thing you cannot do without is "tribute"—that is, food and luxury items.

In recent years, the only ones visiting the master were me and Ozu, Akashi, and a dental hygienist named Hanuki, but by one analysis, he was getting 90 percent of his dietary needs met via the tribute we brought him. For the other 10 percent, he must have been subsisting on mountain mist.

If we all cut ties with him, what would he do? "If he ran out of food, he would take some sort of action" is amateur thinking. Even if his food ran out, he simply waited with confidence; that attitude was the invincible state he attained at the end of his strenuous training. If running out of food was enough to upset him, he would have been upset long ago by his poor finances and dearth of college credits. Our master wouldn't be troubled by such trifling matters. If it came down to running around to procure food for himself, he'd surely rather starve to death— making us think this was one of the techniques at which he excelled.

I actually had the deluded thought that even if we didn't deliver him food, he wouldn't get hungry. He seemed to have enough mystical aptitude to limitlessly delay his starvation to the point that he would forget to die. There aren't many students who have attained this state.

I can't really imagine anything Master Higuchi would be afraid of. But there was just one time he uttered the word "scared."

The master not only failed to return the book I lent him, he failed to return his library books. When I said, "These are half a year overdue," he replied, "I know. That's why I'm scared of the Library Police."

"There are Library Police?" I asked Ozu.

"There are," he said with a frightened look on his face. "It's an organization that will resort to all manner of inhumane methods in order to force the return of overdue books."

"You liar," I said.

"You got me."

• • •

Kyoto, Sakyo Ward, the approach to Yoshida Shrine. A secret meeting at midnight . . .

Yoshida Shrine is known as a shrine so responsive to prayer that if you pray to pass your classes you will absolutely fail. Every year, scores of high school and college students pray for academic success and instead experience the misery of repeating a year or having to retake their entrance tests; surely their bitter tears would fill half of Lake Biwa. I had always kept a respectful distance from Yoshida Shrine, but even with that precaution, credits eluded me like sand slipping through my fingers. So yes, Yoshida Shrine's powers are fearsome.

In those days of meager credits, I had no interest in setting foot inside the grounds of Yoshida Shrine. But various circumstances had compounded, and I was stuck attending a secret midnight meeting on the path leading to them.

It was May, two years since I had started college.

During the day it was hot, but the night air was cool. The university's clock tower shone solitary in the darkness; there was almost no one along dimly lit Konoe-dori. About the only people passing by were nocturnal students reminiscent of deep-sea creatures.

If this were a sweet, late-night rendezvous with an innocent black-haired maiden, I wouldn't have been averse to waiting all alone on the approach to Yoshida Shrine. I would have enjoyed the profoundly charming self-conscious giddiness that came with it. But the one showing up on this night was Ozu—a scheming yokai with a filthy Y chromosome. I considered just breaking the promise and going home, but then there would be no way I could face Master Higuchi. Thus cornered, I waited. Ozu had said he would come in a car he borrowed from Aijima, an upperclassman from a club he was in. I killed time by imagining him getting turned into wisps of shredded flesh in a self-contained car accident that inconvenienced no one.

Eventually a little bug of a car came down Higashi-Ichijo-dori and parked next to the university's gate. A dark figure got out and walked toward me. Unfortunately, it was Ozu.

"Good evening to you. Did you wait long?" he said cheerily.

The reason his expression was extra intense, his face like he had just come around the corner from the first block of hell, had to be that he was just so excited for the night's plan. This was a man who fueled himself on the misfortunes of others. Bear in mind that this shameless, vile operation came straight from his underbelly; none of it was my idea. I'm the exact opposite of him. I'm a saint. I'm a man of virtue. I participated against my will for the sake of our master.

We got into the car and entered the maze of a residential area that spread out to the south. Ozu was in a buoyant mood as he drove.

"Arrrgh, Akashi not agreeing to the plan really puts a wrench in things. Her compassion comes out in the most unexpected situations," he said.

"No sane person would want to assist in this endeavor. I don't want to, either."

"Oh, come on. I know you've actually been looking forward to it."

"Who would look forward to this? I'm just here on Master Higuchi's orders—and don't you forget it," I snapped back. "You understand this is a crime, right?"

"Is it?" Ozu cocked his head. The cuteness of the motion disturbed me.

"It's a bunch of crimes! Unlawful entry, larceny, abduction . . ." I listed them.

"It only counts as abduction if it's a human, right? We're stealing a love doll."

"Do you have to say it like that? Have some tact, man."

"You say that, but I'm sure you want to see what it's like. I've known you for years, so I know. You don't just want to look, you want to touch, too. Your horndoggery is out of control."

There was no excuse for the obscene face he made with this comment.

"Okay, I'm going home."

When I took my seat belt off and tried to open the door, Ozu said, "Ohhh, come on," in a coaxing voice. "I crossed a line there. Don't be cranky. This is for our master, right?"

• • •

The beginning of it all is already buried in the darkness of history, but Master Higuchi called the battle the Masochistic Proxy-Proxy War. Still, all you can glean from that vague title is that it appears to be some kind of dishonorable competition.

About five years ago, a deep rift occurred between Master Higuchi and one Jogasaki; the dishonorable war pitting impure essence against impure essence was triggered. And it was continuing even now in this very neighborhood.

From time to time Master Higuchi suddenly remembered to perpetrate some sort of harassment, and Jogasaki would retaliate; this was the cycle that repeated over and over. The warriors who became Master Higuchi's disciples in turn were all ensnared in this war, and the utter fruitlessness of it rode roughshod over their human dignity. And I was no exception. The only one who was perky as a fish in water was Ozu.

Jogasaki had been the head of a film club, and despite being enrolled as a PhD student, he boasted quite an influence behind the scenes. Unfortunately for him, Ozu was also a member. The previous fall, Ozu had schemed for all he was worth and ousted

Jogasaki. Ozu is rotten to the core, so of course he played dirty. He incited Aijima to mount a coup d'état. Jogasaki still blamed Aijima as the ringleader behind his downfall, having no idea that it was actually Ozu pulling the strings.

Perhaps not knowing what to do with all his vitality after losing his position in the club, Jogasaki began harassing Master Higuchi again. After some mild skirmishes, a tragedy occurred at the end of April: Master Higuchi's beloved navy yukata was dyed pink. Master Higuchi ordered Ozu to mastermind a retaliation. Ozu put his talents for wicked intrigue on display and drew up this indefensibly cruel plan.

We would kidnap Kaori.

• • •

Jogasaki lived at the foot of Mount Yoshida in Yoshida Shimoojicho. It was a recently renovated two-story apartment building with a bamboo grove next door and some atmosphere. Under cover of night, Ozu and I got out of the car and pressed ourselves against the apartment building's concrete-block wall. I felt like I, too, had become a messenger from hell, and from Jogasaki's point of view, it was true. We had come to abduct—with the cruelest intentions—something he loved, so if we got labeled gods of death, we deserved it.

Ozu looked up along the wall. Jogasaki's room was on the southern end of the second floor. His light was still on.

"Huh? What's he doing? He's still in his room," Ozu said in frustration. "We need him to keep his promise to Akashi."

"She's got blood on her hands, too. We shouldn't have put her up to it."

"Eh, she's a fellow disciple, so it's not like this is so much to ask. Idiocy doesn't discriminate between sexes."

We stood in an alley sandwiched by concrete-block walls. Fidgeting in the darkness the streetlights didn't reach, we gave free rein to the sketchiness that would have led anyone who saw us to report us on the spot.

As we huddled there in the shadows, it seemed as though Ozu's dark essence had melted into the night and seeped into my body. If it had been a black-haired maiden, I'd have been willing to endure some huddling in the dark, but it was Ozu. Why did I have to be cuddling with this sinister-faced guy? Did I make a mistake somewhere along the way? Was I at fault? I wanted at least to be with someone whose spirit was a bit more kindred (or a black-haired maiden).

"Jogasaki being here complicates things. It's quite a wrench in our plan," Ozu said.

"We can't make Akashi an accessory to the crime. Let's call it off for today."

"That won't do. I even borrowed Aijima's car; we can't quit now." Ozu frowned and pressed himself to the wall like a gecko.

"What the hell happened between Master Higuchi and Jogasaki anyway? Why do they prolong this pointless conflict? And why do we have to take part in this stuff?" I asked.

"It's the Masochistic Proxy-Proxy War."

"What's that?"

"Who knows?" Ozu cocked his head. "I sure don't."

"Should we really be wasting our precious youth facilitating someone else's beef if no one even remembers how it started? Don't we have better things to do?"

"This is training in order to become a bigger person. That

said, standing here in the dark with you is obviously pointless, yes."

"That's my line."

"Why are you looking at me like that?"

"Hey, don't hang all over me," I said.

"But I'm *looonely*. And the night breeze is so cold."

"You're always lonely."

"Eek!"

Eventually, imitating senseless lovers' talk to kill time wore thin as well. And somehow I had the feeling we'd had a similar exchange before, which swept me up in an anger that had nowhere to go.

"Hey, didn't we have this conversation before?"

"I think not. We're not that dumb. You're just having déjà vu, that's all."

Ozu suddenly crouched down, and I followed his lead.

"The light went off," he said.

As we held our breath in darkness, a man's footsteps clanked as he came down the stairs. He brought a scooter out of the bicycle parking area. I had seen Jogasaki a few times before; he was a handsome guy who almost certainly had better things to do than pour his energy into the Masochistic Proxy-Proxy War. He was so handsome, and what was I? Basically just the nasty palm sweat.

"He's gorgeous," I groaned.

"You mustn't judge people by appearance. He may have a nice face, but all he thinks about is tits."

"You're one to talk."

"How rude. Tits are just one of the many areas I'm proficient in."

Without noticing us pressed against the wall talking about tits, Jogasaki put his helmet on, mounted his scooter, and drove off to the east.

We slid out from our hiding place and went around to the staircase.

"He won't be back for a while now," snickered Ozu.

"Where did he go?"

"To the Karafuneya Coffee on Shirakawa-dori. Well, he'll drink a barrel of coffee and wait for probably like two hours. Without realizing that Akashi will never show up. The fool."

"We seriously suck."

"Okay, okay, let's get to work."

Ozu went up the stairs. And so we illegally entered Jogasaki's place of residence, but it's not as if I'm an experienced lock-picker. Ozu had gotten ahold of a key through Jogasaki's ex-girlfriend. And not only a key: Ozu had acquired knowledge of even the most personal details of Jogasaki's life. He was so meticulous in his craft that he even had in his possession letters Jogasaki had been writing to a certain woman. Ozu would say grandiose things like "the one who rules the information rules the world," and in reality, he was a regular Enma, king of hell. His register was packed so densely it was like a Heibonsha World Encyclopedia of people's embarrassing secrets. Every time I thought of it, I got impatient to cut ties with this warped guy.

When we opened the door, there was the kitchen, a room about the size of a four and a half tatami mats, but with flooring. A glass door led into the next room. Ozu entered ahead of me and turned on the kitchen light, as if he lived here. He seemed to know the apartment inside and out. When I mentioned this, Ozu nodded.

"I mean, we're in the same club. Even now I sometimes come over to let him vent at me. It's a pain, though. Once he starts complaining, he doesn't stop," he said with a totally complacent face.

"You're a heinous fiend."

"I prefer 'tactician.'"

I didn't want to do anything that would land me in prison, so after entering like a gentleman through the door, I stayed where I was.

"C'mon, this way."

Ozu pressed, but I stood my ground.

"You go find it. I'm staying put. I at least want to have some manners."

"It's a bit late for that, no? There's no point in acting like a gentleman now."

We argued a bit, but eventually Ozu gave up and went into the back room on his own. The sounds of him rummaging around in the darkness suddenly turned into the sound of him knocking something over by accident. "Ee-hee-hee." His joy grated on my ears as he fooled around. "C'mon, Kaori, don't be shy. Leave Jogasaki, and let's get out of here."

When I saw the woman he eventually carried into the kitchen, I was astounded.

"This is Kaori," Ozu introduced her. "But dang, I had no idea she'd be this heavy."

• • •

Surely many people are aware of the heartbreaking object known as a "Dutch wife." Even I am. My basic understanding of Dutch wives was that pitiful men driven by unstoppable urges purchased one against their better judgment and then sobbed tears of regret—i.e., it was incredibly prejudiced.

According to intel Ozu obtained in May, Jogasaki secretly owned one of these Dutch wives. He emphasized that this wasn't just any Dutch wife, but an extremely high-end silicone one that cost tens of thousands of yen. Nowadays they're called "love dolls," he explained.

If, after being ousted from the club he had once lorded over and losing his girlfriend at the same time, Jogasaki hit the rock bottom of despair and, spurred by loneliness, ended up shelling out for a love doll, there was a logic to it even if it seemed highly unlikely. But that wasn't the case. Word was he had had her for at least two years. During that time he was also associating with real women, so in a sense he must be a true love doll fan. It was something I couldn't quite fathom.

"There's meaning in living alongside a doll you care for. Owning a love doll is entirely different from dating a woman. A barbarian like you who only sees them as tools for sexual gratification probably can't understand, but what we're dealing with here is a highly evolved form of love."

This was Ozu talking, so I didn't believe it one bit.

But that night, when Ozu pulled this doll, Kaori, out of the back room, she was so beautiful and delicate that she didn't seem doll-like at all. Her black hair was smoothed nicely down, and her refined blouse even had a proper collar. Her dreamy eyes were looking my way.

"That's the doll?!" I blurted in admiration.

"Shh, not so loud!" Ozu said, laying a finger against his

lips. Then, "Right, this is the one. Careful or you'll fall for her," he quipped with a proud grin.

She must have been awfully heavy; Ozu had a tough time setting her on the floor. The scene that played out before my eyes—this weird, oh-so-loathsome yokai crouched next to a pristine beauty lying on the ground—was like an illustration from some tale of the bizarre from the early Showa era.

"C'mon, we gotta carry this to the car," he said, all business despite his nasty appearance. Then he urged me to pick her up.

She had an adorable face. Her skin was completely human in hue, and when I gently touched it, there was a springy firmness. She had well-kept hair and was immaculately dressed. She looked like a lady of noble birth—except she didn't move at all. It was as if she had been frozen the instant she cast her eyes into the distance.

As I gazed at her, I got turned on—no, I got riled up.

I didn't know Jogasaki personally, but though this was a very closed-off kind of love, I was also forced to admit it was indeed evolved. Take Kaori's elegant expression. It wasn't the face of someone lost in an immoral lifestyle. Her smooth hair and neat clothes indicated the depth of Jogasaki's love. A barbarian like Ozu who only saw her as a tool for sexual gratification probably couldn't understand, but destroying this delicate world Jogasaki and Kaori had built together, even on our master's orders, would be unforgivable, the height of inhumane brutishness. Taking Kaori away would be too cruel for words.

So, despite having diligently walked the fruitless path where not even weeds grow, never defying our master's teachings, I couldn't approve of this heartless endeavor. *O Master, I am incapable of it.*

Ozu was about to eagerly touch Kaori's hands, but I grabbed him by the collar.

"Don't."

"Why?"

"I won't let you take Kaori," I said.

Jogasaki, keep right on walking your path with your head held high. There is no road before you, but there will be one in your wake. I sent him a passionate cheer in my head. And, of course, Kaori, too.

• • •

That night, I dragged Ozu, who protested by shrieking like a little animal, out of there and repaired to Shimogamo Yusuiso.

My base of operations was a room at Shimogamo Yusuiso in Shimogamo Izumikawacho. From what I had heard, it had been standing there since being rebuilt after burning down in the disorder accompanying the last days of the Tokugawa shogunate. If there hadn't been light seeping through the windows, the building would have been taken for abandoned. I thought I must have wandered into the walled city of Kowloon when I first visited the place on the university co-op's introduction. The three-story wooden structure caused all those who saw it anxiety; it seemed ready to collapse at any moment. Its dilapidation was practically Important Cultural Property level. Certainly no one would miss it if it burned down. In fact, there was no doubt in my mind that this would be a load off for its landlady, who lived just to the east.

It was already the dead of night.

Ozu and I climbed the stairs. I lived in 110 on the first floor, but Master Higuchi's room was the far one on the second floor, room 210.

Light spilled out from the little window above the door facing the hallway; apparently he was waiting for us to return from our successful operation. To be honest, it pained my conscience to betray his expectations and abandon the proxy war. I would have to present him with something I knew he liked.

When we opened the door, Master Higuchi and Akashi were seated politely on their knees facing each other. I figured the master was admonishing his disciple, but it turned out that Akashi was the one doing the admonishing. When we entered empty-handed, Akashi looked relieved.

"So you gave up on the plan."

I silently nodded, and Ozu sulked.

"Hey there. Welcome back, fellows," said Master Higuchi, his butt fidgeting on his ankles.

I shoved Ozu aside and explained everything.

Master Higuchi nodded casually, took out a cigar, and emitted a huge cloud of smoke. Akashi also puffed on the cigar he had given her. It appeared that, while we were gone, the two of them had gotten into some kind of argument, which ended with Akashi unquestionably on top.

"Well, that's fine for tonight," said our master.

When Ozu tried to express his discontent, Master Higuchi snapped at him. "Shut up! There's a limit to these things. Getting my yukata dyed pink was one of the rare truly regrettable incidents of recent years. But I must say that ripping apart Jogasaki and Kaori, who have had a good relationship for years, in such a despicable way would be entirely too merciless a retaliation, even if Kaori is a doll."

"Huh? That's not what you said last time we had this conversation."

When Ozu protested, Akashi said, "Ozu, please shut up."

"In any case," continued Master Higuchi, "this goes against the rules of the fight Jogasaki and I have been maintaining. Not only that, it also deviates from our greater purpose of attaining the lightness of not having our feet on the ground and coming and going freely between the earth and skies. I was simply upset about my yukata and let it get my blood up." With that, he expelled a huge cloud of smoke. "Will that do?" he asked Akashi.

"I think so." She nodded.

Thus, the plot to abduct Kaori was aborted. Under everyone else's chilly glares, Ozu hurriedly gathered his things to leave. "I have a club party to go to on the delta tomorrow. So much to do, so much to do," he murmured out of spite, huffy as a piping hot fish burger.

"Sorry, Ozu. I can't make it tomorrow," said Akashi. She was one of the younger members of Ozu's club.

"How come?"

"I have an essay to prep for. I need to find sources."

"Which is more important, school or the club?" Ozu arrogantly lectured. "You should be at the party."

"No," she replied flatly.

Ozu didn't seem to have a comeback. Master Higuchi was smirking.

"You're an interesting one," he said in praise of Akashi.

● ● ●

It was the evening after our aborted attempt at abducting Kaori.

Finally the mugginess of summer had eased and a cool breeze was blowing. As I walked across Sanjo Ohashi, I thought about the various things that had happened in the past two years. There were countless "If only I hadn't . . ." moments, but I'm positive that meeting Master Higuchi at the clock tower was the decisive one. If I hadn't met him, who knows, but I'm pretty sure things would have turned out all right. I could have joined the Ablutions film club, or if not that, then the Mellow softball club; that underground organization Lucky Cat Chinese Food was another option. No matter which I had chosen, it's clear that I would have been a more useful, wholesome person than I am now.

The streetlights sinking into the twilight only spurred those thoughts on, but in any case, I crossed Sanjo Ohashi and entered a retro scrub brush shop on the west side to acquire a Kamenoko Tawashi to present to Master Higuchi.

This is just me repeating what he said, but apparently these scrub brushes were first sold by Nishio Shoten a hundred years ago. They're usually made with palm or hemp fiber. According to Master Higuchi, in the confusion following the Pacific War, a medical student stole Nishio Shoten's method and began selling Kamenoko Tawashi made from a special type of hemp fiber grown in Taiwan. Because the tips of the tough, unimaginably fine fibers form molecular bonds with the dirt constituents via the van der Waals force, these brushes can remove any grime with a light touch, no muscle necessary: the ultimate kitchen weapon. They remove grime so well, corporations fearful that even their soap sales would be scrubbed away put pressure on the brush's creator, and now they aren't sold very widely. Still, those fishy-sounding Kamenoko Tawashi continue to be made in secret.

The filthiness of Master Higuchi's room was insufferable. Especially the filth of the sink, which was enough to send a young lady of gentle birth into a fainting spell after just one look. When I pointed out that in one corner of that sink, a life form hitherto unknown on earth seemed liable to forge a unique line of evolution, Master Higuchi told me that he needed that luxury scrub brush in order to clean it and that I should stop at nothing to get one. If I didn't, I would be expelled.

By all means, please expel me. The words were in my mouth; I just didn't say them.

Thus I found myself at this shop filled with tons of Kamenoko Tawashi, but as I timidly explained the elusive scrub brush I was searching for, a wry smile appeared on the shopkeeper's face. Of course it did. Even I had to laugh.

"Hmm, yeahhh, we don't carry anything like that," the shopkeeper said.

Fleeing that wince, I exited into the crowd on Sanjo-dori.

We had already failed to abduct Kaori. *Maybe it would be better to just expel myself?*

From there I wandered toward Kawaramachi-dori. I passed the famous pachinko parlor where long ago the Shinsengumi attacked masterless samurai conspirators. Why the samurai chose to do their conspiring at a pachinko parlor is a mystery that won't be solved so easily.

I couldn't go back to Shimogamo Yusuiso like this. Even if I couldn't get my hands on one of those elusive scrub brushes, I had to find something to humor Master Higuchi with. *How*

*about a luxury cigar from Cuba? Or maybe I should get some
tasty seafood from Nishiki Market?*

Having fretted and fretted, I walked unsteadily south down
Kawaramachi-dori. Night was drawing near, and the atmosphere grew charged with energy despite my lack of excitement,
which spurred my irritation.

I stopped by the used bookstore Gabi Shobo and thought I
would buy a book. When I went inside and started searching
the shelves, the owner, with a face reminiscent of simmered octopus, didn't even smile as he said, "We're closing—out, out,
out!" and chased me off as if I were a poisonous bug. The fact
that even though we know each other to some extent, he wasn't
the slightest bit flexible, pissed me off; it was very admirable, but
it still pissed me off.

With nowhere to go, I slipped between buildings and walked
to Kiyamachi.

Ozu had said he had a club party tonight. He was probably
surrounded by cute underclassmen, doing just fine; I, however,
failed in my quest to find the weird scrub brush born of Master
Higuchi's fantasies, had been thrown out of the used bookstore
that should have been a place for me to rest, and was walking
alone in a bustling crowd. Isn't that just the height of injustice?

As I stood sulking on the little bridge over the Takase River,
I saw Hanuki's face among the people coming and going in the
neighborhood. I hurriedly pretended to be a pedestrian having
trouble lighting a cigarette and covered my face.

Hanuki was a mystifying dental hygienist who often visited
Master Higuchi's place. Eight or nine times out of ten, if she was
on the prowl in the Kiyamachi area, she was after ethyl alcohol.
Once I ran into her in town, and just like a weakling lassoed and

dragged over the ground by an outlaw on a horse in a Western, I was dragged from Kiyamachi all up and down the Pontocho district, and the next thing I knew, I was sprawled out alone next to the Ebisu River power plant. It was summer, so not a big deal, but if it had been winter, I'd have frozen to death beneath a row of leafless trees. I had absolutely no intention of being dragged into an endless night and kept in a half-alive state with coffee shochu. I ducked my head and avoided Hanuki's gaze.

Though I was relieved when she passed, it wasn't as if I had anywhere to go.

Just as I was getting seriously tempted to expel myself, I met an old woman.

• • •

Among the bars and sex shops crouched a dark house.

Under its eaves, an old woman sat before a wooden table covered with a white cloth—a fortune-teller. A sheet of paper hanging from the table was crammed full of kanji whose meaning I couldn't fathom. Something like a little lantern glowed orange, bringing the woman's face into view. There was something strangely intimidating about her. She was a yokai licking her lips at the souls of the people passing by. *Get a single fortune read and forevermore the shady old woman will haunt you day and night, nothing you try to do will go well, the one you're waiting for won't come, your lost items will never turn up, you'll fail the classes that should have been easy credits, your graduation thesis will spontaneously combust just before you hand it in, you'll fall into Lake Biwa Canal, you'll be solicited on the street by one of those people on Shijo-dori*—I was resolutely imagining all of this terrible luck while staring at her, so eventually she sensed my presence. From the depths of the darkness, she flashed her eyes at me. The unearthly atmosphere she emitted ensnared me. That atmosphere was persuasive. I considered it logically: there was no way someone giving off supernatural vibes this potent for free would tell a fortune that missed the mark.

I've been alive in this world for nearly a quarter century, but I can count on my fingers the number of times I listened so humbly to another person's opinion. Maybe that was how I ended up purposely taking this thorny path there was no need to walk down at all? If I had abandoned my own judgment sooner, my life as a college student would have turned out very differently. I wouldn't have become the disciple of this weird guy, Master Higuchi; I wouldn't have met Ozu with his labyrinthine character; and I probably wouldn't have wasted two years, either. I would have been blessed with good friends and upperclassmen associates, employing my overflowing talents in full to excel in both the literary and military arts, the result of which would have been a beautiful black-haired maiden at my side and, before me, a shining future of pure gold; if things went well, perhaps even that elusive, supreme treasure—a rose-colored, meaningful campus life—would have been within my grasp. For a person of my caliber, such a stroke of luck wouldn't be even a little unusual.

Right.

It's not too late. With all possible haste, seek an objective opinion and escape into one of the other lives you could have!

I stepped forward as if drawn by the old woman's otherworldly aura.

"Well, my boy, what would you like to know?"

She spoke in a mumble as if her mouth was full of cotton, which really made me feel like I was speaking with a wise elder.

"Hmm. Good question."

When I remained lost for words, the old woman smiled. "From the look on your face right now, I gather you're terribly irritated. Dissatisfied. It seems that you aren't making full use of your talents. Your current environment doesn't appear to be a good fit for you."

"Yes, that's right. That's exactly it."

"Let's have a look."

The old woman took my hands and pored over them, nodding to herself.

"Mm. You seem to be extremely hard-working and talented."

I was already impressed by her keen insights. Just as in the proverb "a clever hawk hides its talons," I had modestly kept my good sense and talents hidden so no one would find them, but I did such a good job that I hadn't been able to locate them myself for the past few years; for her to spot them within five minutes of our meeting meant she couldn't be any ordinary fortune-teller.

"It's essential that you not let chance pass you by. What I mean is a good opportunity. Do you understand? But chance is rather hard to seize: sometimes something that doesn't look like a chance at all is one, while other times what you were sure was your chance turns out, in retrospect, to not have been it at all. But you must perceive your chance and act on it. It looks like you'll have a long life, so I'm sure you'll be able to seize one at some point."

Profound words befitting her otherworldly aura.

"I can't wait that long. I want to seize my chance now. Could you explain in a bit more detail?"

When I pressed her, the old woman's wrinkles warped slightly. I wondered if her right cheek was itchy, but apparently this was a smile.

"It's difficult to speak in particulars. Even if I tell you now, your fate might change, and then it won't be your chance anymore. Wouldn't I feel bad about that? Fate can change from second to second, you know."

"But what you said is so vague I have no idea what to do."

When I cocked my head, the old woman said "Hmm-hmm!" with a sniff. "Very well. I'll refrain from talking about the too distant future, but I'll tell you something very near."

I opened my ears as big as Dumbo's.

"*Colosseo*," she whispered suddenly.

"Colosseo? What's that?"

"Colosseo is the sign of your chance. When your chance appears, there colosseo will be," she said.

"You're not telling me to go to Rome, are you?" I asked, but the old woman only grinned.

"When your chance comes, don't miss it. When it comes, you can't go on idly doing the same things you've always done. Be bold, and try seizing your chance by doing something completely different. If you do that, your dissatisfaction will disappear, and you'll be able to walk down a new path—though there may lie a different dissatisfaction. I'm sure you understand."

I didn't understand one bit, but I nodded anyway.

"Even if you miss this chance, you needn't worry. You're a fine person, so I'm sure you'll be able to seize one someday. That I know for sure. There's no rush."

With that, she ended the reading.

"Thank you."

I bobbed my head and paid her fee. When I stood and turned to go, Akashi had appeared at some point and was standing behind me.

"Playing little lost lamb, are you?" she said.

• • •

Akashi had begun visiting Master Higuchi the previous autumn. After Ozu and myself, she was his third disciple. She was a newer member of the club Ozu was in, basically his right-hand girl. Because of that, their ties were hard to cut, and she ended up a disciple of Master Higuchi.

Akashi was a year behind me and belonged to the engineering department. As someone who didn't mince words, she seemed to be given a wide berth by her peers. She had straight black hair cut short, and when something didn't make sense, she would furrow her brow and argue back. Her eyes were rather cold. She wasn't the vulnerable type. Why did she end up getting close to a man like Ozu? Why did she end up visiting Master Higuchi's four-and-a-half-mat tatami room?

The summer of her first year, one of the kids in her club asked her, like a dope, "Akashi, what do you do in your free time on the weekends?"

Akashi replied without even looking at him.

"Why should I tell you?"

No one asked Akashi about her weekend plans after that.

I heard the story after the fact from Ozu, and it goes without saying that I sent her a passionate mental cheer: *Akashi, you keep running right down your own path!*

This girl, tough like a medieval European castle town though she was, had one weakness.

The previous autumn, back when Akashi had first started coming around to Master Higuchi's place, I met her at the entrance to Shimogamo Yusuiso and went up the stairs with her to visit him.

Walking ahead of me, her silhouette as resolute as a wartime censor, Akashi suddenly screamed, "Gyoaehhh!" like you'd see in a manga, bent backwards, and fell. I swooped in to catch her with a precise motion. That is, I didn't manage to get out of the way in time, and she landed on me. With her hair in a mess, she clung to me. I couldn't keep my balance in that posture, and we both fell down the stairs.

A moth overhead feebly fluttered away. Apparently, as she had been climbing the stairs, that huge moth had landed on her face. She was more frightened of moths than anything.

"It was so squishy, it was so squishy."

She said it over and over as she trembled, her face as pale as if she had seen a ghost, and there was something about it impossible to capture with words—the charm of that moment when someone who usually has such a solid outer wall exposes a vulnerable part. Even I, who should have known my place as an elder disciple, nearly fell in love. I remember consoling her like a gentleman as she repeated "It was so squishy," as if delirious: "All right, calm down."

• • •

As we walked, I mentioned that elusive scrub brush, and Akashi made a face. "Master Higuchi always makes such difficult demands," she grumbled.

"He must be upset about the aborted abduction," I said, but Akashi shook her head.

"I don't think so. That plan was out of character for him. When I told him that last night, he thought better of it."

"Huh."

"You gave up on the plan, right? If you hadn't, I would have had no choice but to despise you from the pit of my stomach."

"But you cooperated with Ozu and invited Jogasaki out, didn't you?"

"No, no. I didn't, in the end. Master Higuchi called him," she said.

"Oh?"

"Doing something like that and having dark, nasty feelings is against Master's teachings in the first place."

"It carries some weight when you say it."

She smiled wryly at my comment. Her short, neat black hair swayed pleasantly as she walked. She had the slickest of vibes.

"The abduction failed, I can't find the scrub brush. Maybe I'll finally be expelled?" I said.

"No. It's too soon to give up."

With that, Akashi pulled ahead of me. The brave, confident way she carried herself made me think of Sherlock Holmes. Like a client at his office on Baker Street pressing their palms together in supplication with no other option but to rely on him, I followed her.

"I've always wondered what exactly happened between

Master Higuchi and Jogasaki." She cocked her head as we strolled down an alley that led from Kiyamachi to Kawaramachi.

"Jogasaki is an upperclassman in your club, right? You don't know anything about it?"

"Not a thing."

"All I know is that it's called the Masochistic Proxy-Proxy War," I said.

"I suppose whatever happened wasn't something you could forgive and forget."

We were chatting like that when she stopped in her tracks. We were in front of Gabi Shobo, where I had gone earlier.

The owner wore a cranky frown as he prepared to close up, but when he saw her, he beamed; this old fart with a mug reminiscent of simmered octopus suddenly looked as soft as the old bamboo cutter must have when he found Princess Kaguya. Akashi had become friends with the owner after working at his stall at the used book fair, and it seemed she made a point of stopping by to chat when she was on Kawaramachi-dori. But, wow, his melted marshmallow softness was no joke. Compared with his attitude when he threw me out earlier, the difference was night and day.

While I looked at the *Complete Works of Akinari Ueda* in the window, Akashi was talking to the owner, and the old bamboo cutter nodded as he listened. After a little while, he shook his head apologetically. Then he pointed west of Kawaramachi-dori and told her something.

"Here's no good. Let's try somewhere else," Akashi said; the search for the Kamenoko Tawashi changed course for west of Kawaramachi-dori.

We crossed Kawaramachi-dori going west on Takoyakushidori and entered Shinkyogoku, which was bustling with the evening crowd. Akashi turned into an alley that headed toward Teramachi and strode into a secondhand shop with worn luggage and lamps lined up under its eaves. While I toyed with a tin submarine model in one corner of the shop, she asked for info about the scrub brush and got the name of a gift shop in Nishiki Market.

When I obediently followed her, she went into a dimly lit gift shop on the western end of Nishiki Market and, after talking about this and that with the couple who ran it, learned that the owner of a gift shop on Bukkoji-dori might know something.

The sun was going down as we crossed Shijo-dori, headed south along Bukkoji Temple, and this time turned east. Unlike in the Shijo area, there weren't as many people on the streets here, and it was quiet.

There was a gift shop with its shutter half down. Akashi poked her head inside and called, "Excuse me." She mentioned the gift shop in Nishiki Market, and apparently that worked. I was also invited inside.

All sorts of things were crammed together on the dark room's earthen floor. When the owner, thin as a crane, flipped a switch, an orange light came on.

"Where did you hear about that?" he asked, and I mentioned Master Higuchi and said I wanted to get ahold of the scrub brush if at all possible.

The chiseled features of the lean shopkeeper were thrown into even sharper relief by the orange glow, giving him an intimidating air. His aura alone overpowered me into speechlessness, and after a little while he went into the back room and came back momentarily with a paulownia wood box. I looked inside when he wordlessly removed the lid and saw what at a glance appeared to be a perfectly ordinary Kamenoko Tawashi.

"This is it," the shopkeeper said, handing me the box.

"How much is it?" I asked, and he took a good look at my face.

"Hmm. I suppose I'll take twenty thousand," he said decisively.

No matter how special the palm fibers were, twenty thousand yen was exorbitant. If I were going to spend that much on a scrub brush, I'd rather choose glorious expulsion.

I got through the moment by making the excuse that I didn't have enough on me, and on the way home I thought I might just let Master Higuchi expel me.

"What's your plan? Are you going to buy it?" Akashi asked as we walked down Shijo-dori.

"Would you? I don't care what kind of brush it is, twenty thousand is insane. That's probably the sort of thing they use at Shimogamo Saryo; it's for cleaning at a fine establishment, not a mucky four-and-a-half-mat-tatami-room sink."

"But Master told you to get it, right?"

"I'm finally going to be expelled."

"Really? I doubt he'd cut you off over a scrub brush," she said.

"Nah. He has you now! And Ozu is there. Maybe he's about ready to put someone like me out to pasture."

"Please don't lose hope. I'll talk to him."

"Thanks."

• • •

Since becoming a disciple, I'd navigated many of Master Higuchi's unreasonable demands.

When I think back on them now, I wonder why I wasted my time on such things. All of his challenges were pointless.

There are a lot of universities in Kyoto, so there are also a lot of students. Our master declared that as students living in Kyoto, we should contribute to the city. For a while, Ozu and I would sit on a cold stone on the Philosopher's Path, even in the wind or rain, poring over Kitaro Nishida's *An Inquiry into the Good* and debating all sorts of things without even understanding what he meant by "perception is a kind of impulsive will" and whatnot. We were attempting to be tourism resources for the city. It was the most pointless thing ever. Not only that, but I messed up my stomach. I did my best as long as my mental and physical strength held out, but by chapter 3 of part I, "Will," I had burned out completely. Ozu's face had been focused at first but immediately went slack, and by the time we read, "Originally, organisms perform various movements to preserve life," Ozu murmured, "movements to preserve life . . ." with a lewd grin and got unreasonably excited. He must have been dazzled by shameless fantasies unleashed by his Y chromosome. As a result of Ozu's being forced to read philosophy texts he didn't understand in a place as quiet as the Philosopher's Path, his dark urges seemed about as ready to burst as ripe Kyoho grapes, and *An Inquiry into the Good* transformed into an elaborate collection of dirty jokes. Needless to say, our plan didn't work out. If we had gotten to part IV, "Religion," everything that would have come out of our mouths would have been so blasphemous that we wouldn't have been able to show our faces in public any longer. That our mental strength, endurance, and intelligence weren't up to the task was fortunate for Kitaro Nishida's reputation as well.

Our master was a Ferrari fan, so on the occasion of Ferrari's winning the Formula One championship, I ended up having to run diagonally across the Hyakumanben intersection carrying a huge (probably two tatami mats huge) red flag with their rearing horse logo and nearly got hit by a car. I was going to make Ozu do it, but since it was Ozu who had procured the flag somehow, I was at a severe disadvantage; on top of that, Ozu ran away after egging Master Higuchi on. So yeah, I got stuck having to brandish Ferrari's power for all to see. I got cussed out by drivers, and pedestrians glared at me in contempt; it was a tremendously awful experience.

• • •

Our master desired all sorts of things. He bragged that great men had great big appetites, but it was always Ozu and I who had to do the acquisition.

It wasn't only food, cigarettes, and alcohol that we gifted him. My tribute included a coffee grinder, a folding fan, a Carl Zeiss spotting scope I'd won in a shopping street raffle, and more. The copy of *Twenty Thousand Leagues Under the Sea* he'd been reading for a year was originally something I had purchased at the Shimogamo Shrine used book fair. I had set the book carefully aside because I thought chilly autumn evenings should properly be spent staying up late reading a classic adventure novel, but before I knew it, I had given it to Master Higuchi.

Mame mochi from Demachi Futaba, fresh cinnamon mochi from Shogoin Yatsuhashi, sea urchin rice crackers, or cookies from Nishimura Eisei Boro were doable, but when he asked for stuff like a banner from the used book fair or a Keroyon figurine, I was pretty stumped. By the time he was asking for a life-sized Kamen Rider V3 figure, a square of fish cake as big as a tatami mat, a seahorse, and a giant squid, I had given up. Where was I supposed to get a giant squid?

Once he told us to leave immediately for Nagoya and buy just the miso they put on miso katsu, and Ozu really did go to Nagoya that very day. I've got to give him props for his dedication. Incidentally, I did once go to Nara just to buy deer crackers.

When Master Higuchi mentioned that he wanted a seahorse, Ozu got his hands on a big aquarium somehow. As he was filling it with water and adding in gravel and water plants, there was suddenly an ominous *fwoosh*, and all the water flooded out with the force of Niagara Falls. Our master laughed watching Ozu and I running around the soggy four-and-a-half-mat tatami room in a panic. After a little while, Master Higuchi said, "I suppose the water is leaking downstairs?"

"Ah, right. This place is falling apart."

Ozu smacked his forehead. "We're gonna have trouble if the person downstairs comes up to bitch at us. What'll we do?"

"Wait a minute—*I* live downstairs!" I shouted.

"Oh. Then who cares? Leak away!" Ozu didn't bat an eye.

The leak from Master Higuchi's apartment had soaked into my room, number 110. The water dripped down to make all of my precious documents—both obscene and not—soggy. But that wasn't the only damage I suffered. All my precious data—both obscene and not—was lost from my waterlogged computer, vanished into the electron sea. It goes without saying that this incident hastened the decay of my academic life.

After all that, before Master Higuchi even got his seahorse, he started asking for a giant squid, so rather than getting repaired, the aquarium gathered dust in the hallway. To distract the master from his feelings toward marine life, I lent him my copy of *Twenty Thousand Leagues Under the Sea*, but it had been almost a year and he hadn't returned it.

In other words, there wasn't much in this relationship for me.

• • •

Among our many foolish endeavors was the fierce Masochistic Proxy-Proxy War with Jogasaki.

Following orders from our master, we did things like rewrite the name plaque outside Jogasaki's place, set a fridge someone was trashing in front of his door, and send him a string of nasty chain letters. Jogasaki retaliated by, for example, gluing Master Higuchi's sandals to the floor, planting a black pepper balloon, and ordering sushi for twenty people in Master Higuchi's name. By the way, when the twenty people's worth of sushi arrived, Master Higuchi accepted it without batting an eye. Then he invited the study-abroad kids and us to a sushi party. While I can't fault his ability to roll with the punches, it was Ozu and I who split the bill.

After two years of training, if you were to ask me if I shed my immaturity to become an upstanding young man, I would only be able to say that unfortunately, the outcome was unfortunate.

So then why did I spend my days on such futile training? For no other reason than I wanted to see our master's smile. When we did these pointless idiotic tasks, Master Higuchi's whole being rejoiced. When we brought him the sorts of things that would satisfy him, he would smile and praise us, saying, "You're getting the hang of it, huh?"

Our master was never servile, only arrogant. Even so, when he smiled, he was as open as a child. This ingenious art of manipulating Ozu and me with smiles was what Hanuki called "Higuchi magic."

• • •

The day after the search for the Kamenoko Tawashi, at seven a.m.—a time, it isn't an exaggeration to say, that most college students still consider night—I was woken up by someone banging at my door. When I jumped up to see what the issue was, I found Master Higuchi standing outside practically ripping his hair out, eyes blazing.

"What's going on? It's so early," I said, but Master just stood there in the cold hallway without saying a word, clutching something square inside his yukata. Soon huge tears began to fall. His eggplant-esque face crinkled up, his mouth frowned, and he cried, using the back of his hand to wipe his eyes with all his might like a bullied child. Then he told me, "My good man, it's over. It's over."

I tensed up instinctively and pressed him, "What's over?"

"This." He brought the thing he was carrying so carefully out of his breast pocket. It was Jules Verne's *Twenty Thousand Leagues Under the Sea*. "This year-long voyage ended this morning. I was so moved, I thought I should tell you. And I needed to return the book, too."

I felt all the tension go out of my body, but Master Higuchi was so moved as he wiped his eyes that even I was somewhat touched that his epic twenty-thousand-league journey had come to an end.

He returned *Twenty Thousand Leagues Under the Sea* to me.

"Sorry it took so long, really. But it was a pleasant time, so thank you." Then he said, "I've been reading for a while now on an empty stomach, so I'm hungry. Wanna go get gyudon or something?"

Thus we went in the crisp morning air to a beef bowl shop at the Hyakumanben intersection.

• • •

We ate breakfast at the beef bowl shop, and as I was settling the bill for both of our meals, Master Higuchi had already leisurely strolled off from Hyakumanben toward the Kamo River. When I caught up to him, he said, "Nice weather, huh?" He looked up, stroking his unshaven chin. A slightly hazy, blue May sky spread out overhead.

We had arrived at the Kamo River Delta. Master Higuchi went through the pine grove and down the bank. Once we were out of the trees, the sky opened up, and it felt as if I might be sucked into it. Right in front of us stretched Kamo Ohashi with cars and people busily coming and going in the bright sunlight.

Master Higuchi stood at the point of the delta as if standing at the bow of a ship sailing the sea. Then he lit a cigar. The Kamo River coming from the right and the Takano River coming from the left mingled before us to become one Kamo River that flowed vigorously south. It had been raining for a few days previously, so the river seemed to be running high. The bushy green underbrush along the banks was submerged, so the river was wider than usual.

As Master Higuchi smoked his cigar, he said, "I want to go somewhere far away."

"That's unlike you."

As far as I knew, our master had never left his four-and-a-half-mat tatami room for more than a few hours.

"I'd been thinking about it for a while, but I made up my mind after reading *Twenty Thousand Leagues Under the Sea*. It seems the day I set out into the world has come."

"Do you have money for traveling?"

"Nope," he said, smiling as he puffed his cigar.

Then he continued as if he suddenly remembered something.

"Speaking of which, the other day I went to school and saw a guy I used to drink with back in my junior year. I greeted him with a 'Hey, hello there,' and he looked terribly uncomfortable. He asked me what I was doing, and when I said, 'Retaking German,' he skedaddled."

"If he was in the same year as you, he's probably doing his PhD by now. So I guess running into you would be awkward."

"What's he got to be embarrassed about? It's not like he's the one doing extra years . . . I don't get it."

"That's why you're the master, Master."

He put on a smug face.

In my first year, Master Higuchi lectured me, "My good sir, you must never repeat years, become a gamer, or play Mahjong. If you do, you'll be wasting your life as a student." *Here I am, following your teachings to the letter, not repeating years, not playing video games or Mahjong, so why is my life as a student still going to waste?* I considered asking Master Higuchi, but I couldn't make myself bring it up.

We sat on a bench on the bank. It was Sunday morning, so there were people walking and jogging along the riverbed.

"While I was looking for the Kamenoko Tawashi around Sanjo, I consulted a fortune-teller," I said out of nowhere.

"Your life hasn't even started yet and you're already lost?" He looked amused. "Your college years are still an extension of your esteemed mother's womb."

"I can't spend the two years I have left searching for scrub brushes, fighting the Masochistic Proxy-Proxy War, searching for scrub brushes, listening to Ozu's obscene chatter, searching for scrub brushes, and otherwise wasting my life. There's just no way."

"If you mean the Kamenoko Tawashi, it's okay. No worries, I won't expel you over that." He consoled me. "You'll be fine. Haven't you hung in there the past two years? Why stop at two more? You'll do a fine job of wasting the next three or four years, I guarantee it."

"I'd rather you didn't." I sighed. "If I hadn't met you and Ozu, I would have lived more purposefully. I would have applied myself to my studies, dated a black-haired maiden, and relished every moment of my untarnished student life. That's right. I'm sure of it."

"What's gotten into you? Still half asleep?"

"It hit me how completely I've wasted my time here! I should have given more thought to my possibilities. I made the wrong choice as a freshman. I need to seize my next chance and escape into a different life."

"And what chance is that?"

"Apparently it's 'colosseo.' That's what the fortune-teller said."

"Colosseo?"

"I don't get it either."

Master Higuchi looked at me as he scratched his stubbly chin. His sharp eyes suggested nobility. It made a four-and-a-half-mat tatami room in a building on the verge of collapse seem completely unsuitable. All I could think was that he was a young lord from some family with good lineage who suffered a sailing accident in the Seto Inland Sea and was washed up on the remote island that was a messy four-and-a-half-mat tatami room, but there he was, still wearing that worn-out yukata, lingering in that room covered in tatami that looked as if it had been simmered in a soup.

"You can't use the word 'possibilities' without qualification. What defines us as beings are not our possibilities, but our impossibilities," Master Higuchi said. "Could you be a bunny girl? Could you be a pilot? Could you be a carpenter? Could you be a pirate who sails the seven seas? Could you be the thief of the century going after the pieces in the Louvre's vault? Could you develop a supercomputer?"

"No."

Master Higuchi nodded and offered me a cigar—something he didn't usually do. I held it up with gratitude and then had trouble trying to light it.

"Most of our distress begins when we imagine how different life should have been. Entrusting your hopes to something as flimsy as your possibilities is the root of all evil. You must accept this you of here and now; you are incapable of becoming any-one else. There's no way you could live a so-called rose-colored campus life to the fullest. I guarantee it, so best dig in your heels."

"I think there's a nicer way you could have phrased that," I said.

"Stand tall. Follow Ozu's example."

"That's the one thing I'd rather not do . . ."

"Oh, don't be like that. Just look at him. Sure, his idiocy knows no bounds, but he's stable. In the end, a stable idiot will live with more significance than an unstable genius."

"Is that really true, though?"

"Yes . . . Well, every rule has its exceptions."

After that, we smoked our cigars in silence and gazed at the sunlight streaming through the pine needles. Since I could boast that I get an average of ten hours of sleep per night, I hadn't slept nearly enough, so when the sun started to warm up the area, I started to get drowsy. Master Higuchi hadn't slept a wink, so he was looking sleepy, too. Two weird fellows hovering between dreams and wakefulness on the Kamo River Delta were probably enough to ruin people's precious week-end morning.

Master Higuchi yawned. I yawned. We were both yawning forever.

"Shall we head back?" I asked.

"I suppose."

On our way back to Shimogamo Yusuiso, we took the ap-proach to Shimogamo Shrine.

"We've got to get you stable, my good sir," he said, as if he were talking to himself. "If we don't, how am I supposed to have you take my place?"

"What place?" I asked in surprise.

Master Higuchi smiled as he puffed on his cigar.

• • •

In life, the future just past your nose is shrouded in darkness. From that bottomless darkness, we must unerringly seize those things that will benefit us. For the purpose of learning that philosophy firsthand, Master Higuchi proposed Blackout Hot Pot. He said that the skill of plucking the ingredient you want out of a hot pot even in pitch darkness is one that is essential for surviving our dog-eat-dog contemporary society, but that can't be true, right?

Gathered that evening at Master Higuchi's four-and-a-half-mat tatami room for Blackout Hot Pot were Ozu, Hanuki, and me. Akashi had an essay due soon, so she didn't come. I contended that I also had an extremely troublesome lab report to turn in, but that contention was rejected out of hand. Terrible sexism no matter how you look at it. "You'll be fine. I'll have the Printing Office whip something up for you," said Ozu, but relying on Ozu to acquire forged reports from the Printing Office was what made my academic decay definitive.

We were each to bring ingredients, but there was a rule to keep their nature a secret until they were done simmering. Ozu was apparently still steamed over the aborted plot to abduct Kaori; "It's Blackout Hot Pot, so anything goes, right, everybody?" he said with a nasty grin and laid in some shady foodstuffs. This was Ozu, who fueled himself on other people's misfortunes, so I was beside myself with anxiety that he would add something unspeakable.

Ozu hated vegetables, and I knew that mushrooms, specifically, he didn't count as fit for human consumption, so I brought a ton of tasty mushrooms. Hanuki had a mischievous look on her face as well.

In the four-and-a-half-mat tatami room, so dark we couldn't really see each other's faces, the first round of ingredients went into the pot. Master Higuchi immediately said, "Dig in, dig in!"

"It's not done cooking yet," I said.

"Listen, everyone. When your chopsticks touch something, you have to take responsibility and eat it," ordered Master Higuchi.

It seemed Hanuki was drinking beer. "In the dark, it doesn't really feel like beer," she grumbled. "I don't see how I'm supposed to get drunk if I can't even see it."

• • •

I met Hanuki for the first time through Master Higuchi in the summer of my first year. Since then I had often encountered her in his room.

She was beautiful, but she had a face like the wife of a Sengoku-era warlord—no, you could say she had the face of the commander himself. That was how full of ambition her features were. I always felt that if the era had been right, it was the face of someone destined for feudal lordship. She had the power to slice Ozu or me in half with a single slash if she felt like it. Her favorite foods were ethyl alcohol and castella.

She worked as a dental hygienist at Kubozuka Dental next to the Mikagebashi Bridge. I'd been invited a few times, but I'm not about to lie there unresisting while someone sticks random rods and pipes into my mouth, and the idea of Hanuki doing it came attached to the image of her removing the plaque from my teeth with the blade of a naginata. It made me wonder about my chances of getting out of there without ending up a bloody mess, and I couldn't convince myself to go.

I had debated about this with Ozu many times: Hanuki gave off vibes like she might be the master's lover, but it wasn't clear; yet she wasn't a disciple, and of course she wasn't his wife, either. She was a mystery.

Hanuki had been in the same year as Master Higuchi, and she had known Jogasaki for a long time, too. Jogasaki even went to Kubozuka Dental for regular checkups, so he and Hanuki saw each other a few times a year.

It wasn't clear what kind of history Master Higuchi, Jogasaki, and Hanuki had, but I was convinced Hanuki knew the story behind the Masochistic Proxy-Proxy War. Ozu and I once waited till she was drunk and tried to get her to tell us, but we were outplotted. Never again did we try to get her to tell us anything.

• • •

Eating things you can't see is creepier than you might think. It's even creepier when one of the four people seated around your hot pot is the crystallized essence of ill will known as Ozu.

Once the pot had simmered, we ate, and every new mystery food—or food-like item—that appeared was overwhelming. "This thing is squirming!" shrieked Hanuki, and I groaned when the thing she hurled away hit me in the forehead—"Ugyah!" I threw the squirmy thing in the direction Ozu seemed to be and heard a muffled scream from over there, too—"Uhyoh!" Later we learned it was just a curly noodle, but in the dark, it seemed to be a long, thin worm.

"What's this? An alien's umbilical cord?" asked Ozu.

"You were probably the one who put it in, so you should be the one to eat it."

"No."

"Gentlemen, we mustn't waste food," Master Higuchi intoned like the head of the household, and we quieted down.

Eventually Ozu appeared to have grabbed a shiitake; "Ugh, it's a clump of fungus!" he screeched, and I smiled. Meanwhile, my heart nearly stopped when I picked up something like a thumb-sized yokai, but when I calmed down to investigate, it turned out to be a firefly squid.

By the time we reached the third round, the ingredients had gotten bizarrely sweet. And there was a beery smell in the air.

"Hey, Ozu. You added sweet bean paste!" I screamed at him.

"Ee-hee-hee," Ozu laughed. "But Hanuki put beer in."

"You knew it was me? I thought it would add some depth to the flavor."

"It's so deep I can't tell what's what anymore," I said.

"A hot pot abyss."

"Just so we're all clear, it wasn't me who put the marshmallows in," Ozu declared quietly. Apparently he had grabbed a marshmallow.

I ate a shrimp that tasted like sweet beans and some cabbage covered in marshmallow goo. When I checked on Master Higuchi next to me, he was eating everything happily, panting to dispel the heat, a feat that was certainly to his credit.

I talked about how Akashi had put a stop to the Kaori abduction plan. Hanuki burst out laughing.

"Akashi is right. Abducting the doll would be vicious," she said.

Ozu was disappointed. "Seeing as I planned this whole operation, please consider my perspective: Jogasaki dyed Master's yukata *pink*!" he argued. "That's a low blow if I ever saw one."

"But it's funny, isn't it? Jogasaki's prank had some charm."

Disappointed, Ozu clammed up and harmonized completely with the darkness. Ozu was always such a dark presence to begin with, it was impossible to tell where he was.

"I've known Jogasaki for such a long time, too." Hanuki waxed nostalgic. "He got kicked out of his club, right? I think that was just as overkill as the abduction plot. Wouldn't you say you got carried away, too, Ozu?"

Hanuki must have been glaring in the direction Ozu might have been, but Ozu stayed hidden and didn't reply.

"Jogasaki's in no position to be spending all his time on club activities, anyhow," said Master Higuchi. "He's getting older."

"That's not very persuasive when you say it, Higuchi," Hanuki said.

Having eaten a bunch of mystery objects, we got full faster than usual, so from then on we quit eating and chatted about this and that. Hanuki seemed to be knocking back the drinks still. Ozu's embittered silence was eerie.

"Ozu, why aren't you saying anything?" Master Higuchi asked, perplexed. "Are you still here?"

He didn't answer, so Hanuki said, "If Ozu isn't here, then let's talk about Ozu's girlfriend."

"Ozu has a girlfriend?" I asked.

"They've been going out for two years! They're in the same club, and I've heard she's so sophisticated and charming, you'd think she was some kind of aristocrat. I've never actually seen her, though. One time she threatened to dump him, so he called me for advice and cried all night . . ."

Ozu lurking in the darkness kicked up a fuss. "Lies! All lies!"

"So you are here!" Master Higuchi said gleefully.

"Things are going well with her then?" Hanuki asked.

"I exercise my right to remain silent," Ozu declared in the darkness.

"What was her name again?" Hanuki was thinking. "I'm pretty sure it was something like Kohi . . ."

She got that far before Ozu started wailing, "I reserve the right to remain silent!" and "I'm gonna call my lawyer!" so she stopped, laughing.

"You bastard, how are you getting freaky while I'm getting nothing!" I got swept up in my anger, but Ozu feigned ignorance: "Whatever are you talking about?" As I glared at the darkness in Ozu's direction, Master Higuchi was poking recklessly at the hot pot next to me.

"Oh? I got a big one," he mumbled. "It's kinda squishy," he intoned, and then he must have tried to take a bite. "This doesn't seem to be food," he said quietly. "Surely putting inedible objects in is against the rules."

"Shall we turn the lights on?"

When I stood up and turned on the light, Hanuki and Ozu both had stunned looks on their faces. A spongy little bear plushie was relaxing all plump on Master Higuchi's plate. It was soggy and hot pot–soup colored.

"What a cute plushie," said Hanuki.

"Which one of you put this in the hot pot?" asked Master Higuchi. "I couldn't eat this even if I wanted to!"

But neither Hanuki, Ozu, nor I knew anything about it. The reason I didn't think Ozu was lying was that he clearly didn't have even a fraction of the purity required to come up with something so adorable.

"I'll take it," said Hanuki, and she took it and gave it a careful wash in the sink.

• • •

Hanuki is a pleasant person, but when she drinks too much, she's a handful. Her face gets paler and paler, her eyes glaze over, and suddenly she's licking people's faces.

As Ozu and I scrambled away from Hanuki, who was trying to get us up against the wall to lick our faces, I was strangely aroused, but a gentleman can't get horny just because a woman licks his face. And Master Higuchi was watching the whole thing as if we were a fascinating party trick. Hanuki made the incredibly selfish proposition "I'll give you this whole castella the dentist gave me, so spoon with me!" but I firmly rejected her.

Eventually Ozu fell asleep, resulting in an even more indecent than usual expression on his indecent face. Hanuki had relaxed as well and was nodding off.

"I'm going on a trip," Master Higuchi said in a singsong voice. He doesn't drink much, but there's a strange mechanism by which, when Hanuki drinks like a fish, he seems to get drunk, too.

"Where are you going to go?" Hanuki said, looking up sleepily.

"My plan is to circumnavigate the globe—though I don't

know how many years it'll take. Wanna come with, Hanuki? I know you speak English."

"Don't be ridiculous. How stupid."

"Master, do you speak English?" I asked.

"I scoff at the idea of learning English without putting up a fight."

"But Higuchi, what about the thing?" asked Hanuki.

"Don't worry. I have a plan. But hey, it's already after midnight. We need to go eat Neko Ramen."

"Should I wake Ozu up?" Hanuki asked, but Master Higuchi shook his head.

"Let's let him sleep. Just the three of us is fine." He grinned. "We're going to meet Jogasaki."

• • •

Master Higuchi leisurely strolled down Mikage-dori past Shimogamo Shrine. Since it was late, things were quiet; the only sounds were the rustling of Tadasu no Mori's trees and the occasional car coming down Shimogamo Hon-dori. I followed silently behind Master Higuchi. Hanuki was walking unsteadily, but she seemed to have sobered up to some extent.

"My good sir," Master said, putting smile wrinkles in his eggplant face. "I'm going to make you a proxy, just so you know."

"A proxy for what?" I asked in surprise.

"Hoo-hoo. Just be ready."

"Why not Ozu?"

"Don't worry about Ozu. He has a different role."

Neko Ramen is a ramen stand rumored to make its soup from

cats. Regardless of whether that's true or not, the flavor is unparalleled. I was stuffed with weird things from the Blackout Hot Pot, but remembering the taste of the ramen, I thought a bowl would fit.

In the chilly darkness stood a lone stall with a shining lightbulb. Despite the cold night air, it had an aura of cheerful warmth. Master Higuchi snorted in amusement and gestured with a jerk of his chin. Looking where he indicated, I saw someone had arrived ahead of us. He was sitting on a stool chatting with the owner.

When we approached, the owner looked up with a "Yo." Then the guy sitting on the stool sat up and looked our way. His chiseled features were illuminated by the orangey glow of the lightbulb.

"You're late," said Jogasaki.

"Sorry," said Master Higuchi.

"Haven't seen you in a while, Jogasaki. How've you been?" Hanuki bobbed her head.

"I'm the very picture of health, thank you for asking." He flashed his straight, white teeth.

We took three stools next to him, sitting in a row. I wasn't quite sure what to do with myself and shrank into the far corner. What was this gathering about, anyhow? For one thing, I had never seen Master Higuchi and Jogasaki together before, so I wondered whether this wasn't actually something very important.

Thus opened the Higuchi-Jogasaki Reconciliation Conference.

"Well, maybe it's about time we end this," said Master Higuchi.

"Yeah," nodded Jogasaki.

Thus ended the Higuchi-Jogasaki Reconciliation Conference.

• • •

"It was a long one this time," said the Neko Ramen owner. "Five years? Longer?"

"I forget," Jogasaki said with an air of indifference.

"Pretty much exactly five years, right? The previous proxies' reconciliation conference was around this time of year," said Master Higuchi.

"I see, I see. So five years on the dot, then," said the Neko Ramen owner. "What are your predecessors up to?"

"Mine works at the courthouse in Nagasaki. That's his hometown."

"How about yours, Jogasaki?"

"I wonder. He was so random, I have no clue what happened to him," said Jogasaki. "We haven't talked since he dropped out."

"Your predecessor was a lot like Higuchi. Detached from the world. How did he end up being your master, anyway?" the owner asked.

"I don't know. That's just the direction things went, I guess."

The owner laid out our ramen bowls in a row.

The four of them had a mysterious sense of fellowship, and I wasn't in on it. For starters, I wasn't even aware that the owner of Neko Ramen had known the masters for so long. Surprised, I modestly, quietly slurped my ramen.

"Him?" Jogasaki said, looking at me.

"Yeah, he's my proxy." Master Higuchi cheerfully clapped me on the shoulder. "Is yours not coming tonight?"

"That dumbass—he said he had plans so he couldn't come."

"Hmm."

Jogasaki smiled. "He's a hardcore weirdo, but I'm sure he'll be a proper proxy. Yours had better be prepared."

"Something to look forward to," Master Higuchi said.

"He'll definitely be with me on the day of the duel."

The owner winced beyond the steam. "Huh. You're really gonna do the duel?"

"We sure are. The duel on Kamo Ohashi is part of the whole tradition," said Master Higuchi.

• • •

The mysterious conference ended amicably, and Jogasaki zipped away on his motorbike.

"It's about time to kick Ozu out and get some good sleep," said Master Higuchi with a considerable yawn.

"Master, I have no idea what's going on . . ." I said. "What's all this proxy business?"

"I'll explain in detail tomorrow. I'm too sleepy right now."

He went back to Shimogamo Yusuiso.

I was ordered to escort Hanuki back to her apartment along Kawabata-dori. She walked along the dark road toying gently with the unidentified bear plushie that had come out of the Blackout Hot Pot. Perhaps due to the girlish fidgeting she was focused on, the Sengoku-era warlord ambition was less noticeable; on the contrary, she seemed rather lonely, more like a damsel in distress.

Puzzled, I walked alongside her down quiet Mikage-dori.

"Jogasaki is pretty, uh . . . chill, huh?"

When I said that, she giggled. "He's honestly not all that different from Higuchi."

"Really? He certainly doesn't seem the type to carry on a prank war with him, but . . ."

"He gets a kick out of it, he just doesn't show it."

"I find that hard to believe," I said.

"He hasn't really had any friends besides Higuchi for a long time."

After that, she fell silent. She squeezed the bear. The spongy plushie made a terribly heart-wrenching face.

Eventually we came upon the Takano River. Mikagebashi is a round little bridge, and if you look east on it, you can see Mount Daimonji. During the Bon holiday, the bridge apparently fills with a crowd of people looking up at the burning kanji character. Incidentally, I've never seen the okuribi ritual.

Hanuki was very quiet. Was this the calm before the storm? I had a bad feeling I couldn't shake. It was later than one would have expected, but was something evil nested inside her beginning to writhe, trying to burst out? When I looked over, her face was an anxious pale color, her lips were tightly pursed, and while it might have been my imagination, she seemed to be shaking slightly. It was as if she had wagered her life on this resolve.

"Hanuki, are you by any chance not feeling well?" I asked cautiously, and she grinned.

"It's that obvious, huh?"

With that, she abruptly clung to the bridge's railing. Then she vomited in the most casual, gorgeous way I've ever seen. She watched the Neko Ramen she had just eaten sorrowfully fall into the Takano River with what seemed like great interest.

When she had thus let her guard down, the bear plushie she'd been holding rolled—tragically—off the railing like a rice ball.

"Ah," she said and leaned over the railing, and I used all of my nonexistent strength to pull her back. We nearly both went after the ramen and the plushie. The bear plushie gracefully spun as it fell toward the water's surface, putting all of its inherent cuteness on display in its last hurrah. Eventually a tiny *splish* sounded.

"Ahhh, it fell," she grumbled in regret and rested her chin on the railing. "I wonder how far he'll float," she said in a singsong voice.

"He'll go toward the Kamo River Delta, enter the Kamo River, then the Yodo River, and then Osaka Bay," I broke it down for her.

Hanuki sniffed, "Hmph," and stood up. "Fine. Go wherever you want," she said in a strangely theatrical way and hocked a loogie.

That poor, unfortunate bear plushie.

• • •

After making sure Hanuki got to her apartment, I headed back to Shimogamo Yusuiso.

I thought for a second there was a horribly filthy beast sitting outside room 110, but it was Ozu. "Go the fuck home," I said, but he replied, "Oh, don't be so mean," as he barged into my room and lay down in a corner of my four-and-a-half-mat tatami room like a corpse.

"Where did you all go off to without me?" he asked.

"Neko Ramen."

"No fair. I'm so sad. I'm so sad I might disappear."

"Perfect."

He mewled a little longer, but then he seemed to get sick of it and went to sleep. When I did my best to push him into a dusty corner of my four-and-a-half-mat tatami room, he protested, "Mrrmrr."

I burrowed into my futon and became absorbed in my thoughts.

Somehow, I ended up designated as our master's successor, but what is the Masochistic Proxy-Proxy War, even? What happened in the past between Master Higuchi and Jogasaki? What's this duel that's happening tomorrow on Kamo Ohashi? What does the owner of Neko Ramen have to do with it? Or does he have nothing to do with it? Will I have to carry on this unproductive prank battle with the successor Jogasaki will bring? Is escape no longer a possibility? And what kind of guy will my opponent be? What if he's the type to kick those who are down and butter up anyone stronger than him—someone selfish and arrogant, lazy and contrary, who never studies, has not a crumb of pride, and fuels himself on other people's misfortunes? What then?

I sat up and listened to Ozu's sleeping breath.

I had such an unambiguously bad feeling—awful, really—that I couldn't look away even if I wanted to; it spread like a bitter juice through my breast and any efforts to deny it were futile. I was so dissatisfied with my state that I had even sought an interpretation from a fortune-teller, so what was I doing? I was supposed to be seizing my due chance and escaping into a new life, but far from seizing anything, wasn't I actually just driving myself further into a bottleneck there was no coming back from?

Paying no mind to my worries, Ozu slept, his face irritatingly innocent.

• • •

The next day, I kicked half-asleep Ozu out of my room and went to school.

But the thought of the evening's duel on Kamo Ohashi made me antsy. I hurried through my labs and returned to Shimogamo Yusuiso. I tried going to Master Higuchi's room, but a chalkboard hanging from his door read, "At the bathhouse." He must have been purifying his body for the coming battle.

I went back to my room, and as I listened to the coffee burble, I stared at the castella Hanuki had given me after the Blackout Hot Pot. Hanuki sure could be cruel. I felt that it was actually quite depressing to eat this much castella on one's own—wrong as a human being—and it would be better to enjoy it more gracefully with someone pleasant, sipping some tea or something, someone like—I was surprised to find myself thinking—Akashi. Indulging in such reprehensible fantasies despite having had the horrible fortune to be selected as a successor in the mysterious Masochistic Proxy-Proxy War and forced to stand at the gateway to an even more unproductive future, whether I wanted to or not, was pretty hardcore escapism. I needed to learn a thing or two about shame.

Overhead, a big moth that had slipped into my room at some point was fluttering around the fluorescent light. *Oh, yeah, Akashi hates moths*, I recalled, and, like an idiot, became absorbed in the sweet memory of us falling down the stairs together. I sliced the castella with a fruit knife and groaned as I crammed the pieces into my mouth one by one. Just as I was reaching for my porn library to keep myself from being seized by a reprehensible fantasy impulse, I heard a knock.

When I opened the door, Akashi, who had been standing in the hallway, shrieked and recoiled. I wondered if I had a face like a gross monster driven by lust, but she was just afraid of the moth in my room. I calmly repelled the moth and welcomed her in like a gentleman.

"Master Higuchi called and told me to come this evening, but he doesn't seem to be home," she said.

I briefed her on Master Higuchi and Jogasaki's reconciliation conference.

"Wow, sounds like an awful lot happened while I was writing my essay. I'm disqualified as a disciple."

"Don't worry. It was all very sudden."

I poured a cup of coffee and handed it to her.

After taking a sip, she said, "I brought you something." The paulownia box she took out of her bag I had seen somewhere before. When I took the lid off, that elusive scrub brush we had searched for together was nested inside. "Now you won't be expelled, right?" she said with a straight face, but the compassion of this junior disciple for her senior nearly obliterated my tear ducts.

"Sorry. I'm so sorry," I moaned.

"It's fine," she said.

"Anyhow, would you like some castella?" I offered her some cake. She took a slice and bit into it. "You were busy with your essay, right? I feel so bad," I said.

"Yeah. I just barely made the deadline."

"What was the essay about? You're in the engineering department, right?"

"I'm in the engineering department, but my major is architecture. The essay was about the history of architecture."

"The history of architecture?"

"Yes, I wrote about Roman architecture. Temples, the Colosseum, and so on."

Colosseo.

Just then, we heard a knock.

"Are you there, my good sir? It's duel time."

It was Master Higuchi's voice.

• • •

The master's face was gleaming after his bath, but his stubble
remained. "I went and had a soak with Ozu," he said.

"Then where's Ozu?"

"He went to Jogasaki's place. Ozu has been Jogasaki's henchman all along. What a character, that guy." He pulled a hand
inside his yukata and cackled. "He was the one who dyed my
yukata pink."

Of course, I'm sure you had all realized this by now, gentle
readers.

The fall of the previous year, when Jogasaki was dethroned
as head of his film club and was lamenting his isolation, Ozu
began frequenting his place, listening to his complaints and con-
demning the inferior oafs who had driven him out. Of course, as
I have already mentioned, the ultimate villain who had incited
those inferior oafs was Ozu. Thus, Ozu slipped into Jogasaki's
heart like the devil himself and secured the status of right-hand

man. Hanging out with nothing in particular to do for days on end, they got along well, so when Jogasaki found out that Ozu was a disciple of Master Higuchi, he said, "Why don't you act as my agent, then?" and Ozu grinned like an unscrupulous salesman and agreed, saying, "We're a couple of bad boys, aren't we, Jogasaki?"

Thus, the most strange and pointless stage ever was set thanks to Ozu's behind-the-scenes machinations of dubious intent.

Ozu took Master Higuchi's orders and stuffed a dozen types of insects into Jogasaki's mailbox, meanwhile taking Jogasaki's orders and dyeing Master Higuchi's yukata pink—repeating these bizarre comings and goings, displaying the operational capacity of ten men, enjoying his repulsive double agent–hood. You don't even have to think very hard to see that Ozu was the only one running around so busy. What on earth did he mean to accomplish by giving all of his vitality over to this dangerous game played with nigh virtuosic skill? It was a mystery that wouldn't be solved so easily, but neither was it necessary to solve.

"I figured out that Ozu was Jogasaki's agent, but his antics amused me, so I left him alone," said Master Higuchi.

"So you're saying he rigged everything?" I said. "That means he had you and Jogasaki dancing in the palm of his hand."

"I'm impressed," said Akashi.

"Yeah." Master Higuchi didn't seem pissed off at all. "His idiocy knows no bounds. One might even say this is unprecedented in all the annals of the Masochistic Proxy-Proxy War. His name will go down in history." Then he said, "Oh, castella!" and dug in before I could even offer him any. Finally, with an exuberant air, he said, "Now then, tonight is the night of the Kamo Ohashi duel."

"Master, could you please slow down for a second?" When I expressed my bewilderment, he nodded.

"You probably want to know what it's all about. Perhaps it's time I explain the Masochistic Proxy-Proxy War."

· · ·

What is the Masochistic Proxy-Proxy War?

This fruitless yet noble battle has its roots in the pre-war period.

The trigger is said to be a clash of high schooler hearts, or possibly a drinking contest featuring unrefined sake, but the details have already sunk into the dark corners of history.

The initial fight dragged on for a long time. They battled all throughout their student days. The fight went on so long that it hadn't reached a conclusion when their graduation came around. These men whose names have been lost to history gave up on reaching an outcome while they were in school. They could have simply made up, but these two were stubborn, so they refused. Still, they were tired, so they also refused to continue fighting. Yet they were also proud, so they also refused to let this matter go unsettled. Thus trapped, the novel measure they came up with was to have two underclassmen unrelated to their argument carry on the fight as their proxies.

Thus began this generations-long current flowing through the university's history.

There are no records of how the fight was carried out in

those early days, but if one thing is certain it's that the unwritten law that proxies must devote themselves to unproductive pranks had been established. The underclassmen forced to be proxies had no personal grudges against each other. They were merely handed the format: "You must fight." They continued the battle, but didn't force a conclusion. They didn't know whether it was theirs to conclude. They, as their seniors had done, passed their battle on to some underclassman. They postponed a decision.

Paying absolutely no mind to the eventual Pacific War, the loss of it, the postwar recovery period, the student protests, or any other social movement, the battle was inherited in an unbroken chain. The reason for it was forgotten, and only the format remained, then the format was repeated until it became tradition, codifying the actions of the proxies.

In the late 1980s, Neko Ramen was established as the venue for reconciliation talks and meetings about succession. The outgoing proxies have a final duel on Kamo Ohashi, and that completes the handoff. The newly appointed proxies must drag the fight on for as long as they can, find promising successors, and get them to carry on this traditional battle.

From that day on, Ozu became Jogasaki's proxy and I became Master Higuchi's.

In the sense that proxies do battle via unproductive bullying against each other, people started calling it the Masochistic Proxy-Proxy War at some point. Technically, it would be the Masochistic Proxy-

Proxy-Proxy-Proxy-Proxy-Proxy War, since we were the thirtieth proxies.

Master Higuchi and Jogasaki were merely the twenty-ninth proxies. There was no horrific strife deeply rooted in their past. It was just that no one wanted to be the one to let the tradition lapse, and no one knew how to end it.

In other words, there was no reason for this fight.

• • •

"Is that true?" I asked.

"If you won't be my proxy, my reconciliation with Jogasaki can't go forward. I'm sure it'll be worth your while, given how twisted Ozu is."

"That's not funny."

Master Higuchi abruptly prostrated himself.

I didn't think the protection of this tradition was worth getting so worked up about, but if my master was planting his forehead on the ground, I couldn't say no. Still, sensing that my rose-colored campus life was receding to a place where I would never be able to reach it again, I was crying on the inside. "Understood," I said quietly, and Master Higuchi looked up and nodded in satisfaction.

"Akashi, bear witness. I want you to keep an eye on them and make sure they carry this out properly and as gentlemen. Should they begin to actually quarrel, find a way to step in."

"Understood." Akashi bowed her head respectfully.

My path to retreat had been cut off.

Master Higuchi seemed satisfied and sighed as he relaxed

his posture. "Now I have no regrets," he murmured. He took out a cigar and lit it. Having missed my chance and ended up as successor to this mysterious tradition, I was already feeling drained by the responsibility when I noticed that Akashi was poking me. She was pointing at the box with the scrub brush in it.

"Master, here; it's a Kamenoko Tawashi. Akashi acquired it for me."

When I handed it out to him, his eyes went wide and he moaned, but almost immediately he looked apologetic. "Sorry for the trouble," he said. "Once the duel is decided I'm making myself scarce."

"What?" gasped Akashi.

"Are you really planning on taking a trip around the world? That sounds pretty reckless to me," I said, but he shook his head.

"But it's why I chose a new proxy. I won't return to my room for a while. My good sir, would you kindly clean it with this brush?"

"It's just one order after another, huh."

"Oh, don't be like that." He grinned. "Hey, we need to start heading over to Kamo Ohashi. My final battle with Jogasaki is upon us."

Just as we were about to leave Shimogamo Yusuiso, Hanuki came running over, nearly out of breath.

"I'm so glad I made it in time," she said. "I came straight from work."

"I was beginning to think you wouldn't show," Master Higuchi said.

"Oh, I'm going to see this through to the end. Not that this fight is going to be worth watching, but still."

Then we all headed to the bridge.

• • •

On the eastern end of Kamo Ohashi . . .

Master Higuchi had rolled up the sleeves of his yukata and was looking at an old-fashioned wristwatch.

The area was submerged in indigo twilight by this time. The Kamo River Delta was occupied by lively college kids. They must have been having new student welcome parties. Come to think of it, I'd spent two years completely removed from that scene. The river was running high from the rain that had lasted until just the other day, and it rushed noisily past; in the lights reflecting here and there, the surface of the water looked like a sheet of metallic paper being waved like a stage prop. Imadegawa-dori was busy, and the bridge was packed with brilliant head- and taillights. The orange lights affixed at intervals along the bridge's thick railing shone with a hazy, mystical air in the darkness. Kamo Ohashi felt larger than usual on this night.

"He's here," Master Higuchi said cheerfully and strode toward the center of the bridge.

Looking over, I saw Jogasaki approaching from the opposite end. Walking next to him was Ozu.

We strode forward, glaring at each other, until we met right in the middle. Peering over the railing, I could see the surface of the Kamo River, which was sending up spray, it was flowing so hard. Glancing south, farther down the dark river's course, I saw the distant Shijo neighborhood's lights gleaming like jewels.

"Hey, if it isn't Akashi!" Jogasaki said with a suspicious look.

"Hi," she said with a bow.

"You're one of Higuchi's friends?"

"I joined as a disciple this fall."

"She's, well, a witness. Here's my proxy, the one I introduced you to the other day." Master Higuchi pointed at me. "By the way, could it be that your proxy is my disciple Ozu?"

Jogasaki put a smile on. "You may have thought he was your disciple, but he was my spy. Tricked you, huh?"

"You got me." The master crinkled up his eggplant face in laughter.

"Anyway."

"I suppose we should do the thing," the master said.

With everyone gathered, a faint tension hung in the air.

Bathed in our gazes, Jogasaki and Master Higuchi stared each other down. Jogasaki's chiseled features were pale in the light of the old lamp next to the footpath; he had the threatening aura of a Bakumatsu-era Kyoto assassin. The fact that the gloomy smirk on the face of Ozu, next to him, just accentuated his intensity could only mean they were a good match for each other. Intercepting them, Master Higuchi did everything he could to make his eggplant-shaped face stern. He stood firmly, haughtily, in his navy yukata with his arms crossed, and the energy coming off of his back was no ordinary determination. It was a real tiger-versus-dragon scenario.

What kind of duel was about to unfold? We looked on with bated breath.

Eventually Hanuki stepped between Jogasaki and Higuchi

and gestured with her hand as if it were a sword slicing through a string between them.

"All right, hop to it."

It was a bit flavorless for a line being used to signal the start of a duel that would be the culmination of a five-year battle.

Jogasaki took an oblique stance. Ozu skittered to the rear. Akashi and I also moved back. Master Higuchi didn't move a muscle. Jogasaki thrust his left palm out, face up, and balled up his right fist on his hip. In response, Master Higuchi uncrossed his arms and performed hand seals as if he were reciting a Shingon mantra.

"Here I come, Higuchi," Jogasaski said in a low voice.

"Come, then," said Master Higuchi.

After one breathless instant, they clashed.

"*Janken . . .*"

"*Pon!*"

Jogasaki collapsed dramatically.

"Okay, that's it! It's over!" Hanuki applauded. A beat later, Akashi began to clap. As for me, I just stood there dumbfounded.

"I won, so you'll deliver the first attack," said Master Higuchi.

The duel on Kamo Ohashi was a game of Rock Paper Scissors to determine which of the successors would strike first.

• • •

"Phew, that's a load off," said Master Higuchi looking up at the indigo sky. He had crossed his arms again and resumed his leisurely air, and who would have expected anything else? Jogasaki stood up as if nothing had happened, seeming unconcerned. Master Higuchi took out a cigar and offered it to him.

"So what are your plans now, Higuchi? We ended this on your request, after all," Jogasaki asked with a smoky exhale.

"I'm going to spread my wings."

"Hey, Hanuki—Higuchi's not making sense."

"Well, he *is* an idiot," Hanuki retorted. Then she said, "Let's go for drinks."

Suddenly, Master Higuchi leaned into my ear with a grin. "So. I probably won't be meeting you again, my good sir."

"What?"

"So I'm gifting you my globe."

"How can you gift me something that was mine to begin with?"

"Was it?"

Was he really planning to disappear?

As I was searching for the right words, a shriek shot up from the Kamo River Delta, north of the bridge. The partying kids had begun running around in a panic.

When I pressed up against the railing to look, I saw something like a black fog eerily spread out from Aoi Park to the Kamo River Delta, swiftly coating the delta's bank below. And within that black fog was a muddle of young people. They were half mad, flailing their arms and ripping out their hair. The black fog glided along the river and seemed to be heading straight for us. We watched as if entranced.

The clamoring on the Kamo River Delta grew even louder.

Black fog poured continuously from out of the pine grove. This was nothing to sniff at. With a trembling, fluttering, rustling, and flapping, the wriggling black fog was spreading out like a carpet below us when it began to rise up from the river's surface before suddenly exploding over the railing and rushing onto Kamo Ohashi.

"Gyoaehhhh!" Akashi emitted a shriek straight out of a manga.

It was a swarm of moths.

• • •

A news item appeared in the next day's *Kyoto Shimbun*, but no one knew exactly why the extraordinary number of moths had appeared. Retracing their flight path, they seemed to come from Tadasu no Mori—that is, Shimogamo Shrine—but this wasn't clear. Even if every moth that lived in Tadasu no Mori had decided to migrate all at once, there wasn't a good reason for it. Apart from the official explanation, there were rumors that the moths had come, not from Shimogamo Shrine, but the neighborhood next to it, Shimogamo Izumikawacho; but that only made the story even stranger. Apparently, it was the area right around my apartment that had been flooded with moths and thrown into an uproar.

When I returned to my room that night, there were dead moths strewn throughout the hallway. My door was half open, as I had forgotten to lock it, so there were moth corpses all over my room, too. I gave them a respectful burial.

• • •

Pushing my way through the swarm of moths as they flapped into my face, sprinkling their scales around, sometimes trying to force their way into my mouth, I moved to Akashi and protected her like a total gentleman. I used to be a city slicker, so I had been above living alongside insects, but after residing in my lodgings for two years, I'd had numerous opportunities to become familiar with all manner of arthropods, so bugs didn't bother me anymore.

That huge swarm of moths, though, was beyond the realm of common sense. The awful sound of their beating wings cut us off from the outside world; it was less like moths and more like little winged yokai passing over the bridge. I couldn't see much of anything. Through the slits of my barely open eyes, I could make out a riot of moths fluttering around the orangey glow of the lamps on the railing and Akashi's shiny black hair. I didn't have the wherewithal to concern myself with anyone else.

Once the swarm had finally gone, a few stragglers had been left fluttering here and there. Akashi stood up with a deathly pale face and screamed, "Are there any on me?! Are there any on me?!" as she frantically brushed off every part of her body before running toward the western end of the bridge at a tremendous speed to flee the moths twitching on the ground. It was in front of a café casting a soft glow into the twilight that she eventually crumpled.

The swarm of moths became a black carpet again and went down the river to Shijo.

I noticed Jogasaki and others scanning the area in a daze. I did the same, looking around the bridge dotted with orangey lamps.

Master Higuchi had vanished; it was as if he had flown

away on the swarm of moths. What a brilliant exit, and entirely worthy of my master. But strangely, Ozu was also missing. I figured Master Higuchi's mysterious disappearance was another of Ozu's underhanded plots.

"Higuchi and Ozu are gone," said Jogasaki. He sounded a little confused as he looked around the bridge.

With her arms on the railing, bracing herself against the evening breeze, Hanuki shouted, "Fine, just leave, then!"

• • •

"All right, I'm gonna get sloppy tonight," Hanuki declared with her hands on her hips. "Jogasaki, let's go drinking."

"Fine by me," said Jogasaki, looking slightly sad. "But Higuchi didn't even say goodbye. He could have savored the moment a little more."

"C'mon, it'll be just the two of us. We haven't gone out for drinks together in who knows how long." Then she sidled up to me and leaned in. "Take good care of Akashi."

The two of them said they were headed to Kiyamachi, and they left.

I walked over to Akashi. She was sitting in the pool of the café's light. "Are you okay?" I asked. "Master Higuchi disappeared."

Hearing that, she raised her pale face.

"Why don't we get some tea or something to calm down?" I suggested.

It's not as if I was thinking anything so rude as stooping to using her weakness against moths to my advantage. Seeing her so pale, I was offering out of concern. She nodded, and we went into the café that was right there.

"I wonder what happened to Master Higuchi. Ozu is gone, too," I said, sipping on a coffee.

Akashi cocked her head and then giggled. "He disappeared like a mountain hermit. Just flew away." She sipped her coffee. "I'd expect nothing less."

"Where do you suppose they went?" I cocked my head. "I'm sure Ozu must have been planning it."

As we were drinking our coffee, I remembered "colosseo" and told her about it. I told her how when she came to my room and said "colosseo," that was my chance. If I had escaped at that point, I could have avoided inheriting the Masochistic Proxy-Proxy War and entered into a new life. Unable to bear the grief of losing my rose-colored future, I heaved a sigh.

"I failed to seize my chance," I said. "I've done the same thing I always do."

"No, you didn't." Akashi shook her head. "I'm sure you seized it. You just haven't realized it yet."

As we were sitting there serenely drinking our coffee, we heard the siren of an ambulance approaching. Just as we thought it had passed, it stopped at the west end of Kamo Ohashi. Then came the noisy rescue. It was an impressive racket.

"Thank you for going out of your way to find the Kameno-ko Tawashi for me." When I bowed my head, a smile appeared on Akashi's face, which was still regaining its color.

"I guess our master is gone now, anyhow. But if you're happy, I'm glad."

It was awfully sudden, but at that moment, I had feelings for Akashi one should never have for a fellow disciple. Speaking about those feelings at length goes against my principles, but suffice to say, after a fierce struggle to connect those feelings to action, I managed to spit out the following line: "Akashi, wanna go get some Neko Ramen?"

• • •

How my relationship with Akashi developed after that is a deviation from the point of this manuscript. Thus, I shall refrain from writing the charming, bashfully giddy details. You probably don't want to pour your time down the drain reading such detestable drivel, anyhow.

There's nothing so worthless to speak of as a love mature.

• • •

Now then, following those events, we never did find out where Higuchi went. I didn't think he would leave so flashily and without so much as a goodbye. It was unclear whether he actually got to go on his trip around the world or not.

A couple of weeks after he left, I reluctantly went to clean up room 210 with the assistance of Akashi and Hanuki. That scrub brush came in very handy, but let the record show it was a battle filled with hardship. Hanuki quickly designated herself out of commission, Akashi pretended to panic due to the utter filth and tried to escape, and when Ozu came to visit on crutches, he vomited in the sink, making our job even harder.

So my storm of regret over becoming a disciple of Master Higuchi's charted its highest instantaneous wind speed immediately following his departure, but once life began without him, it sometimes felt like something was missing. When I looked at the pins he had left in the globe in his room charting the voyage of the *Nautilus*, even I was moved by emotions so strong I longed to embrace that globe and rub my cheek against it, but I was aware how repulsive that would be and thought better of it. Then I took the pins out and wondered where Higuchi was at that moment.

Incidentally, the elusive Kamenoko Tawashi ended up at Akashi's house, where she makes very good use of it.

• • •

I heard from Hanuki that Jogasaki intends to leave his program and get a job somewhere. Speaking of Jogasaki, I wonder how the silent beauty Ozu was planning to abduct, Kaori, is doing. I hope the couple are enjoying their life together.

Hanuki herself still works at Kubozuka Dental. About two months after Master Higuchi disappeared I went to get my teeth looked at. "Bet you're glad you came in, huh?!" Hanuki said; apparently one of my wisdom teeth was rotting away. I also had the honor of having her remove my plaque. To her credit, I must say that regardless of how much her face says "ambitious Sengoku-era warlord," her hands are precise and trustworthy. She's a true professional.

A dense man like me shouldn't even try to guess at Hanuki's feelings following the disappearance of Master Higuchi, but she must be lonely. For that reason, whenever she asks me to go drinking, I make sure to extend the invite to Akashi and Ozu.

And it almost always ends up a total mess.

• • •

Ozu and I took over Master Higuchi's one concern: the Masochistic Proxy-Proxy War. When I think that I must carry on this unsavory battle until I find a proxy, I can't help but feel depressed.

In the duel on Kamo Ohashi, I was awarded the initiative. For my first attack, I took advantage of Ozu's hospitalization to paint his bicycle, Dark Scorpion, pink. It came out looking so shameless, you would never even think it was the same bike.

Ozu hobbled into Shimogamo Yusuiso with his crutches, huffy as a piping hot fish burger, so enraged his hair was standing on end.

"You're awful. You can't go turning things pink."

"Aren't you the one who dyed Master Higuchi's yukata pink?" I asked.

"That was different."

"It was not!"

"Let's have Akashi be the judge. I'm sure she'll understand."

That was how things were going.

• • •

It's not fair for you to assume that I'd naively approve of my past just because there have been some new developments in my student life since Master Higuchi left. I'm not the kind of man who would so readily affirm his past mistakes. Certainly I considered giving myself a big, loving embrace, but regardless of how it would go with a black-haired maiden of a tender age, who would have any interest in hugging a mess of a twenty-something guy? Driven by that inescapable anger, I firmly refused to give my past self salvation.

I can't shake the feeling that I never should have signed up to be a disciple at the foot of that fateful clock tower. I think about what could have happened if I had chosen something else. If I had joined the film club, Ablutions, or chosen the Mellow softball club, or if I had joined that underground organization Lucky Cat Chinese Food, I would have had a very different couple of years. At least, it's clear that I wouldn't be as warped as I am now. I might have attained that elusive treasure, a rose-colored campus life. No matter how I try to avert my eyes, I can't deny the fact that the past two years have been utterly wasted on a pile of mistakes.

More than anything, the stain of having met Ozu is sure to linger for the rest of my days.

● ● ●

In the immediate aftermath of Master Higuchi's disappearance, Ozu was staying in the hospital next to the school.

I have to say, it felt pretty great to see him strapped into a crisp white bed. He always had such a horrible complexion that he looked like a patient with an untreatable illness, but it was just a broken bone. I suppose it's lucky that he got away with just a broken bone. He grumbled that he wasn't able to perpetrate any of the misdeeds he preferred over three square meals a day, but I just thought, *That's what you get*. When his grumbles got to be too much, I crammed the castella I brought him into his mouth to shut him up.

How did he get a broken bone?

We have to go back to the night that swarm of moths flew by Kamo Ohashi.

• • •

Pushing my way through the swarm of moths as they flapped into my face, sprinkling their scales around, sometimes trying to force their way into my mouth, I moved to Akashi and protected her like a total gentleman.

Meanwhile, Ozu, his creepy grin unwavering even as every nook and cranny of his body was fondled by moths, waited for things to calm down. His only concern was that his hair was getting messed up.

Just then, what he saw through the slits of his barely open eyes was Master Higuchi clambering up onto the bridge's railing. Beyond the veil of powdery scales in the air, our master spread his arms atop the railing as if he were going to slip into the swarm of moths and depart the old capital. Ozu yelled, "Master!" in spite of himself. He choked when several moths flew into his mouth, but he still got ahold of the railing and desperately grabbed our master's yukata. Suddenly Master Higuchi's body rose into the air, and Ozu felt his own body float along. Master Higuchi stared down at him. Though he was cocooned in the sound of flapping moth wings, Ozu swears he heard our master say, "You're quite the promising disciple, Ozu."

But this was Ozu himself relaying the story, so it can't be trusted.

With that parting comment, Master Higuchi escaped Ozu's attempt to stop him.

Ozu then lost his balance on the railing and fell into the Kamo River. He broke his leg and was stuck under the bridge like a piece of garbage, unable to move, until a member of the cheer squad partying on the delta found him.

The ambulance that stopped by the west end of Kamo Ohashi while Akashi and I were leisurely sipping our coffee had been on its way to pick up Ozu.

• • •

That explains Ozu's broken bone, but it doesn't hold much water when it comes to Master Higuchi's disappearance. I suspected there was something Ozu wasn't telling us.

"You're saying our master took off on the wings of moths for his world tour?"

"I'm sure that's what happened. It must be," Ozu said.

"I can't trust anything you say."

"Have I ever told a lie?"

"How am I supposed to believe you put yourself in physical danger in order to stop him?"

"I did, though. Our master's important to me," he snapped back.

"If he's really so important to you, then why did you play double agent with Jogasaki? What the hell was that about?" I asked.

• • •

Ozu put on his usual yokai grin and laughed his head off.

"It's my love language."

"Gross—you can spare me," I replied.

THREE

Tatami and the Sweet Life

Let's just say I accomplished absolutely nothing during the two years leading up to the spring of my junior year in college. Every move I made in my quest to become an able participant in society (to associate wholesomely with members of the opposite sex, to devote myself to my studies, to temper my flesh) somehow missed its mark, and I ended up making all sorts of moves, as if on purpose, that need not have been made at all (to isolate myself from the opposite sex, to abandon my studies, to allow my flesh to deteriorate). How did that happen?

We must ask the person responsible. And who is responsible?

It's not as if I was born this way.

Fresh from the womb I was innocence incarnate, every bit as precious as the Shining Prince Genji must have been in his infancy. My smile, without a hint of malice, is said to have filled the mountains and valleys of my birthplace with the radiance of love. And now what has become of me? Whenever I look in the mirror I am swept up in a storm of anger. *How the hell did you end up like this? You've come so far, and this is all you amount to?*

"You're still young," some would say. "It's never too late to change."

Are you fucking kidding me?

They say that the soul of a child at three remains the same even when the man reaches a hundred. So what good can it do for a splendid young man of twenty-one, nearly a quarter century old, to put a lot of sloppy effort into transforming his character? The most he can do in attempting to force the stiffened tower of his personality to bend is to snap it right in half.

I must shoulder the burden of my current self for the rest of my life. I mustn't avert my eyes from that reality.

I can't look away, but it's just so hard to watch.

• • •

After a nigh fruitless two years, I became a junior.

I'm going to attempt to write about some *King Lear*–level drama that occurred that spring between me and three women, but this story is neither a tragedy nor a comedy. If someone sheds tears reading this, it must be that either their sensibilities are overly keen or they got curry powder on their contacts. And if someone laughs from the pit of their stomach, I will hate that person from the pit of my stomach as if they'd insulted my parents and chase them to the ends of the earth to pour hot water over them and wait three minutes.

I'm sure some extremely admirable person has said that if you have the will to learn from even the most trivial matter, there is a way. Naturally, those words apply to this series of events as well.

I, for one, learned all sorts of things. I learned so many things I can't possibly list them all. If I had to pick two, I'd say, "Don't hand over the reins to Johnny so easily," and "Don't stand on the Kamo Ohashi railing."

As for the rest, please glean them from the text as you read.

• • •

On a quiet May night, the witching hour . . .

My base of operations was a room at Shimogamo Yusuiso in Shimogamo Izumikawacho. From what I had heard, it had been standing there since being rebuilt after burning down in the disorder accompanying the last days of the Tokugawa shogunate. If there hadn't been light seeping through the windows, the building would have been taken for abandoned. I thought I must have wandered into the walled city of Kowloon when I first visited the place on the university co-op's introduction. The three-story wooden structure caused all those who saw it anxiety; it seemed ready to collapse at any moment. Its dilapidation was practically Important Cultural Property level. Certainly no one would miss it if it burned down. In fact, there was no doubt in my mind that this would be a load off for its landlady, who lived just to the east.

Sitting upright in my four-and-a-half-mat tatami room, number 110, I scowled up at the light. It was dim and flickering now and then. I'd been thinking I needed to change the bulb, but that was a pain in the ass, so I hadn't yet.

Just as I was carefully making a selection from my library of obscenities, my best friend whom one can't help but hate, Ozu, came over and drummed on the door, ruining this hour of peace and tranquility I love. I pretended not to be home and tried to lose myself in a book, but Ozu emitted a cry like a small animal being tortured and urged me to open the door. Acting without thinking about anyone else is his specialty.

When I opened the door, he put on his Nurarihyon smirk and said, "'Scuse me." Then he called back into the darkness of the hallway, "Okay, Kaori. Apologies for the squalid accommodations . . ."

Loitering around the Shimogamo Shrine neighborhood in the dead of night in the company of a woman and absorbing oneself in profligate diversions is inexcusable. Still, if there was a woman present, I at least had the decency to clean up my library of obscenities.

With a sidelong glance as I hastily stowed the books back in their places, Ozu came in with a petite woman riding piggyback. Her silky, flowing hair was beautiful, and this scene of such a sweet lady entrusting herself to a yokai like Ozu had the aura of indefensible crime.

"What in the . . . Is she drunk?" I asked, worried.

"Huh? This isn't a person," Ozu commented, bizarrely.

He sat the woman down, leaning her against the bookcase. Apparently she was heavy; sweat had beaded on his forehead. When he fixed her hair, I got a good look at her features.

She had an adorable face. Her skin was completely human in hue, and when I gently touched it, there was a springy firmness. She had well-kept hair and was immaculately dressed. She looked like a lady of noble birth—except she didn't move at all. It was as if she had been frozen the instant she cast her eyes into the distance.

"This is Kaori," Ozu introduced her.

"What is it?"

"A love doll. I can't keep it in my room, so I want you to hold onto it for me."

"You've got some nerve barging in here in the middle of the night with this bullshit."

"There, there. It's only a week. I wouldn't do you wrong." That Nurarihyon smirk.

"It's like a pretty flower suddenly bloomed out of your filthy tatami mats," he said. "She'll brighten the place up a bit."

• • •

Ozu was in the same year as me. Despite being registered in the Department of Electrical and Electronic Engineering, he hated electricity, electronics, and engineering. At the end of freshman year he had received so few credits, and with such low grades, that it made you wonder whether there was any point to him being there, but Ozu himself didn't give a damn.

Because he hated vegetables and ate only instant foods, his face was such a creepy color it looked like he'd been living on the far side of the moon. Eight out of ten people who met him walking down the street at night would take him for a yokai goblin. The other two would be shapeshifted yokai themselves. Ozu kicked those who were down and buttered up anyone stronger than him. He was selfish and arrogant, lazy and contrary. He never studied, had not a crumb of pride, and fueled himself on other people's misfortunes. There was not a single praiseworthy bone in his body. If only I had never met him, my soul would surely be less tainted.

On that note, we must say that joining the Mellow softball club in the spring of my freshman year was my first big mistake.

• • •

At the time, I was a fresh-as-a-daisy-man. I remember how exhilarating the vibrant green of the cherry tree leaves was after all the flower petals had fallen.

Any new student walking through campus gets club flyers thrust upon them, and I was weighed down with so many that my capacity for processing information had been far overwhelmed. There were all sorts of flyers, but the four that caught my eye were as follows: the Ablutions film club, a bizarre "Disciples Wanted" notice, the Mellow softball club, and the underground organization Lucky Cat Chinese Food. They all seemed pretty shady, but each one represented a doorway into a new college-student life, and my curiosity was piqued. The fact that I thought a fun future would be waiting on the other side, no matter which door I chose, just goes to show what an incorrigible idiot I was.

After my classes were over, I headed to the clock tower. All kinds of clubs were meeting there to take new students to orientations.

The area around the clock was bustling with freshmen, their cheeks flushed with hope, and welcoming committee members ready to prey on them. It seemed to me that here there were innumerable entryways leading to that elusive prize—a rose-colored campus life—and I walked among them half in a daze.

First, I found several students waiting with a sign for the film club, Ablutions. They were holding a screening to welcome new students and offered to show me the way. For whatever reason, I couldn't make up my mind to approach them, and I ended up going around to the other side of the clock tower. Just then, I caught sight of a student holding a placard that said "Mellow."

Mellow was a club that borrowed a corner of the school grounds on the weekends to play softball. People who wanted to show up to practice could if they felt like it, but aside from the occasional games, you could use your time as you pleased. I was charmed by the carefree name and lax operating policies. And I had heard there were plenty of girls, too.

It wasn't like I played sports in high school, but I hadn't been in any other clubs either. Really, I did my best to lie low and not participate in anything at all; I spent all my time sitting around with equally inactive men.

I thought, *Well, it wouldn't be so bad to get some exercise.* A real sports team would have been too much for me, but this softball club was just for fun. The point was to make friends, so I wouldn't have to worry about chasing that white ball around night after day after night after day to qualify for the All Japan Championship. Farewell, melancholy high school days. There's no downside to making a hundred friends while working up an invigorating sweat. Following a diligent training period, I would surely gain enough social skills to be able to play conversational catch with beautiful women just as easily as tossing a softball back and forth. This was an ability I most definitely wanted to acquire before going out into the world. My objective was to gain skills, not associate with women. But if women came along as the result of my gaining those skills, I had no intention of rejecting them. *Don't worry. Relax, come chill with me.*

The very thought had me trembling in excitement.

It bears repeating: I was an incorrigible idiot.

Thus, having joined Mellow, I became painfully aware of how difficult it is to smile and talk to people and associate in a pleasant way. The atmosphere was laughably relaxed, beyond anything I could have imagined, and I couldn't for the life of me get used to it. It was unendurably embarrassing. Far from mastering flexible social skills, I couldn't even enter the circle of conversation. By the time I realized I would have to study the art of entering a conversation elsewhere, it was too late, and I had failed to fit in.

How easily my dreams were shattered.

But when I was at wit's end, there was one man in the club from whom I sensed some humanity. That man was Ozu.

• • •

Ozu said the manual labor had left him hungry. I was seized by an unstoppable desire for Neko Ramen, so we left Shimogamo Yusuiso and headed for the noodle stall under the cover of night. Neko Ramen is a ramen stand rumored to make its soup from cats. Regardless of whether that's true or not, the flavor is unparalleled.

As Ozu slurped from his steaming bowl of noodles, he explained that he had stolen the doll, Kaori, from someone's lodgings on his master's orders.

"I'm pretty sure that's a crime, I said.

"Is it?" Ozu cocked his head.

"It sure the fuck is. And I'm not about to be made an accessory."

"But this guy and my master have been friends for five years. I think he'll understand. Besides," he continued, with an indefensibly lewd smirk, "you must want to see what it's like to live with her. I can tell."

"You bastard."

"Why are you looking at me like that?"

"Hey, don't hang all over me," I said.

"But I'm *looonely*. And the evening breeze is so cold."

"You're always lonely."

"Eek!"

Eventually, imitating senseless lovers' talk to kill time at the ramen stall wore thin as well. And somehow I had the feeling we'd had a similar exchange before, which pissed me off.

"Hey, didn't we have this conversation before?" I asked.

"I think not. We're not that dumb. You're just having déjà vu, that's all."

As we continued our bullshit, wavering between ecstasy and anxiety over the unique taste of the ramen, a customer came in and stood next to us. I glanced over and noted how strange he was.

He looked perfectly nonchalant in his navy yukata and wore geta clogs like those you might find on a tengu spirit. Something about him reminded me of a mountain hermit. I looked up from my bowl, and as I observed this mystery man, I realized I had seen him a few times around Shimogamo Yusuiso. I'd seen him from behind, creaking his way up the stairs; I'd seen him from behind, out on the balcony sunbathing while getting his hair cut by a foreign exchange student; I'd seen him from behind, washing some mysterious fruit in the common-use sink. His hair looked like Typhoon No. 8 had just blown through, and the eyes set in his eggplant-shaped head had a carefree look in them. His age was unclear; he might have been older, but he could just as easily have been a college student.

"Oh, you came, too, Master?" Ozu looked up as he slurped his ramen.

"Yes, I was feeling a little peckish."

The man sat down and ordered a bowl of noodles. Apparently this eccentric character was Ozu's master. Ozu paid for his meal—a rare act for this parsimonious fellow.

"I'm positive that we've just dealt a major blow to Jogasaki. The idea that Kaori would be gone when he got back from the café can't possibly have crossed his mind," Ozu declared enthusiastically, but his master frowned as he lit a cigar.

"Akashi came by earlier and said that abducting Kaori was going too far."

"Aw, come on. Why would she think that?"

"She insists that trampling someone's loving relationship like this isn't funny. Even if their partner is a doll. She's prepared to expel herself." Ozu's master scratched his sparsely stubbled chin.

"For someone who's usually hard as rocks, she sure chose a weird case to show compassion. But Master, this is when you need to be master-like and tell her what's what. You shouldn't hold back just because she's a girl."

"Telling people what's what isn't really my style."

"Well, I already went to Jogasaki's place and took it. I'm not about to go return it at this point."

"So where is Kaori, anyhow?"

"In his room." Ozu pointed at me. I silently bowed my head.

The yukata man looked at me with an expression that said, "Oh!" and asked, "Aren't you staying at Shimogamo Yusuiso?"

"I am."

"Humm. Pardon our heist."

• • •

After that we went back to Shimogamo Yusuiso, and Ozu drove off in the car he had used to bring the doll over. Ozu's master bowed to me silently and went up to the second floor.

When I went back to my place, the big doll was still leaning against the bookcase with dreamy eyes.

On the way back, Ozu and his master had muttered to each other and apparently reached the conclusion that since she was here now, we just had to wait and see. I had no say, so how did it make any sense for her to be kept in my four-and-a-half-mat tatami room? Having convinced his master to go along with his plan, Ozu wore a triumphant smirk; meanwhile his master seemed to think it was only natural for me to take care of the doll. It was as if I'd been duped by a tanuki and kitsune trickster tag team.

Ever since quitting Mellow, Ozu and I had continued to hang out together. He may have left one club, but he seemed to have plenty of other things to do. He belonged to a secret organization, he was a respected figure in his film club—he led a busy life.

And among his many habits, visiting this person on the second floor of Shimogamo Yusuiso was an important one. He called that person "Master" and had been coming to Shimogamo

Yusuiso since freshman year. So the reason I had such a hard time breaking our fatal bond was not only because we had fled the same club in the same way, but also because he frequented my lodgings. Whenever I asked him who this "master" was, he would only smirk this obscene smirk. I figured they must just talk smut.

I sat down on the tatami and gazed at my unexpected new roommate, Kaori. The whole thing really pissed me off, but I was forced to admit that she was a pretty charming doll.

"Kaori, I know my room's a dump, but—well, make yourself at home."

I said it just to see, but felt afterward like talking to her was idiotic—even for me—so I laid out my futon and went to bed.

• • •

You could say it was when the immobile beauty Kaori intruded on my four and a half tatami mats that things started to go haywire. My quiet life was assailed in the span of just a few days by a torrent of unbelievable turns, and after being buffeted on that raging river like a bamboo-leaf boat, I was hurled in an entirely different direction without even grasping what was happening. It was all Ozu's fault.

The next day, when I opened my eyes a bit, I was astonished to see an immaculate woman leaning against the bookcase.

A woman in my room? An unprecedented, unexpected affair.

Had I played fiery games of passion with some sheltered maiden and let her stay over, and had said maiden then woken up before me and, horrified at her mistakes of the previous night, leaned against the bookcase, unable to move another muscle? Responsibility, discussion, marriage, dropping out of college, poverty, divorce, extreme poverty, a solitary death—the series of events flickered across the back of my mind like shadows cast by a revolving lantern. This didn't strike me as a situation I could handle, and I trembled in my futon like a new-born deer until I eventually remembered what had happened the night before and that she was a doll.

I was so startled, my eyes fully opened.

Kaori hadn't moved at all during the night. I said good morning to her, made coffee, and fried up a leftover third of a fish burger for breakfast. While I was eating, I talked to Kaori without really knowing why.

"But, wow, Kaori. Guess this is a disaster for the both of us. It must be awful to be stuck in this tiny room stewed in manly essence. Ozu is such a jerk. He's never been someone you could call thoughtful or considerate. He fuels himself on other people's misfortunes. Maybe he didn't get enough love from his parents as a kid . . . You really don't talk much, huh? What has you so mopey on such a nice morning? Come on, you can tell me."

It goes without saying, but she remained silent.

I finished my fish burger and drank my coffee.

I had no business chatting with a doll out of boredom on the morning of my day off. There was real life to attend to. The intermittent rain of the past few days had cleared up and I was awake early, so I thought I'd head out to the neighborhood laundromat.

It was just a few minutes' walk from Shimogamo Yusuiso.

I tossed my laundry into the machine and ran it before going out to buy a can of coffee. When I got back, there was still no one around, and the only laundry machine working was the one on the far left that I always used. I drank my coffee and smoked a cigarette in the fine weather.

When the machine stopped and I opened the lid, I was dumbstruck.

There was no sign of my favorite underwear. Inside the machine sat a spongy little bear plushie. I glared at the adorable thing for a few moments.

This was too bizarre.

If a woman's underwear gets stolen from a laundromat, that I can at least understand. But what's so interesting about stealing gray briefs that have spent the past two years loyally serving a dude like me? Wasn't that just asking for needless sorrow? And the fact that the criminal left behind a cute stuffed animal only raised more questions. What were they trying to impart to me with this bear? Was it affection? But I have no interest in the affections of a criminal who would make off with my underwear. I prefer the affections of a black-haired maiden who is soft, delicate, and sensitive, with a head full of beautiful, dreamlike things.

I opened the other laundry machines, and checked the dryers, too, but there was no sign of my underwear. I stomped my feet. It would have been absurd to report this to the police. I didn't want them to uncover the identity of a criminal this weird.

I went home carrying the spongy bear—because it would

have been too infuriating to go home empty-handed. Flames of rage blazed up inside me, but there was nothing I could do. I kneaded the bear to work off some anger.

• • •

After the theft at the laundromat, I returned to my room thoroughly offended and huffy as a piping hot fish burger.

The four-and-a-half-mat tatami room would get muggy in the western sun, but it was still morning, so it was cool. Kaori awaited my return next to the bookcase. I had been trembling with anger, but gazing at her composed profile seemed to calm me down. Ozu had stolen her from someone, and I was sure that unfortunate individual was searching high and low for her with bloodshot eyes. Given how neat and clean she was, I would imagine she was adored in the manner of all pleasant things—butterflies, flowers!

But just haughtily sitting there, she had no humanity about her. I decided to lay the copy of *Twenty Thousand Leagues Under the Sea* I bought at the Shimogamo used book fair open in her lap. That way she'd give the impression of an intelligent black-haired maiden spurring her dreams on in a corner of my room with a nautical adventure novel. It really brought her personality out.

There was no one in this room—and no one would ever want to enter it.

It was just me and her. Even if I perpetrated a bit of mischief, there was no one around to condemn me. But I exercised self-control I could commend myself for and treated her with the utmost respect. In the first place, Ozu had entrusted her to me. My pride wouldn't allow me to try any funny stuff and suffer his complaints.

To soothe my frayed nerves following the theft of my underwear, I sat at my desk and decided to read the letter that had arrived the other day. It was from a woman.

It may alarm you to hear this, wise readers, but I was engaged in written correspondence.

She lived alone in Jodoji, and her name was Keiko Higuchi. She was a young lady who did administrative work for an English school in Shijo Kawaramachi. Her hobbies were reading and gardening. She wrote happily about the flowers she was growing on her balcony. Her handwriting was beautiful, and her prose was also quite beautiful—she was flawless.

But I had never met her.

• • •

It's very old-fashioned of me, but I love writing letters, and I've always longed for a pen pal. Even better if said pal is a woman in the prime of youth. Why would I write to any intelligent life form who *isn't* a woman in the prime of youth? My pure, single-minded appreciation for letter writing is such that I'm firm on this stance.

The crucial points here are that the letters must be handwritten and that under no circumstances—not even if hell's lid blows off or the world is about to end—do you meet your correspondent. The latter rule, especially, must be followed. If you know your correspondent is a woman in the prime of youth, it's surely natural for the desire to meet her to bubble up within a man. But this is a moment to exercise self-restraint. If you're not careful, the refined relationship you've cultivated will go poof.

My dream was to someday receive a chance out of the blue and embark on a refined correspondence—I had the itch. But embarking on a correspondence with a woman in the prime of youth whom you've never met is harder than you might think. Sending letters to random addresses praying that a woman in the prime of youth lives there is boorish, if not perverted. But consulting an organization like the Kyoto chapter of the Society for Letter-Writing Enthusiasts in Japan just because I feel like writing letters to someone goes against my aesthetic.

When I divulged these hidden feelings to Ozu, he mercilessly teased me for being a creep. Eyes upturned in an indefensibly lewd expression, he said, "I bet you get off on writing dirty stuff to women you've never met. Whatever are we going to do with your uncontrollable eroticism, you prompt yet porn-penning bastard!"

"I would never commit such an unpardonable offense."

"Sure, sure. But I know the truth—that you're fifty percent eros."

"Shut up."

Despite all of that, it was Ozu who presented me with the ideal correspondence opportunity.

In the fall of our sophomore year, Ozu, who was generally only interested in erotic prose, read a normal novel, or so he claimed, which he then gave to me. He said he had bought it on a whim from the hundred-yen bin at a used bookstore on Imadegawa-dori. And then he grumbled, thinking only of his own convenience, that he had finished it and it was dirty, so he didn't need it anymore.

The novel, which went on and on portraying the hardships of an old-fashioned student who had no luck with girls, was far from elegant and not very good, but my eyes were riveted to the final page. A name and address were printed there in beautiful handwriting. Normally, you would erase this sort of thing before you sold the book to a used bookstore, or the bookstore would do it on their end to avoid any trouble. But this case seemed to have slipped through.

I immediately thought, *This is a perfect opportunity. Is this what they call "divine providence"? Isn't this a one-in-a-million chance to embark on correspondence with a new acquaintance of the female persuasion?*

If you consider the situation more rationally, it's clear there was not enough information to determine her youthfulness. And if I was going to go as far as to judge her a woman in the prime of youth who loved reading, was a bit shy, and didn't realize how beautiful she was, well, no wonder I'd get called a creep. But I'm not averse to bearing the stigma of "creep" when the situation calls for it.

I hurried over to the Demachi shopping street and purchased stationery both beautiful and—to counteract the perversion of my endeavor—overflowing with sincerity.

I was sending a letter out of nowhere, so I had enough good sense to make the content benign. If I sent a letter dripping with who knows what juices, she would have every right to report it to the police. I started off by apologizing politely for writing out of the blue, then I smoothly and without any sarcasm added that I was a student engaged in serious academics, honestly stated that I had always wanted to exchange letters with someone, gave my neither complimentary nor disparaging impressions of the book, and specifically avoided saying anything about hoping for a reply. Writing on and on for too long would reek of perversion, so I revised, and revised my revisions, until it all fit on a page and a half of stationery. Rereading the letter after I finished writing, I found it fragrant with sincerity and unblemished by the slightest hint of wickedness—enchanting, if I did say so myself. *Letters really are meant to be written from the heart*, I thought.

In this world of corrupt public morals, replying to a letter from a stranger requires considerable determination. Especially for a sheltered maiden adored in the manner of all pleasant things—butterflies, flowers! I had resolved that I wouldn't be hurt even if I didn't get a letter in return, but one came, so I was ecstatic.

That was the unbelievably simple beginning of my six months of correspondence, which would end in the worst way imaginable that May.

• • •

Greetings,

It feels like Aoi Matsuri was only yesterday but it's already getting muggy out. It's as if we skipped the rainy season and jumped straight to summer.

I don't like the heat, so I hope we get some rain soon. Lots of people hate the rainy season because it's so damp and gloomy, but I find days of continuous drizzle relaxing. There are a lot of hydrangeas at my grandparents' house, and when I was a kid, I always loved watching them bloom from the porch through the veil of rain.

I've been reading Jules Verne's *Twenty Thousand Leagues Under the Sea* ever since you recommended it, and I've just reached part III. I always thought it was a story for kids, but it's actually pretty deep, huh? I like Captain Nemo's air of mystery, but I think my favorite character is the harpooner Ned Land. I feel bad for him being cooped up in the submarine with no way to use his skills. The professor and Conseil are also trapped, but they seem to be sort of having fun; Ned is the only one who's irritated, so that must be why I find myself sympathizing with him. Or maybe I just love to eat as much as he does.

If I were going to recommend something, I suppose it would be Stevenson's *Treasure Island*. Maybe you've already read it; I did when I was little.

Work is the same as always, no major incidents.

A teacher is leaving after three years with us, so we held a going-away party for him the other day at the Irish pub on Oike-dori. I don't drink, but I enjoyed the Irish food. The fried fish was very tasty.

The man who is leaving is from San Francisco, and he said we should meet up if I ever find myself there. He's in his mid-thirties, but I guess he's going back to school. I'd like to study abroad, but I can barely keep up with daily life, so I doubt I'll be able to.

I hope I don't come across as a busybody, but I think it's wonderful that you can explore so many different subjects while you're a university student. I'm sure you'll be able to take advantage of the opportunities you're given and improve yourself immensely. Since you're a junior, I bet you have a lot on your plate this spring, but please believe in yourself and work hard.

That said, your health is most important, so make sure you don't overdo it.

You wrote that you like fish burgers, but please don't eat only fish burgers; balance out your diet and take care of yourself.

Well, I think that's about it for this letter.

I'll be waiting for your reply.

Sincerely,
Keiko Higuchi

• • •

By afternoon, my four-and-a-half-mat tatami room was a sauna. When I get hot, I get irritated, and the anger I felt toward the underwear thief in the laundromat surged up again. Kneading the bear I'd gotten in exchange for my briefs, I gazed at Kaori silently reading in the corner.

To clear my head, I applied myself to my studies.

But as I faced my textbooks, it started to feel like it was too little, too late to make up for the two years I had wasted. Being that pitiful is against my aesthetic, so I gracefully gave up on studying. I have pretty high confidence when it comes to this sort of grace. In other words, I'm a gentleman.

And so, I had no choice but to rely on Ozu for the paper I had to turn in. There was a secret organization called the Printing Office through which you could get a paper written for you by placing an order. I'd been relying on this shady org for my every need for so long that it had gotten to the point where I couldn't make it through a crisis without getting their help via Ozu. Both my body and soul were rotting away. This was one major reason I couldn't break our fatal bond.

It was only the end of May, but it was already muggy enough to be summer. I had my window open as far as I could without risking someone being offended by my porn collection, but the air wasn't moving. The various secret ingredients contained in the stagnant air were slowly maturing like the amber whiskey at a Yamazaki distillery; anyone who entered my four-and-a-half-mat tatami room would become altogether intoxicated. Still, when I opened the door to the hallway, the cat that prowled around Yusuiso came right in and meowed at me, the cute little bugger. It was so cute I wanted to eat it up, and I thought I just might, but of course I couldn't do something so barbaric. A man must be a gentleman even when wearing nothing but his underwear. After cleaning the mucus out of the cat's eyes, I shooed it back into the hall.

Eventually I flopped down and at some point fell deep asleep. I had woken up early, so I guess I didn't get enough rest. When I awoke with a start, the sun was already slanting quite a lot, and my day off was about to end as a total waste. The only thing significant enough to save this day from being a complete wash was English conversation school, and it was almost time for it. I got ready to go.

After having such a miserable time as a member of Mellow, I found myself unable to trust clubs any longer. As a result, I had more time than I knew what to do with. Inspired by Keiko

Higuchi revealing that she worked at an English school, I had been taking lessons at a school in Kawaramachi Sanjo since the previous fall. Incidentally, there was no woman by the name of Higuchi working at the school I attended.

"All right, Kaori. I'm counting on you to hold the fort down," I said as I was leaving, but she was completely absorbed in *Twenty Thousand Leagues Under the Sea* and didn't look up. The profile of a woman absorbed in a book is a truly beautiful sight.

• • •

I sped away from Shimogamo Yusuiso on my bicycle.

The area already had the air of evening about it, and the sky covered with soft clouds glowed pink. A chilly breeze was blowing.

I passed by Shimogamo Shrine, crossed Mikage-dori, and exited the shrine's approach road. Where I came out was between two bridges, Kawaibashi and Demachibashi—right where the Kamo River from the west and the Takano from the east merge into one Kamo River. This area was commonly known as the Kamo River Delta. At this time of year, it was often crowded with college kids holding parties to welcome new students. I remembered being a freshman and attending a barbecue here with those weird softball people, but my inability to join the conversation meant I was left with only sad memories of throwing stones into the river.

As I rode along the cool embankment between the west end of Demachibashi and the west end of Kamo Ohashi, I was seized by some masochistic urge and was staring at the friendly gatherings of students enjoying themselves when I noticed Ozu among a group of chatting kids on the riverbed. There was no mistaking that odd character. I stopped my bike in spite of myself.

Ozu was surrounded by a group of what appeared to be new students, and he seemed totally comfortable. I suppose he was living it up with his bosom buddies from his club, with zero regard for my barren day. With the Kamo River between us, it felt like the flow separated light and darkness, and I was infuriated. What was the world coming to if a bunch of purehearted youngsters would warmly cluster around a creepy yokai like him? Their souls were bound to be polluted, and I had no way of stopping it.

For a while I glared angrily at Ozu from the opposite shore, but that accomplished nothing besides making me hungry. I switched gears and got back on my bicycle.

• • •

After my English lesson, I walked around the dark streets.

To fill my stomach, I stopped by Nagahama Ramen in Sanjo Kiyamachi to slurp a bowl and then strolled through the neighborhood.

As I walked, I thought about Ozu, and my full stomach started to feel a bit sick as my mood fell into it. These two years he had sat complacently in the center of my infinitely small social circle, always finding some way to ruin the tranquility of my four-and-a-half-mat tatami room. Like the way he barged in during the middle of the night to dump Kaori on me and blew out of there like the wind—he was so selfish. But the fundamental problem was that Ozu was polluting my once innocent soul. Mingle with darkness and you turn to the dark side. While I associated with Ozu and his warped character, was my own character not being adversely affected right under my nose?

Smoldering with irritation toward Ozu, I strolled along the Takase River.

Before long, I came to a halt.

Among the bars and sex shops crouched a dark house.

Under its eaves, an old woman sat before a wooden table covered with a white cloth—a fortune-teller. A sheet of paper hanging from the table was crammed full of kanji whose meaning I couldn't fathom. Something like a little lantern glowed orange, bringing the woman's face into view. There was something strangely intimidating about her. She was a yokai licking her lips at the souls of the people passing by. *Get a single fortune read and forevermore the shady old woman will haunt you day and night, nothing you try to do will go well, the one you're waiting for won't come, your lost items will never turn up, you'll fail the classes that should have been easy credits, your graduation thesis will spontaneously combust just before you hand it in, you'll fall into Lake Biwa Canal, you'll be solicited on the street by one of those people on Shijo-dori*—I was resolutely imagining all of this terrible luck while staring at her, so eventually she sensed my presence. From the depths of the darkness, she flashed her eyes at me. The unearthly atmosphere she emitted ensnared me. That atmosphere was persuasive. I considered it logically: there was no way someone giving off supernatural vibes this potent for free would tell a fortune that missed the mark.

I've been alive in this world for nearly a quarter century, but I can count on my fingers the number of times I listened so humbly to another person's opinion. Maybe that was how I ended up purposely taking this thorny path there was no need to walk down at all? If I had abandoned my own judgment sooner, my life as a college student would have turned out very differently. I wouldn't have joined the weird softball club, Mellow, and I probably wouldn't have met Ozu with his labyrinthine character. I would have been blessed with good friends and upperclassmen associates, employing my overflowing talents in full to excel in both the literary and military arts, the result of which would have been a beautiful black-haired maiden at my side and, before me, a shining future of pure gold; and if things went well, perhaps even that elusive, supreme treasure—a rose-colored, meaningful, campus life—would have been within my grasp. For a person of my caliber, such a stroke of luck wouldn't be even a little unusual.

Right.

It's not too late. With all possible haste, seek an objective opinion and escape into one of the other lives you could have!

I stepped forward as if drawn by the old woman's otherworldly aura.

"Well, my boy, what would you like to know?"

She spoke in a mumble as if her mouth was full of cotton, which really made me feel like I was speaking with a wise elder.

"Hmm. Good question."

When I remained lost for words, the old woman smiled. "From the look on your face right now, I gather you're terribly irritated. Dissatisfied. It seems that you aren't making full use of your talents. Apparently your current environment isn't a good fit for you."

"Yes, that's right. That's exactly it."

"Let's have a look."

The old woman took my hands and pored over them, nodding to herself.

"Mm. You seem to be extremely hard-working and talented."

I was already impressed by her keen insights. Just as in the proverb "a clever hawk hides its talons," I had modestly kept my good sense and talents hidden so no one would find them, but I did such a good job that I hadn't been able to locate them myself for the past few years; for her to spot them within five minutes of our meeting meant she couldn't be any ordinary fortune-teller.

"It's essential that you not let chance pass you by. What I mean is a good opportunity. Do you understand? But chance is rather hard to seize: sometimes something that doesn't look like a chance at all is one, while other times what you were sure was your chance turns out, in retrospect, to not have been it at all. But you must perceive your chance and act on it. It looks like you'll have a long life, so I'm sure you'll be able to seize one at some point."

Profound words befitting her otherworldly aura.

"I can't wait that long. I want to seize my chance now. Could you explain in a bit more detail?"

When I pressed her, the old woman's wrinkles warped slightly. I wondered if her right cheek was itchy, but apparently this was a smile.

"It's difficult to speak in particulars. Even if I tell you now, your fate might change, and then it won't be your chance anymore. Wouldn't I feel bad about that? Fate can change from second to second, you know."

"But what you said is so vague I have no idea what to do."

When I cocked my head, the old woman said "Hmm-hmm!" with a sniff. "Very well. I'll refrain from talking about the too distant future, but I'll tell you something very near."

I opened my ears as big as Dumbo's.

"*Colosseo*," she whispered suddenly.

"Colosseo? What's that?"

"Colosseo is the sign of your chance. When your chance appears, there colosseo will be," she said.

"You're not telling me to go to Rome, are you?" I asked, but the old woman only grinned.

"When your chance comes, don't miss it. When it comes, you can't go on idly doing the same things you've always done. Be bold, and try seizing your chance by doing something completely different. If you do that, your dissatisfaction will disappear, and you'll be able to walk down a new path—though there may lie a different dissatisfaction. I'm sure you understand."

I didn't understand one bit, but I nodded anyway.

"Even if you miss this chance, you needn't worry. You're a fine person, so I'm sure you'll be able to seize one someday. That I know for sure. There's no rush."

With that, she ended the reading.

"Thank you."

I bobbed my head and paid her fee. When I stood and turned to go, a woman was standing behind me.

"Playing little lost lamb, are you?" said Hanuki.

• • •

Hanuki went to the same English school as me. I had known her for about six months, since I had signed up the previous fall, but we were just classmates, nothing more. I had made repeated attempts to steal her superior techniques, but they all ended in failure.

Hanuki spoke extremely fluid, extremely messy English. The fragments of what seemed to be English that she hurled forth one after another danced in the air and, despite their broken grammar, joined together in a way that transcended the rules to somehow make sense in the mind of the listener. It was profoundly mysterious. Meanwhile, while I revised my revisions in my head, the conversation would move on, and by the time I had confidently completed some lines I could pronounce with my dignity intact, it was too late. This was the pattern I tirelessly repeated. Rather than speaking grammatically bankrupt English, I would choose the glory of silence. I am a man who looks before he leaps.

From what I had gleaned in her self-introduction at school, I knew she worked at a dental office. In our English class, we all spoke on topics of our choice, and she almost always talked about teeth. Her dentistry vocabulary had grown by leaps and bounds even just during the six months since we'd met. And her classmates' knowledge of dentistry had also grown by leaps and bounds—a very good thing.

My speeches were always about Ozu's evil deeds, because Ozu occupied the core of my social life. Honestly, I hesitated to publicize his unproductive activities in an international context, but when I referred to one of them out of necessity one day, my classmates applauded for some reason, and I ended up giving regular "Ozu News" reports. I guess it was funny because it was all happening to someone else.

After a few rounds of these anecdotes, Hanuki approached me one day after class. I was surprised to learn that she was acquainted with Ozu. He was a patient at Kubozuka Dental, where she worked—not to mention that the "master" Ozu was always visiting also happened to be an old friend of hers.

She said, "Small world, huh?"

We got to talking about Ozu's unscrupulous nature and hit it off right away.

• • •

After I ran into Hanuki out by the fortune-teller, the two of us decided to get a drink at an izakaya together.

Hanuki had come to Kiyamachi because she had made plans with someone after English class, but she was suddenly filled with loathing for him, and not only that, but she wanted a drink, and she didn't want to see him, and actually she wanted to drink like there was no tomorrow; these were the troubles she was carrying when she found me wondering what to do with my life. "Perfect timing, perfect timing!" she sang in a chaotic melody as she briskly led me off on a voyage into the night.

Since it was the weekend, the izakaya was hopping. There were always a lot of college kids around, but especially during the new student welcome party season. Here and there I saw people who looked so young they had probably been high schoolers until just the other day.

We toasted to the dark future spreading out before Ozu. As long as we were bad-mouthing him, we could keep the conversation going, so that was handy. There are infinite types of slander in this world.

"He's made my life hell," I said.

"I bet. I mean, that's his hobby."

"More like his purpose in life. He's always interfering in other people's business for no good reason . . ."

"And then he turns around and keeps his own secret."

"Seriously. I don't even know where he lives. He won't tell me no matter how many times I ask. Yet he's shown up at my place a zillion times . . ."

"Oh? I've been to his place," she said.

"Really?"

"It's over in the Jodoji area, a little ways off Shirakawa-dori; he lives in a studio in a fancy building that looks like candy. Ozu gets loads of money from his parents. They have my pity."

"Wow, and I thought he couldn't piss me off any more."

"But you're his best friend, aren't you?" she said, and then cackled. "He talks about you all the time."

"What does he say about me?" I asked, envisioning Ozu grinning ominously in the gloom. It was possible he was feeding

Hanuki outrageous lies, in which case I would need to firmly deny them.

"All sorts of things. Like how you escaped a weird club together."

"Oh . . ."

That was true.

• • •

The club I had strayed into, Mellow, was—as its name implied—as mellow as a cloud hanging in a sky veiled with spring mist. There was no hierarchy among members; students in all years treated each other with mutual respect. No senior or junior members, no hatred or sadness—everyone tossed love back and forth the same way they tossed the white ball; they all wanted to have a fun time and help each other out. Yes, join for a week and you'll want to flip a table.

As we played catch on the school grounds on the weekends, grabbed food, and generally hung around together, May passed by, June passed by, July passed by. Would these tepid interactions allow me to master basic social skills? No. My patience was on its last legs.

I just couldn't get used to the other members. They were always smiling and speaking in gentle tones, never arguing or talking smut. Everyone and their brother made the same impression, so I couldn't tell them apart or match any names with faces. Every time I said anything, everyone would fall silent with their kind smiles still plastered on their faces.

The only person I felt any affinity with was Ozu. He had his own unique powers of conversation that secured him a position within the group, but he seemed to have a hard time with the innocent smiling bit and always ended up smirking like a yokai, so the impression he made was that he was incapable of hiding the evil lurking just beneath his skin. He was the only one whose name and face I was able to remember. Frankly, I wish I would've forgotten them.

That summer, the club took a trip to a forest on the prefectural border between Kyoto and Osaka for two nights and three days. There was softball practice for amusement, but we were mainly there to get to know each other. *You're always smiling and getting along, so I doubt there could be any more ice to break at this point,* I thought unkindly.

But then on the second day, after a meeting in one room of the outdoor activity center where we were staying, a middle-aged man I had never seen before was suddenly introduced by one of the upperclassmen. It was so sudden. He was on the fat side, with a face that looked like he'd been stuffing it with marshmallows, and his glasses were too small, so they looked like they were embedded in his head.

Before long, he began to speak. He was putting an awful lot of effort into talking about love, and the ills of contemporary society, and how "This is your fight!" His slippery, exaggerated remarks went on and on, but I had no idea what he was trying to say. *Who is this?* I thought, but when I looked around, everyone else was listening appreciatively. The only ones yawning were me and Ozu, sitting diagonally in front of me.

After a little while, at the man's urging, club members stood up, one after the other, to talk about all sorts of personal matters. Some confided their anxieties; others expressed gratitude for the club's existence. Some said they were happy to be invited. One girl stood up to talk and ended up bursting into tears. The plump guy consoled her in a syrupy tone: "You're not wrong, sweetheart. I believe you—all of us here believe you."

Ozu stood when he was called on. "I was so nervous about everything when I started college; I think I was only able to adjust because I joined this club. I feel so at ease with everyone here. I really think this is an amazing group." He spoke so artlessly it was as if he hadn't been yawning at all.

• • •

"And then what happened?" Hanuki pressed me for the rest of the story. Maybe it was because she was a little drunk, but she sounded sort of affectionate.

"I got called on and said whatever, but then the plump guy said he would come to my room to talk later; that's when I realized I was in for some trouble. On the way back to my room I ducked into the bathroom and killed time until there was no one left in the lobby; then I headed down to the entryway and went outside."

"And you ran into Ozu there."

"Exactly."

When I snuck out of the outdoor activity center and saw Ozu appear out of the darkness, I thought I had encountered an ancient, forest-dwelling yokai. After quickly realizing that it was Ozu, I still didn't lower my guard—because I figured he was an assassin sent by Mellow. He would wind a rope around me and present me to the plump man to foil my escape. I could be locked in a basement torture cell that reeked like nukazuke pickles and grilled about every last detail of bittersweet memories, such as my first crush in high school. I wasn't about to let them get away with that so easily.

As I scowled at him, he whispered, "Hurry! You're running away, right? I'm going with!"

Having no choice, then, but to sympathize with each other, we went through the dark forest.

To descend from the outdoor activity center to the farming village at the base of the mountain, we had to walk a truly pitch-black road, but Ozu had a flashlight, which was a big help. He was the kind of guy who was prepared for any eventuality. I had left my luggage in my room, but I wasn't concerned, as I hadn't brought anything important. Cars went by now and then, and each time one passed, we dove into the trees and hid.

"What a big adventure," Hanuki said with exaggerated admiration.

"I dunno. I'm not sure whether our desperation was warranted. It's possible that if we had stayed that night, nothing would have happened," I said.

"But it was a religious club, no?"

"Well, yeah. But after that, I just got one phone call—no repeated soliciting. Maybe they never considered me a promising target to begin with."

"Hmm, maybe not. So you walked down the mountain road, and then what?" she asked.

"Well, we got off the mountain and went through some fields. We figured once we got to the national highway we would be able to get a lift, but since it was the middle of the night, there were almost no cars, and we couldn't get anyone to stop. Not that I would stop for two creepy, empty-handed guys in the middle of the night, either."

"That's rough."

"So after that we just walked a ton, found a sign, and headed toward the nearest station. It was so far away, because we were in the middle of nowhere. We finally arrived at around four a.m., but we were paranoid that someone would come looking for us there, so we walked along the tracks to the next station. It was very *Stand By Me*. We bought canned coffee to kill time outside the station and then boarded the first train."

"Dang."

"I slept like a dead man on the train. My legs were totally shot."

"And that's how you became tight with Ozu . . ."

"No—we're about as tight as a loose screw," I said, and Hanuki cackled.

"But Ozu does have an innocent side," she said.

"Not that I've ever seen."

"Oh, come on. You've never heard about his girlfriend?"

That caught my attention. I leaned forward in spite of myself. "What, what, *what*? Ozu has a girlfriend?"

"Yeah. A girl he met his freshman year in the film club. He hasn't introduced her to his master, and I've never met her, either. I guess he doesn't want her to see how he is in other settings. It's pathetic but also kind of cute, don't you think? He even asked me for advice about her once."

"Damn it all to hell."

Seeing me quaking in anger, Hanuki seemed terribly amused. "What was her name, again? Mmnh . . ."

• • •

Hanuki took me to a place in Pontocho where she was a regular, Bar Moon Walk, and as we talked all kinds of shit about Ozu, we got along better and better. Bad-mouthing really brings people together.

Eventually I told her about what happened at the laundromat.

"They wanted your underwear that badly?" She cocked her head, laughing.

"Not even joking, it really sucks when all your underwear suddenly goes missing at once."

As we carried on like that, the night deepened, but Hanuki didn't lose any momentum. Buffeted by the nightlife racket, I grew tired. I couldn't go on drinking alcohol forever, either, and I felt that I needed some air. When Hanuki's drunk eyes started to twinkle alluringly, I began to miss my four-and-a-half-mat tatami room. *I want to go home ASAP. And when I get there, I want to select something from my library of obscenities without mulling over this or that and then dive straight into my futon.*

But things proceeded in a way that betrayed expectations.

Since we lived in the same neighborhood, we ended up grabbing a taxi back together, and the way her eyes were gleaming, I lost faith in my ability to steer reality. Hanuki had been watching the night scenery go by outside, but when she turned to me and laughed quietly to herself—"Heh-heh"—she looked like she was about to eat me.

Her apartment was near Mikage-dori, facing Kawabata-dori. Her feet were unsteady. By the time I had decided to escort her to her place, and she invited me in for tea, I no longer had any idea who I was, where I had come from, or where I was going; I felt as helpless as if I had been left behind in the eternal flow of time. I trembled like an abandoned cat out in the rain.

• • •

Ever since passing through the cursed gates of puberty, I've been keeping my Johnny miserable. Among the Johnnys of other men were surely a countless lot that did what they pleased without any regard for respectability. But with an owner like me, my Johnny was unable to show off the full extent of his mischief in broader society, and his true powers were kept under tight wraps. Though a clever hawk hides its talons, it wasn't as if hot-blooded Johnny could tolerate such empty circumstances forever. If given an opening, he would confirm his raison d'être by throwing off my restraints and haughtily rearing his head.

"Hey, hey, my turn's coming up, right?" his fearless voice would say over and over.

And each time, I would reply, "Your chance has not yet come," and scold him harshly with a "Stay where you are!"

I'm a respectable, civilized member of contemporary society. I'm a gentleman, and I have lots of other things to do. I argue that I don't have time to occupy myself with sexy-time games just to give Johnny space to do what he pleases.

"Is my chance ever going to actually come?" Johnny would

grumble. "Don't patronize me with your half-assed consolations."

"Oh, don't be like that. I can't help but look down on you; you're down *there*."

"Hmph. I know you care more about your brain than me. Shit. I wish I lived upstairs."

"Don't pout. It's pathetic."

"I guess good things don't actually come to those who wait, huh?"

With that, he would loll to the side and sulk.

It's not as if I don't care for him, so it pained me to watch him waiting with no sign of any opportunities on the horizon.

The naughtier he got, the more I saw myself in him—barking like a lone wolf, unable to come to an understanding with the world. My compassion only grew. *Is he doomed to frolic only in the occasional fantasy world, wasting his precious talents?* The thought had me holding back tears.

"Don't cry," Johnny would say. "Sorry, I was being selfish."

"No, I'm sorry," I would say.

Thus, Johnny and I would make up.

Well, if that's how you imagine my days going, you wouldn't be wrong.

● ● ●

Hanuki's room was tidy. There weren't many extraneous objects. I got the feeling she could pick up and go wherever she liked at the drop of a hat, which made me jealous. It was like night and day in comparison to my chaotically chaotic four-and-a-half-mat tatami room.

"I'm sorry. I think I had one drink too many." Hanuki cackled as she made some herbal tea. Her eyes were giving off that dubious light. At some point she had taken off her jacket and was wearing only a blouse on top. I had no idea when she did that.

She opened the window to the balcony. Since it faced Kawabata-dori, we could see the trees lining the Takano River.

"Nice location next to the river, right? Though the cars are a little loud," she said. "If you go up to the roof, you can see Daimonji."

But I no longer had any interest in things like Mount Daimonji.

I was facing that classic example of an extraordinary situation—being invited into a room where a woman lives alone and drinking tea alone with her—and thinking how to get through it while maintaining my dignity, like a gentleman. Historyphysicspsychologybiologyliteraturepseudoscience—I mobilized my knowledge from every possible field, and my brain's internal combustion engine roared. *If Ozu were here, I wouldn't have to be so nervous; things would go fine*, I thought.

But jeez, isn't Hanuki being a bit too careless?

Leading me into her room after midnight was dangerous. Certainly I was her classmate from English school, and we had known each other for six months. And I was her acquaintance Ozu's "best friend." But any woman with decent powers of judgment probably wouldn't be able to rest until she had turtletied me, wrapped me in a sheet, hung me from the balcony upside down, and set the whole kit and caboodle on fire. With complete disregard for my worrying about her on behalf of her drunk self, she began to tell me, in a sweet voice, about the person she was supposed to meet that evening.

I was surprised to learn she had been waiting for Dr. Kubozuka himself of Kubozuka Dental. Hearing that he had a wife and children was even more shocking. I found it inexcusable that someone in that position would abuse the powers of his station to plan a rendezvous with her, but she said she had been working for him for a long time, and a dense male student like me could hardly comprehend the intricacies of adult relationships. I was thinking I shouldn't make any reckless comments, but she spoke more and more about her relationship with the dentist and asked for my advice.

"Maybe it was wrong of me to leave him in Kiyamachi," she murmured.

I gradually found less and less to say. And as I grew quieter, Hanuki scooted closer.

"Heyyy, whaddya makin' such a scary face for?" she asked.

"Alas, this is my resting face."

"That's not true. You didn't have wrinkles in those spots before!" she said, leaning her face closer to my brow.

Then she suddenly tried to lick my forehead.

I freaked out and recoiled. She clung to me with a blatantly bizarre look in her eyes.

• • •

As for what I realized at that moment, there are four things I can list.

One was that the swell of her breasts was pressing against me. I tried to accept this fact calmly, but in line with the majority of expectations, that was extremely difficult. I'm someone who has always found it shameful that men are driven into a frenzy by this mystery swell only women possess, and though I had spent long years observing them via video, I hadn't managed to solve the puzzle of how we could be ruled by these things when their only real merit was their soft roundness. Naturally, given the location of Hanuki's breasts at this moment, I was not averse to being aroused, but it wouldn't do to allow my simple heart to be clenched in the thorny talons of such a simple plumpness and squander the chastity I had had no choice but to protect all these long years. My pride wouldn't allow it.

The second was that when I looked up to avoid being licked, I saw a corkboard. Among all the other photos pinned to it was one she must have taken on a trip. It was Italy. Despite the extraordinary nature of the situation I was in, seeing the Colosseo there instantly reminded me of what the fortune-teller in Ki-yamachi had said. Was this the chance I had been waiting for?

The third was that Johnny, that hooligan, began to assert his presence, as if the good things he had been waiting for had come. He reared his head, saying, "Hey, hey, is it my turn?" When I tried to scold him, he made a convincing argument: "But isn't this your chance? I've been holding back for so long— enough is enough. It's about time you let me take the reins."

The fourth was that if I moved left along the wall we were against and went through the kitchen, the bathroom was on the other side. You could say it was the perfect place to hole up, clear my mind, and wait for the situation to blow over.

Hanuki tangled herself around me and kept trying to lick my face. My mind strayed from its straying, and Johnny squirmed ominously as he appealed for a place to shine. Apparently he was plotting to soak up every drop of every type of desire from throughout my whole body and seize hegemony. The General Staff—that is, my brain—hadn't given the go sign yet, but Johnny and his party were crowding the entrance to the office. "What are you doing?!" "I'm pretty sure your chance is right now!" "This isn't what we agreed upon!" they roared.

Sitting deep in the General Staff office, I plugged my ears so I wouldn't have to hear Johnny's voice and then stared down in earnest at the operation map of my life. "Can you call yourself civilized if you let yourself get swept away by a moment's desire? Is it possible to maintain your dignity if you take advantage of a woman you don't even know to do the deed while she's restlessly drunk?" I solemnly said, but that only made Johnny start pounding on the office's iron door. He was virtually half mad.

"If we can do the deed, that's all that matters!" he was shouting. "Surrender control to *meee*!"

"What's the point of doing it just to do it? Nothing should take precedence over one's pride."

In response to my argument, Johnny switched to an entreating tone. "C'mon, what's the point of a man's chastity, anyhow? If you guard it forever, who in the world is gonna be like, 'Nice job, buddy!'? This might be a doorway to a new world. Don't you want to see what's on the other side?"

"I do want to see what's on the other side. But it's not time yet."

"You say that, but isn't this your chance? You saw the Colosseo! It's just like that old fortune-teller predicted!"

"The one who decides whether to seize the chance or not is me, not you," I said.

"Ahhhmahgahhhh, I'm gonna cry. You're gonna make me cry."

I turned my heart to stone. I inched my way along the wall to run away from Hanuki, who was still scooting into me, but she clung all the same. We moved across the room, in tandem, like some strange creature that lurks deep in the jungle, and eventually slid into the kitchen.

"Ah, a cockroach!"

The moment I said that, Hanuki whipped around in surprise. I capitalized on that opening to finally stand up. Then I ran into the bathroom to hole up and locked the door. It's too bad it didn't seem to be the kind of thing you could be proud of doing, even though I was doing it to maintain my pride.

I don't think I need to tell you that Johnny was heartbroken and wailing.

• • •

"Are you okay? Do you feel sick?" Hanuki called to me from outside the bathroom in a carefree voice.

I said, "I'm fine. Just . . ." and listened. She appeared to eventually go back to the main room.

Shut up in the bathroom, I considered the three women I was involved with. One of them was a pen pal whose face I had never seen, one was a doll, and one was someone who licked people's faces when she got drunk.

But in the past two years of my indifferently lived life, my vicinity had never been so full of cheer. Oh, the sweet life. Perhaps the wind changed when Ozu brought Kaori to my room. From now on, I'll meet woman after woman, my planner will be crammed with dates, and I'll have to whisper so many sweet nothings my throat will bleed. Just the thought was enough to make me sick of it. I could just see the nervous breakdown in my future—I'd end up having to race up Mount Hiei.

If I wasn't aiming to be a master of sexy-time games, I would need to settle on one woman.

Of the three of them, one was a literal doll, so I would have to count her out. Another I was forbidden from meeting due to my pen pal philosophy. Obviously, that left only Hanuki.

The Kiyamachi fortune-teller had predicted "colosseo" and, lo and behold, here was a Colosseo photo. This wasn't about Johnny's superficial whining for the initiative to be yielded to my lower half. Precisely because this was my chance, I needed to keep my genteel wits about me and wait for Hanuki to sober up so I could restart merger negotiations through the proper channels.

She wouldn't lick the face of someone she's not even interested in simply because she's drunk, would she? She's rather eccentric herself, so I wouldn't be surprised if she were weird enough to like me. If I turn over a new leaf here, I should be able to manifest enough power to turn my future into gold. I'm confident in my latent abilities. They're just so latent that I lost track of them.

I calmed my mind.

I waited for Johnny to simmer down, and when I finally came out of the bathroom, Hanuki was sprawled on the floor in the middle of the room whooshing like a pair of bellows as she slept.

I sat in the corner to wait for her to wake up.

· · ·

Probably because I was drunk, I did something out of character—that is, I nodded off. I had been leaning against the wall, but at some point, I had slumped over.

I sensed an alarming presence.

Rubbing my eyes as I sat up, I saw a Nurarihyon sitting politely before me. Suppressing the urge to shriek, "Gyah!" and jump to my feet, I saw it was Ozu. That was strange. I should have been in Hanuki's room, but here was Ozu sitting in front of me. I imagined that perhaps the dental hygienist Hanuki had been a disguise, and once that skin was peeled off, it was Ozu underneath. Could it be that I had been getting my face licked by Ozu disguised as a woman, that I had been about to negotiate a merger with Ozu disguised as a woman?

"What are you doing here?" I finally asked.

He smoothed his hair down with an affected air.

"I was having fun with our precious underclassmen in Sanjo when I got the call. I came over in a cab! You should try putting yourself in my shoes."

I didn't know what he was going on about.

"In other words: Hanuki is my master's friend, and I'm close with her as well, so I know she has one weakness. When she drinks too much, her rational mind goes out to lunch, I guess you could say. Well, something like that."

"What's that supposed to mean?" I asked.

"Did you by any chance nearly get your face licked?"

"Yes. I nearly did."

"Usually she manages to restrain herself, but she had so much fun drinking with you tonight she went a tad overboard. That is, please let everything that happened tonight be water under the bridge."

"What."

I was stunned.

"She says she's sorry. Not that it does her any good to start getting embarrassed about it now," Ozu said.

Just then, as if in protest, came an *ullrrghp* from the bathroom. It seemed Hanuki had holed up in there and was receiving just deserts from the alcohol.

"But why are you here?" I asked.

"My role is to explain the situation and console you as her representative. I'd be remiss to ignore my master's friend when she's in trouble."

Hanuki had very nearly licked my face, and I had been under the impression I had found a turning point in my destiny, but once the mechanism was revealed, the whole thing turned out to be idiotic. I was glad I had kept my grasp on the reins of reason. But it pissed me off that Ozu was the one hitting me with this bucket of cold water.

"You didn't do anything, right?" said Ozu.

"I didn't do anything. Just nearly got my face licked."

"Well, a guy of your caliber—yeah, I can buy it. You probably got freaked out by her advances and locked yourself in the bathroom."

"I did not. I looked after her like any gentleman would," I said.

"Yeah, I bet."

"Dammit, I'm so fucking pissed."

"Please don't get too upset with Hanuki. I mean, c'mon, she's in there hugging the toilet. That's punishment enough as it is."

"No, I'm pissed off at *you*."

"How mean. I'm just in the crossfire," Ozu said.

"Pretty much every time something shitty happens to me, you're there, you frickin' god of pestilence."

"Oh, there you go saying such horrible things again. Why do you think I went out of my way to ditch a fun party and come over here? To console you, as your best friend!"

"I don't need your pity. Besides, every time I find myself in an uncomfortable situation like this, you're the one to blame!"

"You should be ashamed of yourself, talking like that. I'm surprised you can blurt out those sorts of accusations with such confidence."

"If I hadn't met you, I would have lived with more significance. I would have applied myself to my studies, dated a black-haired maiden, and relished every moment of my untarnished student life. That's right. I'm sure of it," I said.

"Sounds like you're still drunk."

"It hit me today how completely I've wasted my time as a student!"

"Not that it's any consolation, but I think you would have met me no matter what. I just know it. No matter what happened, I would have done everything in my power to corrupt you. You can struggle against fate all you want, but it's futile." He held up a pinky finger. "We're connected by the black thread of fate."

The horrific image of two men, bound like boneless hams by

a dark thread, sinking to dark watery depths, came to mind, and I shuddered.

"More importantly, I hear you've had a girlfriend for two years. How about it? Bull's-eye, right?"

When I said that, Ozu put on a shady grin. "Hoo-hoo-hoo."

"What's so funny?"

"Not telling."

"It's bullshit that a guy like you can be off having fun and I get nothing," I said.

"Now, now. The fact that I'm happy doesn't matter right now. For today, what's important is that you resign yourself to the fact that this was all a dream and swiftly retreat." Ozu held out a box of cake.

"What's this?"

"It's castella—from Hanuki as an apology. So I hope you'll let this all go without a fuss." Ozu had the face of a cashier plotting to take over the shop.

● ● ●

I walked through town as the sky was growing lighter.

An after-the-banquet sense of desolation hung in the air, and the dawn chill sunk into my bones. Hugging myself in the middle of Mikagebashi, I gazed at the fresh green shrouding both banks of the Takano River. This pure morning scenery was a rare and thus refreshing sight for me, which made my dejection upon arriving back at Shimogamo Yusuiso that much worse. The broken light next to the entryway, the wooden shoe cubbies, and the dusty hallway all felt grimier than usual.

I went down the cold hallway with heavy feet and collapsed

into bed in my four-and-a-half-mat tatami room. In my futon, as it warmed up and softened, I went over all the many events of the previous day. It pissed me off that Ozu had showed up at the end, and it sucked that the future with Hanuki I had sketched out in her bathroom couldn't even last a day, but so what? When you stop to think about it, all that really happened was that I had found myself back at the start of Romance Chutes and Ladders, right? That was practically a daily occurrence. *You got cake in exchange for the wound to your heart; that's a fair trade, and you know it. You gotta just deal with it. Just deal.*

But I couldn't.

The crack in my heart refused to be filled.

From inside my futon, I stole a glance at my nonverbal roommate. Kaori was leaning against the bookcase as usual, quietly reading *Twenty Thousand Leagues Under the Sea*. I abruptly sat up and tried stroking her hair. It felt like I was cuddling with a delicate, black-haired maiden who had given her undivided attention to a book. I was deranged.

"I'm such a stupid bastard . . ." I groaned in spite of myself and retreated to my futon.

It was pathetic of me to have had the fantasy that my campus life was coming up roses. Or maybe if I had acted according to the fortune-teller's prediction, let Johnny take charge, and done the unpardonable with Hanuki while she was drunk, my new life really would have been starting right about now . . . ? No, that could never have happened. Not on my watch. The joining of a man and a woman should be a more solemn affair. Who would want it to be as easy as tying a pair of shoelaces?

I thought the winds had changed when Ozu brought Kaori to my room, but of the three women surrounding me, Hanuki had already dropped out. The dream didn't last even half a day. The two left to me were the pen pal I could never meet and the woman I was living with who wasn't human.

In other words, there might as well have been no one left.

I need to face this heartless reality. It's okay, this is me we're talking about—I can do it.

As I lay in my futon gazing at Kaori's face in profile, Johnny nearly started to wriggle by mistake, but I fell asleep, so that ended without incident.

• • •

I woke up late and decided to go to a café next to Demachi for dinner.

As I passed by the Kamo River Delta, I could see the kanji for "big" on the mountain in the distance, illuminated clearly by the evening sun. *I bet you can see the bonfire really well from here.* I nearly began imagining what it would be like to stand there with Keiko Higuchi and watch the shape of the okuribi burn, but daydreaming out in the evening breeze would only make me hungry again, so I found a good stopping point and cut it out.

I decided to distract myself from these feelings with no outlet by returning to Shimogamo Yusuiso, sitting at my desk, and concentrating on writing a reply to Keiko Higuchi.

Greetings,

These days it's so muggy, it's as if summer came early, huh? My room doesn't get much airflow, so it feels even hotter. Sometimes I get seized by the urge to string a hammock up in the hallway and camp out there, but that would be going too far, I suppose. It's a drag that I can't study in my room this time of year. I imagine I'll be holed up in the library for the next few months. There aren't any distractions at the library, though, so I'll probably make decent progress.

I'm glad you're enjoying *Twenty Thousand Leagues Under the Sea*. I had a map open while I read so I could chart the course of the *Nautilus*. That way, I felt like I was on a sea voyage, too. You should give it a try. I haven't read Stevenson's *Treasure Island* yet. I'll find a copy at the bookstore and have a look. Old adventure novels have their white-knuckle moments, but they also tend to move quite leisurely at points—an exquisite balance. I like that this one is an adventure novel but not bloody.

I don't know what an Irish pub is like, but I'd like to try going sometime. These days I just do laps between school and my lodgings; I don't have much occasion to go out on the town.

Since this spring, I've been busy with labs and lectures. From the outside, my life probably looks bleak, but I can say it has been pretty fulfilling. The world of science is fascinating. But the scope has expanded so much since the nineteenth century when Jules Verne was writing; it's too bad we can no longer get a view of the whole so easily. Still, it's thanks to that expansion that we're able to enjoy our contemporary lifestyles, so I can't really complain.

Regarding what you said in your previous letter, Miss

Higuchi, I fully intend to make good use of the chances given to me and continue improving myself. For that, health is important, so I make a point of exercising whenever I can. I'll take care with my nutrition as well.

But it's not as if I'm chowing down on fish burgers every day. Please don't misunderstand. I'm the sort of man who won't hesitate to down a barrel's worth of aloe yogurt if it will improve my well-being.

I'm sure you're busy, but please remember to take care of yourself, too.

• • •

*Hmm*ing and *Mm*ing as I went, I finished my letter to Keiko Higuchi.

I embellished a few points, but I think this would be rightly called creative direction. Even when I'm writing things I don't actually mean, along the way, I start to feel as though I've been thinking them all along. While I'm writing a letter, I become a model student, and when I'm finished, it's as if I'm waking from a dream; rediscovering the me who has gotten lost down some path of beasts is rather painful. Writing about my intention to improve myself was shameless even for me. I have the will, but the way is shrouded in darkness. *What can I do to improve myself?* I couldn't shake the feeling that I was improving (?) only the parts of me that needn't have been touched.

After putting my finished letter into an envelope, I reread Keiko's letter.

She said she liked the rainy season. She liked to look at the hydrangeas veiled in rain. She pitied the poor harpooner cooped up in the submarine in *Twenty Thousand Leagues Under the Sea*. She told me, of all people, to take care of myself!

What kind of woman might she be?

The letter was supposed to distract me, but ironically, my heart got riled up instead. I clutched her letter to my breast and sighed. That was sickening behavior even for me, so sickening that it brought me back to reality.

I absorbed myself in squeezing the sponge bear I'd picked up at the laundromat. Its soft texture put my mind at ease. This thing got cuter every time I looked at it, so I decided to give it a name. After thinking for five minutes, I dubbed it Mochiguma for its unparalleled softness.

• • •

That night, Ozu came over, his rude reason being to make sure I hadn't done anything untoward to Kaori.

"When are you taking her out of here?"

"Soon, I said—soon!" Ozu smirked. "You whine, but you're actually enjoying life with Kaori, aren't you? You even have her reading *Twenty Thousand Leagues Under the Sea*."

"Shut up this instant. Shut up for the rest of infinity."

"No, thank you. If I can't blather about pointless shit, I'll die in desolation."

"So, just die, then."

"Conversely, as long as I'm blathering about pointless shit, I won't die even if you kill me."

Then he told me about an elusive luxury scrub brush with tips of tough, unimaginably fine fibers that form molecular bonds with dirt constituents via the van der Waals force so it can remove any grime with a light touch—no muscle necessary. Apparently his master told him to go find one.

"Nothing that idiotic could possibly exist," I said.

"No, it really does. But it's no surprise that you've never heard of it. They remove grime so well, soap manufacturers put pressure on the creator, and they aren't sold very widely. At any rate, I have to get my hands on one."

"You sure are burning out your brain on some stupid nonsense."

"Master wants so many different things; it's a lot of work. Mame mochi from Demachi Futaba or chirimen-zansho are doable, but then he asks for an antique globe, a banner from the used book fair, seahorses, and giant squid. And if you bring him something that displeases him, you get expelled. Always gotta be on your toes." Ozu seemed oddly amused. "Oh, so, back when my master wanted a seahorse, I found an aquarium at a garbage dump and took it to him. When I tried filling it up, it sprang a furious leak, and the water came rushing out, causing a whole scene. The master's whole room was soaked."

"Wait, what number is your master's room?"

"It's the one directly above this."

I flew into a rage.

Previously, while I was away, there had been a flood on the second floor. When I got home, the water had dripped down to make all of my precious documents—both obscene and not—soggy. But that wasn't the only damage I suffered. All my precious data—both obscene and not—was lost from my waterlogged computer, vanished into the electron sea. It goes without saying that this incident hastened the decay of my academic life. I thought I would complain, but getting involved with this unknown upstairs resident seemed like a pain, so I had left the matter unresolved.

"That was your doing?"

"So your library of obscenities got a little wet—that's not such a big loss, is it?" Ozu said impudently.

"Just get out already. I have shit to do."

"That I shall. We're doing a Blackout Hot Pot party at my master's place tonight." He was carrying a plastic bag full of ingredients.

As Ozu was about to leave, he caught sight of Mochiguma sitting next to the TV. He picked it up and squeezed it to test its squishiness.

"What are you doing with something this unreasonably cute?" he asked.

"I found it."

"Can I have it?"

"Why?"

"I want to try putting it in the hot pot later."

"You idiot. You may be able to simmer it, but you can't eat it," I said.

"Maybe someone will mistake it for mochi and try to . . ."

"Who would do that?!"

"If you don't give it to me, I'll flood the apartment upstairs again. Your library of obscenities will be ruined."

"Fine, fine. Take it." I relented. Being robbed of one of the few things that brought me peace was upsetting, but I just wanted to get rid of him.

"Heh-heh-heh. You have my utmost gratitude. No funny business with Kaori, now."

"Shut your trap and get out of here."

As soon as Ozu was gone, the fatigue hit like a brick.

I prayed to the gods of Shimogamo Shrine that Ozu would choke on Mochiguma and meet a sudden end rich in nuance.

• • •

The next day . . .

After a full schedule of resistance against my lectures and experiments, I ate mentaiko spaghetti at Café Collection for my evening meal. When I exited onto Demachigawa-dori, I looked up at Mount Yoshida, its fresh, rising green sparkling golden in the setting sun's light.

Ahh.

I wandered down Imadegawa-dori toward Ginkaku-ji.

Sometimes you really do get an evil itch.

Between constantly gazing at the doll Ozu had abandoned in my room and having Hanuki press her breasts against me and try to lick my face, though I knew it was pointless, it seemed I'd loosened the strings of my peaceful heart. In other words, it was getting harder to not have a fit of loneliness.

I weighed Keiko Higuchi against Kaori. I shut my eyes to the reality that neither of them should have been on the scales to begin with. Both "doll" and "human being" may use the kanji for "person," but there's a huge difference between the two. I'd been an acquaintance of Keiko Higuchi, if only through letters, for half a year already. And with Kaori came the obnoxious issue of Ozu's crime. The scales tipped heavily in Keiko Higuchi's direction. Actually, by weighing things out, my heart, previously as calm as the Pacific Ocean, began to sway dramatically.

To get to the point: I ended up going to Keiko Higuchi's

house even though I was never supposed to meet her. Something just came over me. And if I hadn't gone to her place at that time, if I hadn't confirmed the terrifying true form hidden beneath that veil of mystique, it's clear things would have taken a turn for the horrific, so it's hard to know which is worse.

Dragged by my yearning for companionship, I reached Shirakawa-dori. A ton of cars crisscrossed at the broad intersection of Shirakawa and Imadegawa. A chilly evening wind was blowing, exacerbating my loneliness all the more. At the other side of the crosswalk, the Philosopher's Path stretched into the distance, and the sakura trees that were all leaves now, no more blossoms, were illuminated by the setting sun's light.

I'm just going to see what kind of place she has. It's not as if I'm trying to meet her. That was my awkward defense.

Thus, I headed toward a place I had never once approached before: Keiko Higuchi's address at White Garden Jodoji.

• • •

I went south down Shirakawa-dori until I found the Jodoji bus stop. Then I went into the neighborhood.

Though I had learned her address through exchanging letters, it wasn't as if I'd checked the location on a map, so I had to go by my intuition. I wandered somewhat aimlessly through the gradually darkening residential area. Some part of me felt it would be better not to find it, so I made a point of not asking for directions. As I walked the quiet streets, I was able to imagine Keiko Higuchi's peaceful way of life, and that alone provided some solace.

After walking like that for thirty minutes or so, I began to have second thoughts about my ungentlemanly conduct. Yes, it would be better not to find her house. It was almost dark, anyway, so I decided to go home. And that was the moment I stumbled upon White Garden Jodoji.

It was an unassuming little white apartment building that looked like candy. Comparing it to Shimogamo Yusuiso was like comparing the moon to a muddy turtle shell.

I had found her residence, but I had no idea what to do next. I took a casual glance at the mailboxes, but there was no name tag. The lobby had an automatically locking door, so I couldn't go in, but I could see the first-floor hallway where she lived over the wall surrounding the building. Her room number was 102, so it must have been the second door on the left side. Staring at the closed door, I started to get the sense I was doing something awfully wrong and figured I had better leave before she saw me, but then I remembered that neither of us had ever seen each other before and started to have complicated feelings.

As I was wavering incessantly between loneliness and self-hatred, the door to 102 suddenly opened. I tried to hide; I couldn't forsake the chance that had suddenly presented itself to me.

I saw Keiko Higuchi.

She had a very creepy face. She appeared unhealthy, with a complexion like someone who had been living on the far side of the moon. She wore an ominous grin as if she were hoping for misfortune to befall others, essentially like the yokai Nurari-hyon. She was practically like Ozu. She looked identical to him. Actually, it was him. It was Ozu himself.

"Is there no God or Buddha?" is a phrase made for this moment.

I couldn't possible mistake him.

It was Ozu.

With no regard for me or my confusion, Ozu leisurely opened the auto-locking door and went outside. He went around to the bike parking area, pulled out his bicycle, which he called Dark Scorpion, and with a nasty smirk that made it seem like he was scoffing at me, he pedaled off toward Shirakawa-dori.

The whole time I trembled, hiding in the shadow of the wall.

This was definitely the building—White Garden Jodoji— Keiko Higuchi lived in. And I didn't have the wrong room number. I didn't want to think about it, but was it possible that Ozu was an acquaintance of hers? Was their relationship so close that he would visit her room? No, I refused to accept such a coincidence. Ozu intimate with the woman I just happened to be pen pals with? The gods were pulling one prank too many if they were connecting people in such a tangled way.

So then what other reason could there be?

Just then I recalled that I had no idea where Ozu lived. I remembered that this was Jodoji. And I dredged up the conversation I'd had with Hanuki two nights ago at the izakaya in Kiyamachi.

"It's over in the Jodoji area . . ."

". . . in a fancy building that looks like candy . . ."

". . . a little ways off Shirakawa-dori . . ."

If what Hanuki had said was correct, that would mean that White Garden Jodoji number 102 was Ozu's room. And I would have to accept the fact that Ozu lived in the same room as Keiko Higuchi. To swallow the bitter conclusion that followed from that would take an extraordinary amount of mental energy. In order to endure this unimaginable bitterness, I wanted a whole case of sugar cubes.

Keiko Higuchi didn't exist.

For more than six months, I had been writing letters to Ozu.

• • •

Thus my correspondence with Keiko Higuchi met its sudden end.

No crueler finale could be possible.

As night was falling, I staggered back through the city to the university and then headed to Shimogamo Yusuiso. Looming dark in the twilight, Yusuiso had a weird aura that seemed to mirror my frayed internal state.

When I opened the door to the building and walked down the hall, something was making a little puffing noise in the darkness. Upon closer inspection, it turned out to be a rice cooker. It looked as though someone was using the outlet in the corridor—meant for cleaning—to cook their rice. Lacking the space in my heart to forgive even such minor electricity theft, I yanked the plug out of the socket with all my might to ruin someone's dinner, slammed my door, and sat down in my four-and-a-half-mat tatami room.

In a corner of my desolate room, Kaori was sitting as usual, absorbed in her book. With my dream of life with Hanuki vanished all too soon, and the revelation that Keiko Higuchi didn't even exist, the only option left to me was untalkative Kaori.

I took out the castella I'd received from Hanuki as an apology. I confronted the boxy sweet in the center of my four-and-a-half-mat tatami room. I decided it would be best to forget the sensation of Hanuki's breasts pressed against me, the numerous letters I'd exchanged with Keiko Higuchi—all of it—and forge on toward a dinner of cake; I didn't even cut it, just chomped right in.

"This is what you get for not listening to me," scoffed Johnny.

"Quiet, you."

"You should have let me handle things at Hanuki's apartment. At least then you wouldn't have ended up stuck in a little tatami room like this again."

"Yeah, right."

"Well, now the only option left to you is Kaori here."

"Where are you going with this?"

"Whoa, whoa, are you still trying to keep up the gentleman act after all that? Isn't it time to give it up? Let's be happy together. I won't ask for anything more. It seems I overestimated you."

Apparently Johnny was scheming to engage in some inappropriate behavior with regard to Kaori, and I grew frantic to stop his rampage. If I took the easy way out here, then the honor I went so far as to hole up in Hanuki's bathroom to protect would be vaporized. If I took advantage of the fact that Kaori couldn't move to have my way with her like the feudal lord in a period piece and be like, "You're fine with it, right?" there would be no maintaining my pride.

Johnny and I remained locked in a tug-of-war while Kaori quietly continued reading.

"You drive me up the wall," Johnny finally said, no longer caring what happened.

"It's not me, it's Ozu," I groaned and continued to eat the castella by myself.

As I chowed down on the cake, I realized that eating an entire castella alone in silence could only exacerbate my hell of isolation, and as I chewed, my face took on the grimace of a demon. Anger rapidly filled my heart. *Ozu, you fucker.* Come to think of it, between Hanuki and Keiko Higuchi, could it be that I was just dancing in the palm of his hand? That rotten yokai. "What's so fun about that?" is probably a stupid question. I refused to do something so worthless as measure Ozu's behavioral principles using my own yardstick. He was just that sort of man. He was a man who fueled himself on other people's misfortunes. Actually, he must have relished many a fantastic meal with me as the main course over the past two years.

I'd had a vague idea before, but now I understood clearly.

He was a man who deserved to die.

I would put him through a coffee grinder.

Just as I had made up my mind, my ceiling started shaking.

There was a racket going on in Ozu's master's room, above mine. I could hear voices arguing. Someone was stamping their feet. My broken light blinked and swayed; a moth flew out and the room grew brighter and darker. It was like being in a storm. Thus mentally wandering my desolate four-and-a-half-mat tatami room, I shouted curses at Ozu. *Damn it all. What a dark, hectic four days these have been. You probably think I'll cry—how stupid—who would cry? There are plenty of reasons I want to, but I'm not going to cry until I pulverize Ozu. Oh, Johnny, I'm gonna lose it.*

"At any rate, there's nothing you can do at this point. This is what you get for calling me an idiot and putting on gentlemanly airs. You can't say shit to me anymore. It's just you and me in this four-and-a-half-mat tatami world forever for the rest of eternity," said Johnny, who would never leave me. "In a four-and-a-half-mat tatami room, the clever ones and the idiots both end up miserable."

"I agree with you there. What a wretched pair."

"Then who cares if it's fake? Why don't we let Kaori cheer us up?" Johnny argued as if he'd seen his opening.

I looked at Kaori leaning against the bookcase reading *Twenty Thousand Leagues Under the Sea.* Her black hair was smooth, and her clear eyes looked directly at the pages. Love may come in all shapes, but anyone who wanders into such a closed-off maze of love would never be able to find their way back out—especially someone clumsy like me. *Would you really be okay with succumbing to Johnny's whispers and Kaori's silent profile and hurling away what little honor you have?*

Battered by the dizzying storm of self-interrogation, I reached out my hand and tried touching Kaori's hair.

Just then, I heard one of the people who had been banging around rowdily upstairs come down. I assumed they would leave Yusuiso, but instead they headed down the hall toward my room.

The moment I was thinking, *Oh? What's this?* my door was kicked down.

"You!"

A man mad with rage stepped in.

I figured this out after the fact, but the man was none other than Kaori's owner, one Jogasaki, who was fighting the mysterious Masochistic Proxy-Proxy War against Ozu's master.

• • •

The two of us, who should have been putting up a united front against Ozu, met there for the first time, not with a congenial handshake, but with a sparks-flying fistfight. Since I didn't find it very sporting to resort to brute strength, it would be more accurate to describe it as a one-sided beating.

Without knowing what it was even about, I was knocked into a corner of my four-and-a-half-mat tatami room, and the impact shook my favorite maneki-neko figurine off my TV. Johnny, who until a moment ago had been squirming restlessly in Kaori's direction, emitted a childish "Eek!" and took cover. Even my own boy is so fast when making an escape.

Behind the man standing imposingly before me, the yukata-clad fellow Ozu called his master strolled leisurely in. Shoving him aside to rush breathlessly in was a woman. I felt I had seen her somewhere before, but I couldn't remember who she was.

"Jogasaki!" she said. "Punching him out of nowhere is a bit much." She helped me up. "Are you all right? I'm sorry. There's been a slight misunderstanding."

I couldn't think of any reason I deserved the uncivilized treatment of getting my door kicked in and a fist visited upon my face. I finally got up, and the girl pressed a moistened cloth to my jaw. She picked up the maneki-neko that had fallen off my TV and said, "Sorry to barge in on you like this. My name's Akashi."

"Jogasaki, this is a fundamental misunderstanding," said Ozu's master in a relaxed tone.

"Didn't he play some part in this?" Jogasaki looked suspicious.

"No. Ozu just mixed him up in it," said Akashi.

"Sorry, man." Jogasaki apologized to me but immediately turned to Kaori. Seeing her safe seemed to calm him down. He reached out a hand and stroked her hair as if she were his daughter or something. If I had done anything inappropriate . . . The thought alone was terrifying. I think Jogasaki would have blown a gasket and, swept up in his rage, wrapped me in a bamboo mat and drowned me in the Kamo River.

While Jogasaki and Kaori were having their touching reunion, Ozu's master sat in my chair as if it were his own and leisurely puffed on a cigar; he seemed to have no intention of explaining things to me.

I was completely out of the loop.

• • •

"Would you be willing to just chalk this up to Ozu going out of control?" said Ozu's master. "I didn't mean for him to go this far."

"Well, Kaori has come back safely, so, yeah, we can end things here. But I'm going to give Ozu a talking to. He broke the law to get into my room!" Jogasaki stated sternly.

An anger no less virulent than his surged within me, too.

"I'm sure Ozu will be here any minute. You can steam him or boil him, whatever you like. Not that he'd be tasty no matter how you cook him." Ozu's master commented recklessly.

"Yes, Ozu is the one who caused all of this. He needs to learn his lesson," said Akashi.

Once I grasped the situation, I seethed anew at him. And with Jogasaki, who had been so wronged, right in front of me, my anger grew richer and deeper.

"Oh, if it isn't some castella."

Ozu's master had spotted the cake I'd been chomping to pieces all alone. He seemed to want some, and when I found a spot I hadn't bitten into and cut a slice to present to him, he crammed it in his mouth.

Jogasaki glared at the master eating cake. "I've gotta admit though, this is wild. I thought for sure he had defected to my side."

"That's naive. Do you really think Ozu is so simple?" His master chuckled with a smile and stood up. "Now then, I think I'll return to my room for the moment."

"I wonder how I can get Kaori home . . ." said Jogasaki.

"Ozu said he borrowed a car from someone," said Akashi.

"Yeesh, that guy. Sorry, but could I leave her here until I can arrange a pickup? I'll be back sometime tonight for sure," Jogasaki asked with an apologetic bow.

I nodded.

Ozu's master was the first one to step into the hall. He was gazing toward the building's entryway smoking his cigar when he exclaimed, "Oh-ho!" He continued with a beckoning gesture, "If it isn't Ozu! Come this way, right this way."

Jogasaki and I stood up at almost exactly the same time and clenched our fists to pulverize Ozu the second he set foot in the room.

"Master, what are you doing in a filthy place like this?" said

Ozu as he peered into my room; the moment he saw the pair of us standing there swollen with rage, he turned on his heel and dashed down the hall. His flight instinct must have detected the crisis he was in right away. As he ran, he ended up kicking the rice cooker I had unplugged earlier. It bumped and banged loudly as it careened down the hall. "Sorrysorrysorry!" he shouted as he fled. If he was going to have to apologize, he shouldn't have done it in the first place.

"You bastard!" Jogasaki and I went after him with a roar. Akashi and Ozu's master followed us.

• • •

Ozu was unrivaled when it came to one thing, and that was the speed at which he could run away; he skittered through Shimogamo Izumikawacho like a yokai. I ran with all my might, but Jogasaki pulled farther and farther ahead. About the time I had passed the light thrown by Shimogamo Saryo and was heading toward Demachiyanagi Station, I was this close to white-hot burnout.

Akashi caught up to me on a bicycle.

"Let's pincer him on Kamo Ohashi. Go around to the west end." With that levelheaded remark, she sped off with a huge *squee-konk* to get around Ozu. I found myself rather taken by her receding figure.

Suppressing the urge collapse to the ground and commend myself for getting as far as I did, I reached Aoi Park. Jogasaki and Ozu seemed to have already gone around to Kawabata-dori. I went west over the Demachibashi Bridge right in front of the Kamo River Delta and then ran south along the Kamo River's embankment. Then I ran up to the western edge of Kamo Ohashi.

The area was submerged in indigo twilight by this time. The Kamo River Delta was occupied by lively college kids. They must have been having new student welcome parties. Come to think of it, I'd spent two years completely removed from that scene. The river was running high from the rain that had lasted until just the other day, and it rushed noisily past; in the lights reflecting here and there, the surface of the water looked like a sheet of metallic paper being waved like a stage prop. Imadegawa-dori was busy, and the bridge was packed with brilliant head- and taillights. The orange lights affixed at intervals along the bridge's thick railing shone with a hazy, mystical air in the darkness. Kamo Ohashi felt larger than usual on this night.

As I walked, panting, over the bridge, Ozu came running from the other side. Akashi must have successfully lured him onto the bridge. Being able to take him down brought me immense satisfaction. "Ozu!" I spread my arms wide and shouted, and he stopped with a wry smile.

Jogasaki came onto Kamo Ohashi from the east side, but he was also half dead. Akashi showed up with him. Where I cornered Ozu was about the middle of the bridge, and the Kamo River was flowing by directly below. Glancing south, farther down the dark river's course, I saw the distant Shijo neighborhood's lights gleaming like jewels.

"Help me out. We're friends, aren't we?" Ozu said, pressing his palms together.

"Thank you for all the letters, Keiko Higuchi. What fun we had," I said.

For a second he looked as if he didn't know what I was talking about, but he realized soon enough. "I didn't mean any harm," he said. "I never mean any harm."

"You toyed with my innocent emotions. There's no point in arguing; I'm gonna smack you dead."

"Smack me, sure, but dead? Why would you do such a horrible thing?"

That was when Jogasaki and Akashi caught up to us.

"Ozu, we need to talk," Jogasaki said solemnly.

Though Ozu was completely trapped, he put on an invincible smile.

No sooner had he laid a hand on the railing than he jumped nimbly up on top of it. The light from the lamps on the bridge illuminated his face from below, giving him a spookier air than most I'd seen in recent years. He seemed about ready to escape by flying into the sky like a tengu.

"Keep threatening me, and I'll jump!" Ozu said, which made no sense. "If you don't guarantee my safety, I'm not coming down there."

"Do you really think you're in a position to request safety? You numbskull," I said.

"Think about what you've done," Jogasaki added.

"Akashi, please say something. Stick up for your senior disciple," Ozu implored her in a syrupy voice, but Akashi shrugged her shoulders.

"What you did is indefensible."

"I love that you're so blunt," Ozu said.

"Flattery will get you nowhere."

Ozu slid his feet to the edge of the railing. He spread his arms as if he was going to take off into the night sky. "Whatever. I'm gonna jump," he wailed.

"Fine. Jump, then. Jump right now," I said.

Go ahead and get swept up in the muddy flow of the Kamo River. Then I would finally get some peace and quiet.

"There's no way you're jumping," taunted Jogasaki. "Not when you're so precious about yourself."

"What? I'll show you," Ozu declared. But despite the declaration, he wasn't jumping.

As the argument continued, a shriek shot up from the Kamo River Delta, north of the bridge. The partying kids had begun running around in a panic.

"What's that?" Ozu said, bending over slightly with a puzzled look on his face. Without thinking, I pressed up against the railing to look: something like a black fog eerily spread out from Aoi Park to the Kamo River Delta, swiftly coating the delta's bank below. And within that black fog was a muddle of young people. They were half mad, flailing their arms and ripping out their hair. The black fog glided along the river and seemed to be heading straight for us.

The clamoring on the Kamo River Delta grew even louder.

Black fog poured continuously from out of the pine grove. This was nothing to sniff at. With a trembling, fluttering, rustling, and flapping, the wriggling black fog was spreading out like a carpet below us when it began to rise up from the river's surface before suddenly exploding over the railing and rushing onto Kamo Ohashi.

"Gyoaehhhh!" Akashi emitted a shriek straight out of a manga.

It was a swarm of moths.

• • •

A news item appeared in the next day's *Kyoto Shimbun*, but no one knew exactly why the extraordinary number of moths had appeared. Retracing their flight path, they seemed to come from Tadasu no Mori—that is, Shimogamo Shrine—but this wasn't clear. Even if every moth that lived in Tadasu no Mori had decided to migrate all at once, there wasn't a good reason for it. Apart from the official explanation, there were rumors that the moths had come, not from Shimogamo Shrine, but the neighborhood next to it, Shimogamo Izumikawacho; but that only made the story even stranger. Apparently, it was the area right around my apartment that had been flooded with moths and thrown into an uproar.

When I returned to my room that night, there were dead moths strewn throughout the hallway. My door was half open, as I had forgotten to lock it, so there were moth corpses all over my room, too. I gave them a respectful burial.

• • •

Pushing my way through the swarm of moths as they flapped into my face, sprinkling their scales around, sometimes trying to force their way into my mouth, I moved to Akashi and protected her like a total gentleman. I used to be a city slicker, so

I had been above living alongside insects, but after residing in my lodgings for two years, I'd had numerous opportunities to become familiar with all manner of arthropods, so bugs didn't bother me anymore.

That huge swarm of moths, though, was beyond the realm of common sense. The awful sound of their beating wings cut us off from the outside world; it was less like moths and more like little winged yokai passing over the bridge. I couldn't see much of anything. Through the slits of my barely open eyes, I could make out a riot of moths fluttering around the orangey glow of the lamps on the railing and Akashi's shiny black hair.

Once the swarm had finally gone, a few stragglers had been left fluttering here and there. Akashi stood up with a deathly pale face and screamed, "Are there any on me?! Are there any on me?!" as she frantically brushed off every part of her body before running toward the western end of the bridge at a tremendous speed to flee the moths twitching on the ground. It was in front of a café casting a soft glow into the twilight that she eventually crumpled. I found out later that she really hated moths.

The swarm of moths became a black carpet again and went down the river to Shijo.

I noticed Jogasaki was standing next to me; the moths stuck and flailing in his hairdo didn't seem to faze him.

I looked around Kamo Ohashi with its orangey lamps at fixed intervals.

It was as if Ozu had made a magnificent flying exit on the wings of the swarm of moths; he had vanished from where he had been standing.

"He really fell," murmured Jogasaki before he ran to the railing.

• • •

Jogasaki and I ran down to the bank from the western end of the bridge. Before our eyes, from left to right, roared the Kamo River. Since it was running high, areas that were usually underbrush were submerged, so it was wider than usual.

We entered the water from there and approached the area beneath the bridge. Something wriggled in the shadows by the foot of the bridge. Ozu was clinging to it like a piece of litter, apparently unable to move. The water wasn't deep, but the current was fast, and Jogasaki got his feet swept out from under him and was nearly washed away.

It took a lot of effort, but we finally reached the Ozu-like thing.

"You idiot!" I screamed, getting doused in the spray of the river, and Ozu wheezed with half-crying laughter.

"Take pity and forgive me."

"Whatever, just shut it," said Jogasaki.

"Yes, sir. For some reason my right leg is in terrible pain," Ozu confessed.

With Jogasaki's help, I lifted Ozu up. "Ow, ow, ow—be more gentle, please!" Ozu made extravagant demands as we carried him to dry land. Akashi had come down to the riverbed after us. The shock of being buffeted by the swarm of moths had left her pale, but she had called an ambulance without missing a beat. After calling the emergency number, she sat on a bench with her hands over her pale cheeks. We rolled Ozu like a log and shivered as our clothes dried.

"It hurts, it hurts, it really hurts. Do something!" he moaned. "Nnngh!"

"Quit your whining. It's your fault for climbing up on the railing," I said. "The ambulance will be here soon, so just deal till then."

I could see that Jogasaki, kneeling next to whining Ozu, was struggling with what to do with his anger. And even I didn't have the heart to take Ozu and his broken leg back to Shimogamo Yusuiso to put him through the coffee grinder.

Eventually Ozu's master alighted on the riverbed. He must have walked at a leisurely pace from Shimogamo Yusuiso.

"Sheesh. I was wondering where you were," he said.

"Ozu's hurt, Higuchi. His leg is broken," said Jogasaki.

"Pathetic wretch."

"But Master, this was all for your sake."

"You're quite a promising disciple, Ozu," said Ozu's master.

"Thank you, Master."

"But you're supposed to work *to* the bone for your master, not break it. You're an incorrigible idiot."

Ozu cried softly.

It took about five minutes for the ambulance to arrive at the end of Kamo Ohashi.

Jogasaki ran up the bank and came down with the medical techs. The techs wrapped Ozu in a blanket and loaded him onto a stretcher with skills pros could be proud of. It would have been hilarious if they had just thrown him into the river like that, but emergency workers are admirable individuals who sympathize with all injured people equally. Ozu was packed onto the ambulance with a gravity disproportionate to his nasty ways.

"I'll go with Ozu," said his master, and he leisurely boarded the ambulance.

A moment later, it had driven away. Jogasaki seemed to have already forgotten about Ozu and left the riverbed saying he was going to go procure a car to use to pick up Kaori.

The only ones left were Akashi on the bench, holding her pale face, and me, sopping wet.

"Are you okay?" I asked Akashi.

"I really can't handle moths," she groaned, still seated on the bench.

"Why don't we get some tea or something to calm down?" I suggested.

It's not as if I was thinking anything so rude as stooping to using her weakness against moths to my advantage. Seeing her so pale, I was offering out of concern.

I walked to the nearest vending machine and bought two hot coffees, which we drank together. She gradually relaxed. I told her about my fatal bond with Ozu. And I told her about his evil doings I'd discovered in the past few days. I mentioned the name of the fictional maiden, Keiko Higuchi, and said that Ozu deserved to die for the crime of toying with my heart, but then Akashi suddenly apologized.

"I'm sorry. I'm really sorry—but I think I'm partly to blame. I've been writing the letters because Ozu asked me to."

"What!"

"I read the book you recommended, *Twenty Thousand Leagues Under the Sea*." A pleasant smile appeared on her face. "Your letters were good. It seemed like you told a lot of lies. But they were well written."

"You could tell?"

"Of course, I was lying, too, so we're even," she said.

Then with a smile on her still pale cheeks, she said something I never imagined I would hear. "We met at the Shimogamo Shrine used book fair. Do you remember?"

• • •

It happened the previous summer at the Shimogamo Shrine used book fair. The riding grounds stretching north to south alongside the approach to the shrine were crammed full of sellers' tents, and tons of people were strolling around on the hunt for books. It was only a short walk from Shimogami Yusuiso, so I attended practically every day.

After basking in the charms of summer to my heart's content, drinking a ramune in the sunlight filtered through the treetops, I strolled among the bookseller stalls on either side, browsing as I went. No matter where I looked, I saw wooden shelves packed with books; it made me a little dizzy. On the cloth-covered benches set up in rows, people who must have gotten book fair sick like me hung their heads. I had sat down, too, dazed. It was August, which meant it was muggy and hot, so I wiped the sweat off my forehead with a handkerchief.

Straight ahead was the used bookshop Gabi Shobo's stall. Sitting in the folding chair at the entrance was a woman with her intellectual brow furrowed. I rose from the bench, and when I made eye contact with her while looking through Gabi Shobo's stacks, she bowed her head slightly. I bought *Twenty Thousand Leagues Under the Sea* by Jules Verne. I was walking away afterward when she got up and came after me.

"Here, you can use this," she said, handing me a paper fan with the words "Summer Book Fair" printed on it.

That was Akashi.

I remembered fanning my sweaty face as I left Tadasu no Mori carrying *Twenty Thousand Leagues Under the Sea.*

• • •

Jogasaki came over that night to pick up Kaori and resume his tranquil love life.

From what Ozu told me, Jogasaki was also very popular with human women and had racked up experience as the interest took him while in the club. Given his looks, it's no surprise. What I don't understand is why someone who has no lack of relationships with real women would be so attached to Kaori. He had been living with her for two years; he's hardcore.

"There's meaning in living alongside a doll you care for. Owning a love doll is entirely different from dating a woman. A barbarian like you who only sees them as tools for sexual gratification probably can't understand, but what we're dealing with is a highly evolved form of love." That was Ozu's take.

From my four days living with her, I have the feeling I understand, but I realize it's not a realm a clumsy guy like me should go stepping into. Yes, I'll choose a human black-haired maiden. Like Akashi, for example.

Ozu's master continues to live on the second floor of Shimogamo Yusuiso, so I run into him sometimes. He wears that navy yukata and lives a quiet, leisurely life. Akashi continues to visit him. "He is somewhat admirable—key word 'somewhat'—but still" was her appraisal.

He said to me, "Why don't you become a disciple, too?" so I'm considering it. My first reservation is that I have no idea what I'd be a disciple *of*. My second reservation is that I'd be Ozu's junior.

The other day I had hot pot at Higuchi's and saw Hanuki.

"Small world," she said.

I don't know the details of the fight between Higuchi and Jogasaki that led to the plot to abduct Kaori. But stealing Kaori was deemed a rule violation. While Ozu was in the hospital, Akashi took over Ozu's role with aplomb and rebuilt Jogasaki's bicycle into a quincycle in a single night.

• • •

Following those events, Akashi and I grew closer.

So, considering the outcome, Ozu's evil deeds had a silver lining—not that that means I'm interested in forgiving him. All I got out of it was something else to talk about at English school, so it's totally not worth it. But I'm sure my classmates will give me a round of applause for delivering this most recent development.

How my relationship with Akashi developed after that is a

deviation from the point of this manuscript. Therefore, I shall refrain from writing the charming, bashfully giddy details. You probably don't want to pour your time down the drain reading such detestable drivel, anyhow.

There's nothing so worthless to speak of as a love mature.

• • •

It's not fair for you to assume that I'd naively approve of my past just because there have been some new developments in my student life lately. I'm not the kind of man who would so readily affirm his past mistakes. Certainly I considered giving myself a big, loving embrace, but regardless of how it would go with a black-haired maiden of a tender age, who would have any interest in hugging a mess of a twenty-something guy? Driven by that inescapable anger, I firmly refused to give my past self salvation.

I can't shake the feeling that I never should have signed up for the Mellow softball club at the foot of that fateful clock tower. I think about what could have happened if I had chosen something else. If I had chosen the film club, Ablutions, or answered that bizarre ad for a disciple, or if I had joined that underground organization Lucky Cat Chinese Food, I would have had a very different couple of years. At least, it's clear that I wouldn't be as warped as I am now. I might have attained that elusive treasure, a rose-colored campus life. No matter how I try to avert my eyes, I can't deny the fact that the past two years have been utterly wasted on a pile of mistakes.

More than anything, the stain of having met Ozu is sure to linger for the rest of my days.

• • •

Ozu stayed in the hospital next to the school for a little while.

I have to say, it felt pretty great to see him strapped into a crisp white bed. He always had such a horrible complexion that he looked like a patient with an untreatable illness, but it was just a broken bone. I suppose it's lucky that he got away with just a broken bone. He grumbled that he wasn't able to perpetrate any of the misdeeds he preferred over three square meals a day, but I just thought, *That's what you get.* When his grumbles got to be too much, I crammed the castella I brought him into his mouth to shut him up.

"So now you've learned your lesson and can quit meddling in other people's business, right?" I said with my mouth full of castella, but Ozu shook his head.

"No thank you. I mean, what else do I have to do?"

This guy is rotten straight to the core.

"What was so fun about toying with me in my innocence?" I grilled him.

• • •

Ozu put on his usual yokai grin and laughed his head off.

"It's my love language."

"Gross—you can spare me," I replied.

FOUR

Around the Tatami Galaxy in Eighty Days

L et's just say I accomplished absolutely nothing during the two years leading up to the spring of my junior year in college. Every move I made in my quest to become an able participant in society (to associate wholesomely with members of the opposite sex, to devote myself to my studies, to temper my flesh) somehow missed its mark, and I ended up making all sorts of moves, as if on purpose, that need not have been made at all (to isolate myself from the opposite sex, to abandon my studies, to allow my flesh to deteriorate). How did that happen?

We must ask the person responsible. And who is responsible?

It's not as if I was born this way.

Fresh from the womb I was innocence incarnate, every bit as precious as the Shining Prince Genji must have been in his infancy. My smile, without a hint of malice, is said to have filled the mountains and valleys of my birthplace with the radiance of love. And now what has become of me? Whenever I look in the mirror I am swept up in a storm of anger. *How the hell did you end up like this? You've come so far, and this is all you amount to?*

"You're still young," some would say. "It's never too late to change."

Are you fucking kidding me?

They say that the soul of a child at three remains the same even when the man reaches a hundred. So what good can it do for a splendid young man of twenty-one, nearly a quarter century old, to put a lot of sloppy effort into transforming his character? The most he can do in attempting to force the stiffened tower of his personality to bend is to snap it right in half.

I must shoulder the burden of my current self for the rest of my life. I mustn't avert my eyes from that reality.

I can't look away, but it's just so hard to watch.

$$\bullet \bullet \bullet$$

The spring I became a junior, I was living holed up in my four-and-a-half-mat tatami room.

It wasn't as if I felt out of steam after the rush of the new semester starting, and it wasn't as if I was frightened of society. I was shut up in my room, cut off from the outside world, in order to retemper myself in a tranquil environment. Having wasted two years smearing my future with mud, I didn't have enough credits. Heading ambiguously into my third year, the university had nothing for me. I believed that all my rigorous austerities had to be performed on these four and a half tatami mats.

Shūji Terayama once famously said, "Throw away your books, rally in the streets!"

But what I thought at that time was *Rally in the streets for what, exactly?*

• • •

I'm writing this record to ponder the existence of four-and-a-half-mat tatami rooms—something most people have zero need to think about. My reason is that recently, by bizarre chance, I got stuck traversing an endless series of four-and-a-half-mat tatami rooms and was forced to think about them so much I wanted to jump from the Kegon Waterfall.

I'm terribly fond of four-and-a-half-mat tatami rooms and have been known in some circles as a four-and-a-half-mat tatami-ist. Everywhere I went, no one failed to pay their respects; everyone cast admiring gazes my way. "There's the four-and-a-half-mat tatami-ist everyone's talking about," black-haired maidens would whisper to each other. "Oh, my, now that you mention it, he does have a noble air about him . . ."

But there comes a time when even a four-and-a-half-mat tatami-ist like me has to step outside.

What would drive a man who has such an enthusiasm for four-and-a-half-mat tatami rooms to such a measure?

I'm about to tell you.

• • •

Pretty much the only character in this record is me.

Though it's terribly depressing, I really am basically the only one.

• • •

It was the end of May in my junior year.

My base of operations was a room at Shimogamo Yusuiso in Shimogamo Izumikawacho. From what I had heard, it had been standing there since being rebuilt after burning down in the disorder accompanying the last days of the Tokugawa shogunate. If there hadn't been light seeping through the windows, the building would have been taken for abandoned. No wonder I thought I must have wandered into the walled city of Kowloon when I first visited the place on the university co-op's introduction. The three-story wooden structure caused all those who saw it anxiety; it seemed ready to collapse at any moment. Its dilapidation was practically Important Cultural Property level. Certainly no one would miss it if it burned down. In fact, there was no doubt in my mind that this would be a load off for its landlady, who lived just to the east.

I'll never forget—it was the night before I left on that "journey." I was sulking alone in my room, Shimogamo Yusuiso number 110, when Ozu came to visit.

I'd had a fatal bond with Ozu ever since we met as freshmen. After washing my hands of the secret organization Lucky Cat Chinese Food, I was maintaining my solitary status, and the only person I had kept in touch with for any length of time was this rotten hack yokai of a man. Though I loathed how he polluted my soul, I couldn't cut him off.

Ozu frequented the lodgings of one Seitaro Higuchi, who lived above me, and called him "Master," and every time he stopped by there, he poked his head into my room.

"Gloomy as usual," he said. "You don't have a girlfriend,

you don't go to school, you don't have friends. What the hell are you trying to accomplish?"

"You better watch your mouth, or I'm going to smack you dead."

"Smack me, sure, but dead? Why would you do such a horrible thing?" Ozu grinned. "Actually, you were out two nights ago, right? I came all the way here for nothing."

"Yeah, I did go out the other night. I was applying myself to my studies at a manga café."

"I wanted to introduce you to this girl, Kaori. I brought her over, but you weren't here, so I took her elsewhere. Sucks for you."

"On your introduction? I'll pass."

"There, there. Don't get too down on yourself. Here, I'll give you this."

"What is it?" I asked.

"Castella. I got a bunch from Master Higuchi, so I'm sharing."

"Huh, it's not every day I get a gift from you."

"Well, it's because cutting up a huge castella and eating it alone is the far reaches of solitude. I want you to get a good taste of loneliness," Ozu said.

"Oh, that's what you're up to? Sure, I'll taste it. I'll keep tasting it till I'm damned well sick of it."

"By the way, I heard from Hanuki that you went to the dentist?"

"Yeah, I had a thing."

"So you did have a cavity?"

"No, a more profound infection," I said.

"Liar. Hanuki was like, 'Only an idiot leaves a toothache for that long.' Half of your wisdom tooth was gone, right?"

Ozu still belonged to Lucky Cat Chinese Food, the secret organization I had fled, and now he was ruling from on high. On top of that, he hinted that he was involved in all sorts of other things. Most would hope that he would make his energy useful "for society and the world at large," but he said that the moment he considered the world or society, his joints quit working.

"How were you raised that you ended up like this?" I asked him.

"It's another pearl of wisdom from my master."

"What does he teach you?"

"I can't explain it in just a word or two. It's too profound," Ozu said with a yawn. "Oh, so, back when my master wanted a seahorse, I found an aquarium at a garbage dump and took it to him. When I tried filling it up, it sprang a furious leak, and the water came rushing out, causing a whole scene. The master's whole room was soaked."

"Wait, what number is your master's room?"

"It's the one directly above this."

I flew into a rage.

Previously, while I was away, there had been a flood on the second floor. When I got home, the water had dripped down to make all of my precious documents—both obscene and not—soggy. But that wasn't the only damage I suffered. All my precious data—both obscene and not—was lost from my waterlogged computer, vanished into the electron sea. It goes without saying that this incident hastened the decay of my academic life. I thought I would complain, but getting involved with this unknown upstairs resident seemed like a pain, so I had left the matter unresolved.

"That was your doing?"

"So your library of obscenities got a little wet—that's not such a big loss, is it?" Ozu said impudently.

"Just get out already. I have shit to do."

"That I shall. We're doing a Blackout Hot Pot party at Master Higuchi's tonight."

Kicking Ozu and his smirk into the hallway, I finally achieved some calm.

Then I recalled the events of the spring of my freshman year.

• • •

At the time, I was a fresh-as-a-daisy-man. I remember how exhilarating the vibrant green of the cherry tree leaves was after all the flower petals had fallen.

Any new student walking through campus gets club flyers thrust upon them, and I was weighed down with so many that my capacity for processing information had been far overwhelmed. There were all sorts of flyers, but the four that caught my eye were as follows: the Ablutions film club, a bizarre "Disciples Wanted" notice, the Mellow softball club, and the underground organization Lucky Cat Chinese Food. They all seemed pretty shady, but each one represented a doorway into a new college-student life, and my curiosity was piqued. The fact that I thought a fun future would be waiting on the other side, no matter which door I chose, just goes to show what an incorrigible idiot I was.

After my classes were over, I headed to the clock tower. All kinds of clubs were meeting there to take new students to orientations.

The area around the clock was bustling with freshmen, cheeks flushed with hope, and welcoming committee members ready to prey on them. It seemed to me that here there were innumerable entryways leading to that elusive prize—a rose-colored campus life—and I walked among them half in a daze.

That was where I encountered the secret organization Lucky Cat Chinese Food. It's not as if a secret organization writes "secret organization" in big letters on its flyer—don't be alarmed. I learned about the secret part after the fact.

The one who approached me at the clock tower was an executive in one of Lucky Cat Chinese Food's suborgs, the Library Police, by the name of Aijima. He seemed very sharp, and his eyes were chilly behind his glasses. His demeanor was mild, but I somehow got the impression that his politeness was only superficial.

"You get to associate with all kinds of people. Makes life more interesting." Aijima had invited me into the law faculty's courtyard in order to persuade me to join.

I thought about it. It was true that I lived in a small world. While you're in college, it's important to interact with all the people milling about on campus and learn things. And the experiences you accumulate will prepare you for a shining future. Of course, I didn't only think about serious stuff like that; I can't deny the mysterious atmosphere of the organization held some sort of fascination for me. Have I mentioned that I was an incorrigible idiot?

What was Lucky Cat Chinese Food?

Its purpose was shrouded in mystery.

Actually, I'll just say it: it probably didn't have one.

"Lucky Cat Chinese Food" was an ambiguous umbrella term gathering multiple suborganizations. I could list all of them and what they did, but they were all the sorts of things you would have a hard time believing—even just the main ones, which included the Printing Office, which put superior students under what amounted to house arrest and forced them to write mountains of papers for other people; the Library Police, who existed to forcibly recover library books that were past due; and the Happy Bicycle Disposal Corps, who devoted themselves to organizing the bicycles all over campus. Lucky Cat Chinese Food also had connections to a part of the School Festival Office; a handful of eccentric clubs and associations, such as the Eizan Electric Railway Research Association, the Bedroom Investigation Commission, and the Sophistry Debate Club; and some religious clubs that operated in dubious ways.

The commonly held belief was that, historically, the Printing Office was the mother organization. So the Printing Office chief was said to possess overarching authority, but it was unclear whether any such person actually existed. There was much speculation. Some said the chief was a black-haired maiden of a tender age, while others said the chief was a grizzled law professor; and then there were those who said they were a boob-loving weirdo in a mask who had been living under the clock tower for twenty years. In any case, a guy like me running around as a grunt for the Library Police certainly had no occasion to come into contact with whoever they were.

When I joined the Library Police on Aijima's invitation, he

told me, "For now, this guy'll be your partner," and introduced me to someone in the law faculty courtyard. Standing there was a creepy fellow with a terribly inauspicious-looking face. At first I thought he was a messenger from hell only I, with my heightened sensitivities, could see.

That was how I met Ozu.

• • •

There's a famous book that begins with an ordinary man waking up one morning to find he's been turned into an insect. In my case, it wasn't that dramatic. I was still me, and at a glance, the four-and-a-half-mat tatami room steeped in my manly essence was also the same as usual. Of course, some might be of the opinion that I basically started out as an insect, anyhow.

The clock said six, but it wasn't clear whether it was six in the morning or six in the evening. I thought about it as I lay there, but I wasn't sure how long I had slept.

Squirming like an insect on top of my futon, I sluggishly got up.

It was quiet.

I boiled some coffee and decided to eat some castella. Upon finishing my bleak meal, I realized I needed to pee. I headed out into the hallway to the common bathroom located next to the building's entrance.

I opened the door and stepped into my four-and-a-half-mat tatami room.

How curious.

I turned around. My chaotic four-and-a-half-mat tatami room was there. And yet on the other side of the half-open door was also my chaotic four-and-a-half-mat tatami room. It was like looking at my room in a mirror.

I went through the opening and stepped into the four-and-a-half-mat tatami room. There was no doubt about it: this was my room. The feel of the tatami when I flopped on it, the miscellaneous books lining the bookcase, the broken TV, the desk I'd been using since I was an elementary schooler, the dusty sink—a very lived-in scene.

I went back through the door to my room, and that was also, without a doubt, my room. Even I, who through long years of training had tempered my heart to the point that little things wouldn't alarm me, was alarmed. What strange phenomenon was this? My four-and-a-half-mat tatami room had become two.

If I couldn't get out through the door, I would have to open a window.

I opened the curtains I had been keeping shut for ages, but on the other side of the frosted glass, a fluorescent light was shining. When I shoved the window open, I found myself peering into my own four-and-a-half-mat tatami room. I stepped over the window frame and went inside to check the particulars, but it was indeed my room.

I went back to the first room.

I smoked a cigarette and tried to calm down.

Thus began what ended up being eighty days of exploring a world of four-and-a-half-mat tatami rooms.

• • •

This entire adventure takes place almost entirely in essentially identical four-and-a-half-mat tatami rooms. For that reason, before discussing the adventure proper, I'd like to give you readers a clear image of my room.

First, on the north side there is a door about as flimsy as wafer cookies made for babies. It's covered in indecent stickers, traces of the previous resident, so there's a lot going on there.

Next to the door there is a sink that has been left to its filth and a pile of random junk such as a dusty can of hair gel, a hot plate, and whatnot. I guarantee it would kill any cook's motivation. I flat-out refused to prepare food in such a desolate space and had been putting the old saying "boys should stay out of the kitchen" into practice. Most of the northern wall is a closet crammed carelessly with my utterly cheerless clothing, books I didn't read, documents I hesitated to throw out, and the electric heater I used to repel General Winter, among other stuff. It's also home to my library of obscenities.

Most of the eastern wall is the bookcase. Next to the bookcase is a vacuum cleaner and a rice cooker, though I've never felt compelled to use either of them.

There's a window on the southern side, and in front of it is my trusty desk I've been using since elementary school. The drawer doesn't open, so I've forgotten what's inside.

On the eastern side in the narrow area between the bookcase and the desk extends a space where items that have no other place to go get tossed; being put there is commonly known as being "sent to Siberia." I keep thinking I need to get a handle on what lies in that chaotic territory, but it's so horrifying that I haven't started. Once you wander in there, there's a very low chance of coming out alive.

On the western side there's a broken TV and a small refrigerator.

Then we're back on the northern side.

It only takes a few seconds to take a spin around this space, but this four-and-a-half-mat tatami room might as well be my brain.

• • •

So why a four-and-a-half-mat tatami room in the first place?

I knew one person living in a three-mat room. He was even more of a solitary idealist of a student than me and spent his time reading *Being and Time*; he was so strong-willed and self-confident that his unwillingness to accommodate himself to the world took a turn, and last year his parents came from his hometown to retrieve him.

I've heard that two-mat rooms do exist here in Kyoto. It's hard to believe, but apparently there really is a room near Jodoji that is just two tatami mats laid end to end. I'm sure if you sleep in what is basically a hallway, you must get taller.

And then, according to the terrifying rumor around town, there's a building by the name of ——so in the neighborhood of the Kitashirakawa Baptist Hospital that has a one-mat room; a student saw it and, a few days later, that same student disappeared under mysterious circumstances and everyone they knew suffered a string of bad luck.

Now we come to four-and-a-half-mat tatami rooms.

Compared with one-, two-, or three-mat rooms, four-and-a-half-mat rooms are a tidy little package. You lay three mats side by side and then lay the fourth next to them perpendicularly. When you put a half mat in the leftover space, you get a perfect square. Isn't that beautiful? You can make a square with two mats, but it's cramped. If, on the other hand, you make a square larger than four-and-a-half mats, you end up with something as large as the feudal lord Takeda Shingen's lavatory, so if you're not careful, you could get lost.

I've been a staunch supporter of four-and-a-half-mat tatami rooms since starting college.

Are people who live in seven-, eight-, or ten-mat rooms really worthy of lording over that much space? Do they really know every corner of it like the back of their hand? With control of a space comes responsibility. The amount of space we humans are capable of controlling is four and a half tatami mats or less; those villains who would greedily pursue more will someday find themselves on the receiving end of a fearsome counterattack from a corner of their room. That's what I've always maintained.

• • •

My exploration of the tatami world had begun, but my conscience doesn't allow me to act impulsively. I thoroughly analyze, analyze, analyze, until there is no more analysis to be done. Then, I carefully take infallible measures. I'm the type of person who analyzes so much that the infallible measures happen too late.

Having returned to my original four-and-a-half-mat tatami room, I thought about what my next move should be.

A great individual must think with a clear head under any circumstances and never get agitated. After thinking clearly, I decided to make use of the beer bottle Ozu had left in my room two weeks earlier. I was able to regain my composure by urinating into it.

Panicking wouldn't get me anywhere. Ever since becoming a junior—in name only—the vast majority of my existence had been spent in this space. I hadn't shown any enthusiasm for leaving before; so if I got all flustered about it now, how shallow would that be? Barring imminent crisis, a person like me wasn't required to take any action. If I sat tight and kept my wits about me, perhaps things would take a turn for the better.

So that's what I decided to do. I leisurely opened Jules Verne's *Twenty Thousand Leagues Under the Sea* and turned my attention to the far-off world of the sea bottom. When I eventually tired of that, I glanced over my library of obscenities, made an appropriate selection, and turned my attention to the world of sensuality. I paid very close attention. I paid such close attention I wore myself out.

I thought about turning on the TV, but the TV had been on the fritz for ages. The screen spun like a pinwheel in a typhoon, so unless you had exceptional dynamic visual acuity, it was impossible to tell what was on it. After staring at it for a little while, I felt sick. If I had known this situation was going to befall me, I would have taken it to be repaired.

Soon the clock's hands had made one complete turn. After I ate a remnant of fish burger I had fried up, all that was left was castella. There was a chunk of daikon too, but I didn't bother with that for the moment. I checked once more before going to sleep, but outside, both the door and the window were four-and-a-half-mat tatami rooms. I turned off the light, lay down on my futon, and frowned at the ceiling. How had I ended up in this freakish realm?

I came up with one hypothesis: this was the curse of the Kiyamachi fortune-teller.

• • •

A few days earlier, I had gone to Kawaramachi for a change of pace. I stopped into the used bookstore Gabi Shobo and then strolled through Kiyamachi. That was where I met the fortune-teller.

Among the bars and sex shops crouched a dark house.

Under its eaves, an old woman sat before a wooden table covered with a white cloth—a fortune-teller. A sheet of paper hanging from the table was crammed full of kanji whose meaning I couldn't fathom. Something like a little lantern glowed orange, bringing the woman's face into view. There was something strangely intimidating about her. She was a yokai licking her lips at the souls of the people passing by. *Get a single fortune read and forevermore the shady old woman will haunt you day and night, nothing you try to do will go well, the one you're waiting for won't come, your lost items will never turn up, you'll fail the classes that should have been easy credits, your graduation thesis will spontaneously combust just before you hand it in, you'll fall into Lake Biwa Canal, you'll be solicited on the street by one of those people on Shijo-dori*—I was resolutely imagining all of this terrible luck while staring at her, so eventually she sensed my presence. From the depths of the darkness, she flashed her eyes at me. The unearthly atmosphere she emitted ensnared me. That atmosphere was persuasive. I considered it logically: there was no way someone giving off supernatural vibes this potent for free would tell a fortune that missed the mark.

I've been alive in this world for nearly a quarter century, but I can count on my fingers the number of times I listened so humbly to another person's opinion. Maybe that was how I ended up purposely taking this thorny path there was no need to walk down at all? If I had abandoned my own judgment sooner, I wouldn't have holed up in my four-and-a-half-mat tatami castle after getting caught up in that weird organization, Lucky Cat Chinese Food, and being treated so badly, and I probably wouldn't have met Ozu with his labyrinthine character. I would have been blessed with good friends and upperclassmen associates, employing my overflowing talents in full to excel in both the literary and military arts, the result of which would have been a beautiful black-haired maiden at my side and, before me, a shining future of pure gold; if things went well, perhaps even that elusive, supreme treasure—a rose-colored, meaningful campus life—would have been within my grasp. For a person of my caliber, such a stroke of luck wouldn't be even a little unusual.

Right.

It's not too late. With all possible haste, seek an objective opinion and escape into one of the other lives you could have!

I stepped forward as if drawn by the old woman's other-worldly aura.

"Well, my boy, what would you like to know?"

She spoke in a mumble as if her mouth was full of cotton, which really made me feel like I was speaking with a wise elder.

"Hmm. Good question."

When I remained lost for words, the old woman smiled. "From the look on your face right now, I gather you're terribly irritated. Dissatisfied. It seems that you aren't making full use of your talents. Your current environment doesn't appear to be a good fit for you."

"Yes, that's right. That's exactly it."

"Let's have a look."

The old woman took my hands and pored over them, nodding to herself.

"Mm. You seem to be extremely hard-working and talented."

I was already impressed by her keen insights. Just as in the proverb "a clever hawk hides its talons," I had modestly kept my good sense and talents hidden so no one would find them, but I did such a good job that I hadn't been able to locate them myself for the past few years; for her to spot them within five minutes of our meeting meant she couldn't be any ordinary fortune-teller.

"It's essential that you not let chance pass you by. What I mean is a good opportunity. Do you understand? But chance is rather hard to seize: Sometimes something that doesn't look like a chance at all is one, while other times what you were sure was your chance turns out, in retrospect, to not have been it at all. But you must perceive your chance and act on it. It looks like you'll have a long life, so I'm sure you'll be able to seize one at some point."

Profound words befitting her otherworldly aura.

"I can't wait that long. I want to seize my chance now. Could you explain in a bit more detail?"

When I pressed her, the old woman's wrinkles warped slightly. I wondered if her right cheek was itchy, but apparently this was a smile.

"It's difficult to speak in particulars. Even if I tell you now, your fate might change, and then it won't be your chance anymore. Wouldn't I feel bad about that? Fate can change from second to second, you know."

"But like this it's so vague I have no idea what to do."

When I cocked my head, the old woman said "Hmm-hmm!" with a sniff. "Very well. I'll refrain from talking about the too distant future, but I'll tell you something very near."

I opened my ears as big as Dumbo's.

"*Colosseo*," she whispered suddenly.

"Colosseo? What's that?"

"Colosseo is the sign of your chance. When your chance appears, there colosseo will be," she said.

"You're not telling me to go to Rome, are you?" I asked, but the old woman only grinned.

"When your chance comes, don't miss it. When it comes, you can't go on idly doing the same things you've always done. Be bold, and try seizing your chance by doing something completely different. If you do that, your dissatisfaction will disappear, and you'll be able to walk down a new path—though there may lie a different dissatisfaction. I'm sure you understand."

I didn't understand one bit, but I nodded anyway.

"Even if you miss this chance, you needn't worry. You're

a fine person, so I'm sure you'll be able to seize one someday. That I know for sure. There's no rush."

With that, she ended the reading.

"Thank you."

I bobbed my head and paid her fee. Then, like a little lost lamb, I stepped into the Kiyamachi crowd.

I'd like you to commit this old woman's prediction to memory.

• • •

This might be a terrible curse she put on me. Maybe the key to breaking it is hidden in that word she mentioned, "colosseo." I swore I wouldn't rest until I had solved the puzzle, and it was still on my mind as I drifted into a gentle sleep.

When I woke up, the clock was pointing to twelve.

I got up and opened the curtains. No bright daylight streamed in, but neither was I greeted with the darkness of night; instead there was just the pale fluorescent light of the four-and-a-half-mat tatami room next door. I thought if I slept, things would fix themselves somehow, but even when I woke up, the situation hadn't changed one bit. When I tried opening the door, too, it led to the adjacent four-and-a-half-mat tatami room.

Going forward, for your convenience, I'm going to call the four-and-a-half-mat tatami room I was in to begin with FHMTR0. And I'm going to call the one through the door FHMTR1, and the one through the window FHMTR-1.

I sat glumly cross-legged in the middle of the four-and-a-half-mat tatami room listening to the coffee burble. As you might expect, I was hungry. There was no castella left. I had eaten the fish burger. Praying something had appeared out of nowhere when I wasn't looking, I opened the fridge, but all I had was the chunk of daikon, soy sauce, salt, pepper, and shichimi. I didn't even have that college-student essential, instant ramen. This is what I got for relying on convenience stores.

I boiled the chunk of daikon and ate it with soy sauce and shichimi. I sipped coffee to fill my stomach.

I ran out of food sometime on the second day. All I had left was coffee and cigarettes. No matter how gracefully I employed those to delay the feeling of starvation, at some point my stomach would meet my back. I would perish in this four-and-a-half-mat tatami room, without anyone knowing, and shrivel up.

I cradled my head in a corner and tried to endure by insisting I had no idea what was going on, but even with no idea what is going on, you get hungry. I was forced to come up with a plan to solve the food problem on a fundamental level.

• • •

When you think of a college student, you think of filth. When you think of filth, you think of fungus. I wondered whether I could eat the mushrooms that sprouted in closet corners. But when I pulled out my library of obscenities, cardboard boxes, and half-rotten paperwork and scrounged around inside my closet, it was dry—not the sort of environment mushrooms would thrive in. *Should I try to cultivate them systematically by spreading out a layer of dirty laundry and sprinkling water on it?* But given the choice to live a carefree life surviving on mushrooms grown on my own dirty clothes, I would choose honorable hunger.

I also considered boiling and eating the tatami. Given how steeped in manly essence it was, it probably contained some nutrients. But it had too much fiber. My bowels would be moving as smoothly as the Lake Biwa Canal, which would surely only hasten my doom.

I'm not sure what was so fun about my ceiling, but a moth had been hanging out on one corner completely still. After a while, I began to consider it as a source of animal protein. It may have been an insect, but it was still an animal. People who get lost in the mountains grill and eat woolly bears, hornworms, drone beetles—anything. But if I was going to grill and eat this squooshy moth covered in powdery scales, licking the dust in the corner seemed preferable.

If I could extend my life by consuming my body's excess, that would be a sublime survival drama, but I'm fuel-efficient, so my flesh has eliminated anything deemed unnecessary. If I have any excess, I suppose it's my earlobes. Like a spit-roasted sparrow, I'm all bones—a man who can't be eaten. I'm not interested in people pointing at me behind my back and saying, *He survived by eating his own earlobes.*

If it was beneath me to eat homegrown mushrooms, tatami, the moth, and my earlobes, then I would have to survive on whiskey, vitamins, coffee, and cigarettes. I was Robinson Crusoe, washed up on a deserted four-and-a-half-mat tatami room. In his case he had a gun and could go hunting, but the best I could manage would be to catch the moth fluttering around the ceiling. But in my case, I have water on tap, a full complement of furniture, and no need to fear ferocious animal attacks. It was actually a bit unclear whether what I was doing qualified as "survival" or not.

That day, I once again read *Twenty Thousand Leagues Under the Sea*, haughtily relaxing as if to provoke the cruel god watching me. I couldn't see the light of the sun, so I had no idea whether it was day or night. So though I split the time into days, I'm not sure if the divisions were accurate.

If I closed the curtains and shut the door, everything looked as usual, so it felt like Ozu would kick in the door to start some obnoxious trouble. The blessing in this curse was that I had already had my wisdom tooth pulled two weeks ago. If I hadn't, unable to bear the excruciating pain, I would have been running around the four-and-a-half-mat tatami rooms in search of a dentist before dying in agony.

The tooth I had pulled at Kubozuka Dental on Mikage-dori was displayed reverently on my desk.

● ● ●

By the end of April, my jaw was hurting so badly I couldn't sleep properly.

I diagnosed myself with temporomandibular joint disorder. They say you can get it from stress. For someone like me, who's as delicate as dandelion fluff, and once lost himself in thought like a scholarly priest up on Mount Hiei, it's strange that this was my first brush with TMJ. I should have gotten it sooner. That realization was deeply satisfying: this was actually a trial the chosen ones must submit to. Writhing on my tatami floor, I nevertheless became ecstatic.

"There's no way you're stressed. I refuse to believe that."

Ozu looked as if he had spotted a pervert. "You quit the org and have been doing a whole lot of nothing ever since."

On the surface, it might have looked as though I wasn't doing anything, but I was actually laboring day by day on unrewarding meditations; so you could say I was under extreme stress—that's what I argued. This TMJ disorder was clear proof of my strenuous thinking.

"I'm sure it's just a cavity," Ozu commented helpfully.

"Are you stupid?! It's not my tooth that hurts, it's my jaw!"

Seeing me writhing in agony, Ozu recommended Kubozuka Dental. He said a beautiful hygienist named Hanuki worked there. But I was against it. Even if there hadn't exactly been many vicissitudes, that time in my room had been enlightening; I had tempered my heart and tempered it again. Still, I was terrified of the dentist.

"I'm not going to the dentist."

"But a young woman sticks her fingers in your mouth! You should be grateful. How often do you get the opportunity to lick a woman's fingers? I don't think you ever will. Think of it this way: your cavity is a golden ticket to some lady-finger-licking action!"

"Don't lump me in with freaks like you. I have no desire to lick a woman's fingers," I said.

"Liar, liar, pants on a wire!"

"Are you hanging up the laundry, dumbass? You mean 'fire.'"

"Just go to the dentist."

His endorsement was awfully enthusiastic.

One night, the pain oozing from my jaw zapped through both rows of my teeth, creating a sort of resonance that wreaked havoc, as if a ton of fat little fairies were having a Cossack dance contest in my mouth. With no other choice, I gave in to Ozu's persuasion.

The pain in my jaw was due not to my being delicate or to my intense meditations, but to a cavity in a wisdom tooth. Though I was loath to admit it, Ozu's guess was correct. This is what I got for slacking on brushing my teeth after quitting the organization and living a solitary life where I hardly met anybody.

I was absolutely not enticed by the taste of her fingers, but the hygienist Hanuki was indeed charming. Age-wise, she must have been in her late twenties? Her hair was pulled into a bun, making her face with the severity of a Sengoku-era warlord's wife's even more severe. Furrowing her dignified brow, she deftly used an implement that made a horrendous whining sound to do a splendid job of removing the plaque from my teeth. I expressed respect for her confident skills.

After my treatment was finished, I mentioned that I had come on Ozu's recommendation. She seemed to know him well and said, "He's so funny, isn't he?" Then, as if handing me a newborn baby, she gave me my tooth, swaddled in medical cotton.

I folded it up and then placed the memorial tooth on my desk at home. I gazed upon it every day. For some reason, I found it difficult to throw away.

• • •

Somewhere in my mind I was making light of the situation, thinking, *It must just be a dream.*

But even after about three days, on the other side of the door was a four-and-a-half-mat tatami room, and on the other side of the window was a four-and-a-half-mat tatami room. Naturally, at that point I could no longer lie around reading *Twenty Thousand Leagues Under the Sea*. I was out of food, and I only had a few cigarettes left. I preferred to do as little as possible and maintain my pride, but what good would my little bit of pride be if I lost my life?

I poured coffee into my empty stomach and lapped at a little dish of soy sauce to stave off hunger.

I would apologize for bringing up the vulgar topic but it makes no sense to apologize for a little vulgarity at this point, so I won't; but no matter how little food one is eating, the urge to expel waste still arises. Liquids I put into the beer bottle until it was full and I had the brilliant idea to wash them down the sink, so that was no trouble. The problem was what to do about the solids.

Spurred by my need to defecate, I went through the door to invade FHMTR1. That room also had a window. I opened the curtains with a prayer, but it appeared that beyond the window, the four-and-a-half-mat tatami rooms continued with FHMTR2. I went back to the original room and climbed through the window to FHMTR-1 and opened the door there, but as expected, that led to FHMTR-2.

How far do these four-and-half-mat tatami rooms go?

But first I had to avert the current crisis. After some thought, I spread an old newspaper on the tatami, nonchalantly did my business on that, then put it in a plastic bag, which I tightly tied shut.

With that imminent crisis out of the way, the issues of food and cigarettes crossed my mind. At this point, I had no choice but to stand up and work toward a solution myself. No matter what kind of world you're in, you have only yourself to rely on.

• • •

I solved the food and cigarette issues in the following way:

I moved to FHMTR1.

The room through the door was clearly my room, so there was no issue with me using it how I pleased.

When I stepped through the door, I found a pack of cigarettes. And I found things I thought I might never see again: fish burger and castella. There was a chunk of daikon, too. For starters, I fried up the fish burger, seasoned it with plenty of pepper, and heartily savored my first animal protein in three days. A fish burger has never tasted so good. After that I had a slice of castella for dessert. I felt energy well up inside me as if I'd come back to life.

I looked through the window at FHMTR2.

FHMTR3, FHMTR4, FHMTR5 . . . FHMTR∞—could it be that my four-and-a-half-mat room continued on forever? What a miserable infinite sequence of a world. I was living in an apartment larger than the surface of the Earth.

Though the situation was rather hopeless, you could also say I was fortunate. If I ate all the food in one room, all I had to do was go to the next to acquire more fish burger and castella. It wasn't a balanced diet, but it would keep me from dying of starvation in the near term.

And I couldn't ignore the warmth I got from the castella Ozu had given me. After our unintended meeting in the spring of freshman year, we'd had a fatal bond that I couldn't break even if I wanted to; but for once, I felt his existence had been useful.

• • •

After starting college, I worked with the Library Police for a year and a half and then called it quits.

As I mentioned before, the Library Police's purpose as an organization was to chase down villains who don't return their library books on time and forcefully recover the borrowed materials. When necessary, they didn't hesitate to employ inhumane methods—or rather, I should say they *only* employed inhumane methods. Why the Library Police had taken on this role, what relationship they had to the university's library—the answers to these questions were not to be pursued. Pursuing them could put you in danger.

The Library Police did something else besides recover overdue library books. They also collected comprehensive personal information about given targets to use toward various ends. This data collection was originally a way of forcing the return of books. To know where your target was, you had to have an idea of where they went, and in order to recover books from the nasty ones who would ignore you and try to walk away, you needed to grasp their weakness. But as the data piled up, the organization was made captive to the power and charms of intel.

It had been decades since the data collection had deviated

wildly from its original mission and begun to expand. The Library Police network covered campus, of course, but it had also spread north to Sanzen-in Temple in Ohara, and south to Byodo-in's Phoenix Hall, in Uji, reaching all over Kyoto and beyond.

Let's say the Chief of Library Police felt like breaking up a couple, A (male, twenty-one) and B (female, twenty). With a snap of his fingers, they could procure intel that "A's going out with B, but actually he's also involved with C, whom he knows from tennis club. These are C's grades; she doesn't have enough credits and may not graduate on time." The chief would also have no trouble getting additional information that would allow him to remotely manipulate C to deal a critical blow to A and B's relationship.

The only org that could rival the Printing Office, with its enormous revenue from forging massive numbers of reports, was the Library Police. Since the identity of the Printing Office's head was shrouded in mystery, it was no wonder that the Chief of Library Police was considered the de facto leader of Lucky Cat Chinese Food.

At the time, I was an underling with no contact whatsoever with the chief.

Underlings were tasked with recovering library books. That said, I didn't go about it very smartly. I would let the borrower give me excuses, and then we'd hit it off and go drinking together. Talk about uninvested. The reason I still managed to get results was that I had Ozu.

Ozu employed all manner of techniques to recover library books: stakeouts, tears, dirty traps, blackmail, physical assault under cover of darkness—even theft. Naturally he did well, and as his partner, my standing also improved. To someone like me who was half-assing it, wondering if the Library Police even really existed, it was totally annoying.

Additionally, Ozu enjoyed intel collection so much that he continued to expand his mysterious network of connections and rose to become what you could call Aijima's right-hand man.

The spring of my sophomore year, Aijima became Chief of Library Police.

He tried to install Ozu and me in executive positions. But surprisingly, Ozu refused the offer and transferred to the Printing Office. With no other choice, I became an executive, but I had impressively little motivation and just rotted away, day after fruitless day; in no time, my status plummeted to executive in name only.

Aijima despised me and paid so little attention to me, I might as well have been a pebble by the wayside.

• • •

During my Library Police era, I met a curious individual.

It was the winter of my freshman year.

Someone had borrowed a book called *The Month with No Gods*, a biography of a certain painter, and hadn't returned it in over six months. I was ordered to recover the book, so I decided to make contact with the borrower. He lived on the second floor of the building I lived in, Shimogamo Yusuiso, and his name was Seitaro Higuchi. He was a puzzling fellow. He didn't seem like a student, but neither did he seem like a working adult. It was hard to tell whether he was in his four-and-a-half-mat tatami room or not. Even if he was, you didn't see much of him. Suspecting he was in, I once opened his door to find a duck waddling around and Higuchi having vanished somewhere. He wore a navy yukata and his eggplant-shaped face was perpetually unshaven. His peculiar appearance meant it was easy to spot him when he was out, but when I tried to make contact, he would disappear like a puff of smoke. I had lost sight of him a number of times at Shimogamo Shrine and along the Demachi shopping street.

One late night, I finally managed to nab him at the Neko Ramen noodle stall.

"You've been stalking me for a while now," he said with a broad smile. "I keep thinking I should return it, but I just read so slowly."

"Well, it's just so very overdue."

"Yes, I know. I'll give up."

We slurped our ramen together.

I stuck close to him on our way back to Shimogamo Yusuiso. "I'm going to hit the loo quick," he said and ducked into the communal bathroom. I waited a while, but he wasn't coming out. When my patience expired, I stepped into the bathroom to find it an empty husk. When I went up to his room on the second floor, there was light coming through the little window above the door. What a godly move.

I drummed on the door and called, "Higuchi!" but there was no answer. I felt like he was mocking me. As I was losing my temper there, Ozu, who was still my partner at the time, came along.

"Sorry. That man is my master," he said. "Please leave him be."

"You really think you can get away with that?"

"It's not happening. He never returns anything he's borrowed."

If what Ozu said was true, I had no choice but to withdraw. I wondered what exactly Higuchi was a master *of*, but if a guy like Ozu respected him, the chances of him being a decent person were slim to none.

"Good evening, Master. I brought you some stuff."

With a sideways glance at me, Ozu went into Higuchi's room. Turning around as he shut the door, he grinned and said, "*Sorryyy.*"

• • •

For two days, I wandered between FHMTR-3 and FHMTR3.

Things didn't improve.

Anyhow, I had stuff to do. I did push-ups, pseudo-Hindu squats, and whatnot for exercise. I drank a barrel's worth of coffee. I put six castella cakes into my stomach and developed a new cuisine of fish burger and daikon. I read the passage in *Twenty Thousand Leagues Under the Sea* about the *Nautilus*'s tantalizing dinner table over and over, drooling.

Until then, I had holed up in my four-and-a-half-mat tatami room by choice, but I was always confident that I could leave if I wanted. If I opened the door, the dirty hallway was there, and at the end of the dirty hallway was the dirty bathroom and the dirty shoe cubbies, and I could exit this dirty building to go outside. It was precisely because I could go outside whenever I wanted that I stayed in.

Before long, the reality that no matter how many times I went out, I was in a four-and-a-half-mat tatami room, began to grate on me, and the calcium deficiency I developed due to my food situation made me cranky. No matter how patiently I waited, a change in the right direction refused to come. At that point, all I could do was embark on a grand adventure to the ends of this infinite tatami world to solve its mysteries and hopefully escape.

One day, after about a week trapped in this barren land, at six—morning or night, I still didn't know—I decided to set out.

From FHMTR0, I had two choices, the door or the window. I chose the door.

In other words, I decided to traverse FHMTR1, 2, 3, and so on. I decided I would take this four-and-a-half-mat tatami road as far as it went.

There was no need to steel my resolve for anything so epic as aiming for the ends of the earth—because I would just be continually walking across my room. There was no danger of being attacked by a ferocious beast, no chance of blizzards, and I didn't have to think about my food supply. There was no need to prepare, because during every point of the journey, I would be in my own room. If I got tired at any time, I could burrow into my futon.

Though I never did meet a ferocious beast, I would have several horrifying encounters.

The first day, I went through twenty four-and-a-half-mat

tatami rooms. Yet the four-and-a-half-mat tatami rooms continued. Things started to feel stupid, so I slept there for the night.

•   •   •

On the third day, I discovered "alchemy."

When I explained the layout of my four-and-a-half-mat tatami room, I mentioned the space between my desk and the bookcase. On that day, I decided to investigate that territory to see if there was anything useful in it. I found a shabby wallet that had been "sent to Siberia." Feeling around inside it, I found there was one thousand-yen note remaining. I sat in the center of the room and caressed the wrinkled thousand yen. I laughed hollowly. What good was a thousand yen in this situation? In this tatami world completely cut off from our capitalist society, a thousand-yen note had as much value as a scrap of paper.

But when I went to the next room, I found the same old wallet and the thousand yen inside. I felt as though I'd been struck by lightning. If every room had a thousand yen in it, then every time I switched rooms, I could make a thousand yen. Moving through ten rooms would yield ten thousand yen. Moving through a thousand rooms would yield . . . What a great racket. If I ever escaped the tatami world, I would be able to pay for the rest of my tuition and probably cover living expenses, too. A luxurious time out in Gion would no longer be just a dream.

After that I traveled with a backpack.

Every time I switched rooms, I threw a thousand yen in.

• • •

At first, I would get sick of moving after a while, so I spent the rest of my time reading or inflating and deflating my fantasies to distract myself. I was so bored I had the admirable thought that maybe I should study, so I sat down at my desk but ended up getting destroyed by the Schrödinger equation.

From time to time, the old woman's words reappeared in the back of my mind.

What did she mean by "colosseo"?

I believed my hypothesis that she had cursed me. It was clear that "colosseo" was the key to breaking the curse. But there was no way I had one in my room.

As I passed through the vast string of four-and-a-half-mat tatami rooms, I racked my brain for any "colosseo" associations but found nothing.

• • •

On my brutal journey, I thought about the mochiguma, who had soothed my spirit for the past year. Now, with my heart losing warmth, the softness of the mochiguma was a fond memory.

The mochiguma was a spongy bear plushie. I had acquired it at the Shimogamo Shrine used book fair the previous summer, and ever since, it had provided me with invaluable emotional support. The gray bear was as soft and squishy as a baby's cheeks. It was about as tall as a can of soda. As you kneaded it, your face would naturally relax into a smile. I kept that lovable plushie with me at all times. After cutting ties with the organization and holing up in my room to apply myself to rigorous austerities, that half-yokai Ozu was the only one who ever visited me, but even in a solitary life like that, I required a companion.

But my plushie had vanished in a bizarre incident at the laundromat a few days before I set off on this journey. I was washing the mochiguma, since it had gotten a bit grimy steeping in my manly essence, but when I opened the machine, I saw that someone had taken my mochiguma and crammed in a pile of men's underwear. These undergarments had neither charm nor anything else going for them. When I investigated further, however, I discovered they were my usual underwear, saddled with the sad stains I hadn't been able to remove no matter how I tried.

Could it be that I only imagined that I was washing my bear? Maybe I was actually just doing regular laundry. I was probably just so loath to do the banal task of laundry that I averted my eyes from the cruel reality that I was washing my underwear and thus lost myself in a fantasy of washing a cute bear that was never even here? I thought. *The hazards of autopilot!*

When I returned to my room, however, my underwear was there just as it had been. Faced with double the underwear, I had no idea what I was supposed to do. It was a mystery that never resolved. I never did find my mochiguma, either.

Ah, I hope my mochiguma is out there somewhere, thriving.

I wished the plushie well as I aimlessly wandered the four-and-a-half-mat tatami rooms.

• • •

At first, I was tallying the four-and-a-half-mat rooms I had conquered, but after a while I stopped counting.

I opened the door, went through, crossed FHTMRn, opened the window, climbed over the frame, crossed FHTMRn+1, opened the door, went through, crossed FHTMRn+2, opened the window . . . rinse, wash, repeat. I made a thousand yen in each room, but since I could see no way of escaping, the value of a thousand-yen note fluctuated wildly, depending on my hope versus my despair. If I couldn't escape, then all I was collecting were scraps of paper. The only reason I didn't quit gathering them even when their value plummeted was my indomitable spirit, perhaps you could say, or maybe my poverty mentality.

I ate a mountain of castella, fried up fish burgers, and continued my solo march.

I sometimes wondered if I had died, descended into tatami hell, and been forced to perform endless penance without realizing it. Memories of all the various sins I'd committed paraded through my mind, and I was so mortified I fainted in agony. I also occasionally screamed, "Of *course* I would go to hell!"

Finally, I reached my limit and lay down on the tatami like a log. I refused to march anymore.

Instead, I absorbed myself in *The Curious Casebook of Inspector Hanshichi*. I got drunk on cheap whiskey and smoked cigarettes. I shouted at the ceiling, "Why did this have to happen to me?!" I grew frightened of the utterly silent world surrounding me and sang every song I could think of at the top of my lungs. It wasn't like anyone would complain. I might as well have gotten naked, painted myself pink, and marched shouting obscenities the likes of which I had never vocalized before, but though I might have been all alone, my rationality was still in working order. Under the circumstances, it wouldn't have been surprising for someone to lose their grip. I was able to tolerate the situation precisely because I was me.

Anyway, I would be remiss not to mention my various discoveries.

I realized that the four-and-a-half-mat tatami rooms I had thought were identical were actually each a little different. It must have been about ten days since I had started my journey. It was only a slight difference, but the selection of titles lined up on the bookshelves had changed. I was going to read *The Curious Casebook of Inspector Hanshichi*, but the room I was in didn't have it.

What did this mean? I didn't know yet.

● ● ●

I'm going to discuss hygiene issues in the tatami world.

I hate doing laundry, so I was grateful to not have to. There were clothes in each room, so if my clothes got dirty, I could just change. I started changing my underwear every day, so strangely, in this world with no laundromats I was actually wearing clean underwear more often.

Early on I was shaving my beard, but it started to be more and more of a pain until I quit. I couldn't even go to a convenience store, so there was absolutely no need to shave in the first place. My hair became all-you-can-grow. I had the face of Robinson Crusoe washed up on distant four-and-a-half-mat tatami shores.

My beard and hair didn't bother me much, but I was uncomfortable with the dirt my body was accumulating. Shimogamo Yusuiso had a coin-operated shower at the end of the hall, but with the concept of halls removed from the world, it was also impossible for me to use the shower at the end of one. My only option was to boil some water in a pot, put it in the sink, wet a towel, and scrub myself that way. I hummed and tried to make like I was taking a shower, but it was pretty miserable.

• • •

At loose ends, with nothing else to think about, I considered the past two years I had wasted. It was a bit late, but I regretted getting obsessed with playing idiotic games of pretend.

As a sophomore, with my partnership with Ozu dissolved, I became a record-breakingly useless executive, notorious as the laziest slacker in all of Library Police history. Even though I was just bumming around, I never got kicked out or threatened. Perhaps they were tolerating me because of my relationship with Ozu, who continued to visit me frequently even after carrying his brilliant achievements in the Library Police over to the Printing Office, where he was promoted to executive.

I consulted with Ozu about wanting to quit, but he laughed

and paid no attention. "Oh, come on. If you hang around, I'm sure you'll have enough fun to make it worth your while."

What did he know?

Sophomore year is so up in the air, it's irritating. I was over persevering. I *was* an executive, so I attended some secret meetings and did some scheming even if only as a formality, but no matter what I did, it all seemed idiotic. The members of the org thought of me as the idiot exec, and Aijima, from his position as Chief of Library Police, wouldn't even talk to me. My aversion to him only grew.

Soon I was thinking about escape every night. Simply running away would be boring. I wanted to rebel and make a flashy exit that would go down in Library Police history.

In early autumn of my sophomore year, I mentioned something about that to Ozu while we were drinking, and he said, "I wouldn't. It may just be a goofy college game, but the intel network is real. These guys are terrifying when you get on their bad side."

"I'm not afraid."

Ozu rolled around on the tatami squashing my mochiguma. "Fugyuu!" he exclaimed. "This is how you'll end up. That would pain my heart."

"Like you give a shit," I said.

"There you go again. Your rep might be in the toilet right now, but I'm doing some genius legwork to improve it. I'd appreciate some gratitude."

"Who'd thank you?"

"Being grateful doesn't cost a thing, you know."

Autumn's melancholy was just starting to sink into my bones, so the sound of the simmering hot pot warmed my soul. The fact that the only person I had to spend these autumn nights with was Ozu struck me as a serious problem. It was wrong as a human being. This was no time to be rotting away mixed up in some weird organization. Outside the org, a normal campus life was waiting for me.

"You're probably wishing you had spent your time as a student better, huh?" Ozu abruptly struck to the heart of the matter. "You're restless lately. Are you sure you're not in love? When you fall in love, you realize how pathetic you are."

"I don't fall in love."

"Didn't you work part-time at the Shimogamo Shrine used book fair? I think you met someone there."

I ignored his astute observation.

". . . There are a lot of things I should have done differently," I said.

"Not that it's any consolation, but I think you would have met me no matter what. I just know it. No matter what happened, I would have done everything in my power to corrupt you. You can struggle against fate all you want, but it's futile." He held up a pinky finger. "We're connected by the black thread of fate."

The horrific image of two men, bound like boneless hams by a dark thread, sinking to dark watery depths, came to mind, and I shuddered.

Ozu watched me as he cheerfully munched on some pork. "I dunno what to do with Aijima either," he said. "Even though I transferred to the Printing Office, he still comes to me for advice all the time."

"Why would anyone take a liking to a guy like you?"

"My flawless personality, masterful conversation skills,

clear mind, adorable face, copious love for my neighbor that never runs dry. That's the recipe for getting people to love you. Maybe you should take notes."

"Shut up," I said, and he grinned.

• • •

With a backward glance at those memories, I continued my journey through the four-and-a-half-mat tatami rooms.

There's this thing called geologic time. Split broadly, it goes from Precambrian to Paleozoic, Mesozoic, and then Cenozoic heading to contemporary times. The Cambrian period, the first of the Paleozoic era, is famous for the Cambrian explosion, during which a variety of life forms appeared. The Mesozoic's Jurassic and Cretaceous periods remind me of happily looking at pictures of dinosaurs as a kid.

At the end of the Paleozoic era is the Permian period. But the older Japanese for it uses the kanji "two-tatami period," so it always makes me imagine the earth's surface squirming with all kinds of weird creatures getting covered with tatami mats. During that period, the world was made up of countless two-mat tatami rooms. Then came the Triassic period at the beginning of the Mesozoic era—the "three-tatami period"— during which the rooms expanded by one mat. Eventually the dinosaurs arrived and trampled the tatami, ushering in the Jurassic period.

All I could think was that the whole world had become four-and-a-half-mat tatami rooms. The Quaternary period had met its end, and the "four-and-a-half-tatami period" had arrived. A mass extinction event had killed off all the earth's creatures; the only ones left in the endless four-and-a-half-mat tatami rooms were me and the moth sticking to one corner of the ceiling. No such thing as biodiversity.

As the last person in the history of humanity, I vow to forever wander the tatami world. Even if I want to be the Adam and Eve of the next era, there's no Eve, so it's out of the question.

That's what I was thinking, resentfully, when I encountered an Eve most absurd.

• • •

It had been about twenty days since I started my journey.

I don't know what number of four-and-a-half-mat tatami room it was, so let's just call it FHMTRk. I had been on the march for a few hours, so it was about the time of day that I got sick of it. I decided to take a break and crammed some castella, which I had grown to despise, into my mouth.

The light in the next room seemed to be broken; it was flickering pretty bad. There had been some dim rooms among those I had passed through, and I called them the Overcast World; they creeped me out for whatever reason, so I always hurried through.

After my break, I opened the window and looked into the next room.

Someone was sitting in the corner absorbed in a book.

To use a hackneyed phrase, my heart nearly leapt out of my chest, I was so surprised.

I hadn't spoken to anyone in more than twenty days during my journey in this deserted world, but now I had suddenly stumbled upon someone. I was more full of fear than joy.

The person reading the book was a woman. She was quietly looking down, reading *Twenty Thousand Leagues Under the Sea*, which was open on her lap. Beautiful black hair flowed down her back, shining with a glossy luster. She had to be bold to not even look up when I opened the window, so I figured she had to be a witch who ruled this corner of the tatami world. One false move and she'd make me into a fluffy meat bun and eat me up.

"Um, excuse me." My voice was hoarse.

No matter how many times I called out to her, she didn't reply.

I timidly set foot in the room and approached her.

She had an adorable face. Her skin was completely human in hue, and when I gently touched it, there was a springy firmness. She had well-kept hair and was immaculately dressed. She looked like a lady of noble birth—except she didn't move at all. It was as if she had been frozen the instant she cast her eyes into the distance.

"So this is Kaori, huh?" I murmured in spite of myself, astonished.

• • •

It happened at the end of the previous autumn.

Everyone wondered why Aijima, Chief of Library Police, would do such a thing. He mobilized the Library Police for the express purpose of taking down the boss of an insignificant film club. The victim of this conspiracy was one Jogasaki, who had the Ablutions film club under his thumb.

Some said Aijima had some private beef with Jogasaki, while others said he wanted to gain control of the film club to get a girl he liked, who belonged to it, to respect him. Either way, Aijima had decided to drive Jogasaki to destruction.

In all matters, first comes intelligence gathering.

The intelligence network on campus left no page on Jogasaki unturned. One item they dug up was a picture of his girlfriend. At the meeting called to plan how to dethrone Jogasaki, said picture was shown, and an indescribable cry that couldn't really be termed astonishment shot into the air.

"That's our target. This Kaori," Aijima said.

He came up with an utterly indefensible plot, just the worst.

Kaori was the apple of Jogaski's eye. The bet was that if we abducted her, Jogasaki would have to swallow our demands.

The night of the operation . . .

It was carried out the night before the School Festival, so there was festive activity all over campus until late. Jogasaki's lodgings were empty because he was out on film club business. With a passing glance at the lively festival atmosphere and a miserable "why me?" aura, a group of Library Police executives gathered under cover of darkness at Yoshida Shrine. I was among them. We met up with someone called the Key Man and headed to Jogasaki's place.

In the original plan, the Key Man would unlock the door, and the executives would invade and steal Kaori the love doll, but that flow hit a setback outside Jogasaki's building. The reason? One man with neither guts nor a sense of allegiance realized this would be a crime and got cold feet—that man being me.

I threw a fit, whining, "I hate this, I hate this!" and clung to the concrete wall in resistance. The other executives were disinclined in the first place, so everyone hesitated to carry out the operation. My high-minded resistance in pursuit of justice nearly got Aijima's plan scrapped.

Then Aijima himself, whom no one ever expected to see, showed up.

"What are you all doing dawdling out here?"

The moment he snapped at us, the execs broke into two groups. One faction moved urgently to conduct the operation, while the other abruptly attempted to flee. Naturally, the faction attempting to flee was me. But I prefer to call it a "strategic retreat."

Taking advantage of the darkness, I ran off, parting with "What kind of idiot would participate in this shit?!" Aijima's eyes flashed like a snake's. I thought he was going to kill me. I raced through the streets, concealed myself in the prefestival crowd, and regretted making that comment.

My resistance was futile, and Aijima carried Kaori off.

A deal was made in a corner of the university's basement late that night, and Jogasaki yielded to Aijima's demands. A few days later, Jogasaki relinquished control of the club he had founded to Aijima. I heard he spoke extremely well of Aijima and even embraced him in front of everyone.

It was infuriatingly absurd.

This was unacceptable behavior from the Chief of Library Police.

Not to brag, but I can be efficient at times. I made my move without delay. I escaped to the safe house I'd had Ozu procure, lay low so Aijima wouldn't find me, and trembled like a newborn deer.

• • •

That day I slept in FHTMRk.

Even the day after, I didn't feel like moving on. Scratching my beard, which had achieved a harmonious whole with my sideburns, I got to thinking. I stared at the grimy wall behind the TV as I drank some coffee.

Then I had a divine revelation.

These twenty days I had been repeating the monotonous pattern of entering through the door and leaving through the window. When you think about it, isn't that an incredibly closed-minded way to go about it? If I really wanted to escape, why didn't I try to break through the wall? Might that not solve everything? There was a study-abroad kid living next door, but even if I barged in through a hole in the wall, I figured that since he was foreign, he would have an open mind and be able to laugh it off as a curious cultural difference—probably.

The thought was energizing.

I gave the wall a close inspection. The reason I could endure oozing sweat in this room with no air-conditioning wasn't that I was noble and patient. It was that the walls were as flimsy and holey as the set of a school play. The walls were so thin that when the study-abroad kid next door pulled his girlfriend into his room, I could hear the lovers' whispers they exchanged as if I were right next to them. The moment I installed an air conditioner, the cool air leaking through the walls would immediately provide the inhabitant of room 109, next door, with a comfortable living environment. Having chilled room 109, the air would eventually leak into 108, 107, 106, and the chain of comfort would never end. I would end up paying a vast sum to provide the entire floor with a comfortable living environment.

Finally putting up with walls that thin would pay off.

After doing some push-ups and pseudo-Hindu squats, I grabbed a wrench and laid into the wall. It started to dent with hardly any effort, and a crack appeared. Feeling like Hercules, I merrily pounded away for a while, getting covered in dust, but eventually I grew irritated. I kicked the crack with all my might, and a hole about fifteen centimeters in diameter opened up. Through the hole shone fluorescent light.

"Yes!"

I let out a manly roar and widened the hole to pass through.

Then, as you might have expected, I found myself in an identical four-and-a-half-mat tatami room.

• • •

After that I did whatever came to mind: broke a bunch of walls in a row, tried and failed to break through the ceiling, saw my mood inflate and deflate again, opened doors, lapped at soy sauce, opened windows, slept for two days straight, got wasted and puked, and started busting open walls again as if I had just remembered I could. I continued roaming the vast tatami world.

It occurred to me to write a journal, and the following are

excerpts from the next twenty days. Incidentally, the dates count from the day I woke up in the tatami world. It wasn't as if I was measuring time accurately; I tallied days by when I slept and woke up.

DAY 24

Rose at two. Breakfast was salted coffee and a vitamin. I don't know how many walls I broke today. The walls separating the FHMTRs are fragile, but no matter how many I break, it's pointless. Still, busting up walls takes my mind off things. I get the feeling there's a ray of hope peeking out from the other side. In the end, it's just a dream, I suppose. But couldn't this never-ending tatami world be just a dream? Am I dreaming? A dream. A dream. My dream. A rose-colored, meaningful campus life.

Ruminating on it depressed me, so I drank some whiskey, ate some fish burger, and went to sleep. Even in my dreams I was eating fish burgers. Gimme a break. Asleep or awake, it's fish burgers. Right now, my body must be made entirely of fish burgers and castella.

DAY 25

Rose at four. Today I wasn't feeling motivated, so I only moved a few times. I drank some whiskey. It's awful, and the fact that I've gotten used to that awfulness is sad.

DAY 27

It seems like I've built some muscle. I haven't set foot outside my four-and-a-half-mat room, and yet I've built some muscle—

how about that? It must be thanks to destroying walls and the pseudo-Hindu squats I've been doing to beat the blues. But how do you do a real Hindu squat? The ones I'm doing are just a pseudo version I invented based solely on my personal misconceptions, but they may very well be more effective than the real ones. When I get out of here, I should promote them as New Hindu Squats.

DAY 30

I found something interesting in an FHMTR I passed through today. It was a paulownia box, but inside was a scrub brush. I tested it out on the sink, and even though I didn't use any soap, all the grime came right off. It's an extremely high-performance scrub brush. I was only a momentary guest in the room, but I got so into it I scrubbed the sink till it shined. What an idiotic thing to do.

Why are there differences between rooms like that? What causes them? It's the same with Kaori. At a glance, all the rooms are my FHMTR, so where do these little differences come from? I don't have the interest or money to buy a love doll, and I had no idea a scrub brush of this insane caliber even existed.

It's a mystery.

DAY 31

Rose at three.

Is it afternoon or night? Someone tell me. If you tell me, I'll give you three thousand yen. Today I marched like crazy. But I should have chosen a direction. I think from now on I'll quit breaking walls and go from door to window. Although I'm sure after a while I'll get curious about what's on the other side of the walls again.

When I took a nap, I had a dream.

The Great Wall of China was cutting straight through the FHMTR. I must have been able to climb it so easily because I was dreaming. There's no way I could just step over the Great Wall of China; you can see it from space. But it was a dream, so I did. On the other side of the wall was Ozu enjoying some yakiniku. I was about to take a bite of beef tongue with salty green onion sauce when, to fuck with me, Ozu started eating every piece of meat I reached for. He ate even when the meat was still raw, so I didn't have a chance. Eventually I woke up feeling frustrated. Fricking Ozu. The guy's a piece of shit even in your dreams. But I sort of missed him in spite of myself.

O God of FHMTRs, please give me meat. No, I won't make such an extravagant request. Grilled eggplant, or a partially grilled green onion, or even just some yakiniku sauce would be fine.

DAY 34

Today I settled down early and cooked. I mashed up castella and simmered it with fish burger. That produced a strange flavor, but at least it was something new. Coffee is one thing I'll never tire of, but I wonder what kind of nutritional value it has. It's a critical question. That line of thought made me realize I haven't been getting enough vegetables, so I stuffed my face with vitamins. I want to eat something healthy. I want to eat some seaweed.

I washed my hair in the sink and went to sleep. Why does washing your hair in cold water make you feel so heartbroken?

I was so sad I could have collapsed in tears. Maybe because it chills your spirits.

DAY 38

They say when you've been in an accident, you should stay where you are and wait for help, not move around, but how many people would be able to just sit and wait for someone to rescue them in this situation? If I don't move, I immediately run out of food. I'm a nomad who roams the FHMTRs looking for fish burgers and castella. There's nothing grand or free about it.

And in the first place, who would be searching for me? How to even explain my circumstances right now? Is the world missing, or am I?

If I'm missing, then about a month has gone by in the world. June is over. I'm a man lost in time, the FHMTR Urashima Taro. Except Urashima Taro got to chill at the Dragon Palace, so he had the better deal.

I wonder whether my family is looking for me. I feel bad for my parents.

But I bet Ozu has zero interest in trying to find me. He's probably making out with a cute underclassman, like, "Yeah, I wonder where he went . . ." I'm sure of it. I'm still mad at him for eating all the salty green onion beef tongue in my dream.

DAY 39

I thought about what to do if I can really never get out of here.

As the pioneer of this tatami world, I'll have to bravely survive on my own. I'll come up with a diverse array of recipes using fish burger and castella, go into the mushroom cultivation business, and eventually demolish all the walls to build a bowling alley, a movie theater, an arcade—every kind of amusement facility—to create utopia.

Just the thought gets me excited.

I should be excited, so what are these tears?

• • •

During my intense travel adventure, the problem of food tormented me.

I desperately wanted to eat some rice. Even a convenience store onigiri. Cold and hard would be fine. I would trade a hundred fish burgers for an onigiri. If someone put a bowl of freshly cooked rice in front of me, I would cry a waterfall.

Watery co-op miso soup. Soft-boiled eggs. Rolled omelet. Spinach ohitashi. Grilled horse mackerel. Braised burdock. Natto. Eel bowls. Chicken and egg bowls. Beef bowls. Not-chicken and egg bowls. Rice with chicken and veggies. Seaweed. Yellowtail teriyaki. Grilled salmon. Crab omelet rice. Ramen with grilled pork. Udon with egg. Soba with duck. Gyoza with Chinese soup. Karaage chicken. And of course yakiniku. Curry. Red bean rice. Salad. Cucumber dipped in miso. Chilled tomato. Honeydew. Peaches. Watermelon. Pear. Apple. Grapes. Satsuma mandarins.

It's entirely possible that I'll never eat any of them ever again. The thought made me want to eat them more. I seemed to spend day after day in agonizing pursuit of foods that didn't exist in the tatami world.

What I missed the most was Neko Ramen.

Neko Ramen is a ramen stand that is rumored to make its soup from cats. Regardless of whether that's true or not, the flavor is unparalleled. Thick noodles soaked in that soup with its mysterious depth. Back when I could leave whenever I felt like it, I could go out in the middle of the night for a bowl on a whim.

That was what's known as "paradise."

• • •

The other thing I yearned for was a bath.

My breast was tight with the desire to splash into a big public bath and soak. I remembered the old bathhouse in the neighborhood west of Shimogamo Hon-dori. I would go over there with a towel whenever the mood struck. In the early evening, I'd duck under the entry curtain and sit in the empty bath with a dopey, vacant look on my face: paradise.

The thought was so nostalgic I couldn't stand it.

There was one day I quit marching entirely and tried to construct a bath.

I pulled a bunch of cardboard boxes out of the closet, dumped their contents out, and broke them down. Using that raw material, I spent two hours fashioning a bathtub. I knew how much water I could boil in my pot. I made the tub as flat as I could so I would be able to soak as much of my body as possible and then waterproofed it with layers of garbage bags.

I boiled a pot of water and poured it into the bathtub. I did this over and over.

Though I was able to experience the sensation of soaking in hot water, it cooled off right away, I couldn't soak my whole body, and folding my naked body up to fit in the cramped, flimsy cardboard tub was a drag. *What the hell am I doing?* I thought, but there was no escape. Eventually the tub collapsed, and the bathwater drenched the four-and-a-half-mat tatami room.

Worst of all was that despite the fact that I put in all that work like an idiot, not a single soul made fun of me. If Ozu had been there, I'm sure he would have teased me to death.

"What are you doing? Is your neocortex riddled with maggots or something?" I'm sure he would have said.

• • •

One morning, the feeling of someone brushing my face with a duster woke me up.

When I sat up, I saw there were tons of moths fluttering around the room. I was shocked. Usually there was just the one, but today it had invited a bunch of friends. More and more moths were pouring through the hole in the wall I had opened the previous day. When I peeked through the hole, the room next door was a dark frenzy of moths flying every which way, scattering their powdery scales.

I grabbed my backpack in a panic, moved to the next room, and closed the window.

Even if there's only one moth in each room, bunched up, they create a massive swarm. They must have been lonely. Once exchanges between four-and-a-half-mat tatami rooms began to occur, the moths found compatriots for mutual support. Now they traveled from room to room, adding new friends along their way. It was enough to make me jealous.

I sighed.

They could get riled up over dirty jokes and fall madly in love, and others could even jeer at the ones getting riled up over dirty jokes and falling madly in love. Then there was me, who had to tell dirty jokes to myself, fantasize by myself, and then jeer at myself. How self-sufficient do you really want to be?!

Seeing my roommate moths having a glorious time together in the tatami world made me feel that much more isolated.

● ● ●

Back to what happened the previous fall.

After fleeing the plot to abduct Kaori, I was lying low in my safe house, shaking in my boots.

Since I had clearly expressed my will to rebel, I was sure Aijima would mobilize the Library Police to squash me. Jogasaki's fate would also be my own. My embarrassing secrets would be posted all over the campus bulletin boards, I'd be a laughingstock wherever I went, and before long I'd be assaulted by thugs, painted pink, and dumped into Nanzen-ji's aqueduct.

According to Ozu, Aijima was searching high and low for me.

"Aijima's a bit of an issue. He's borderline rampaging, you know?" said Ozu. "I was just thinking the Printing Office should do something."

I didn't take one step outside the safe house.

The safe house was the four-and-a-half-mat tatami room of Seitaro Higuchi (from whom I had previously attempted to recover a library book). When Ozu suggested hiding out on the second floor of Shimogamo Yusuiso, I didn't take him seriously at first. I was thinking I would make a clean escape from Kyoto and reach satori on Cape Muroto to return an enlightened man.

"It's better to stay here than move when you might be detected. It's dark at the foot of a lighthouse, right?"

Ozu persuaded me to freeload at Higuchi's.

I spent days on end playing a homemade version of Battleship with Higuchi. Ozu didn't come around for a while. *Is it okay for me to be obsessing over Battleship like this when my life as a student is about to come to an end?* As I sunk a sub with a gloomy expression on my face, Higuchi took out a cigar and consoled me in a happy-go-lucky tone.

"You can rest easy. I'm sure Ozu will take care of everything."

"He won't betray me?"

"Ah, there is that possibility." He sounded amused. "You never can tell with him."

"That's not funny."

"But he *was* being all heroic and saying he would defend you with his life."

• • •

It's been almost fifty days since I strayed into this world.

It's hard to believe. It must already be midsummer outside.

For twelve hundred hours, all I had put in my mouth was castella, fish burger, daikon, vitamins, coffee, and whiskey. I hadn't gotten any sun. I hadn't breathed any fresh air. I hadn't exchanged words with another human being. I had gotten sick of alchemy and wasn't even seriously collecting thousand-yen notes anymore. I practically wanted to dump the backpack full of cash.

What kind of a world is this? What a world.

The topography was tatami laid out to cover every corner; there was no night or day, no wind blowing, no rain falling. The only things illuminating the world were shabby fluorescent lights. With loneliness as my only friend, I continued to walk recklessly on toward the ends of the earth. I broke through countless walls, climbed up countless windowsills, and opened countless doors.

Sometimes I stayed in one room for several days, reading, singing, and smoking cigarettes. I sulked, swearing I would never walk anywhere again because it was all pain and no gain. But staring up at the crappy ceiling for a whole day, wrapped in a silence that made it feel as though all of humanity had perished, a terrible sadness presses in on you. I could develop dish after singularly strange dish using my limited ingredients, fold dozens and dozens of paper cranes and yakko-san, humor Johnny, write, do push-ups, humor Johnny again, screw around firing a rubber band gun I made, and exhaust every other thing I could think of, but I couldn't forget reality.

Good things come to those who wait.

Since washing my hands of the organization the previous fall, I had stayed holed up in my four-and-a-half-mat tatami castle. I thought I was a person who could tolerate isolation. That was silly of me. I was never isolated. Compared to the way I was now, I wasn't even a bit isolated back then. I was a precocious babe who wetted his toes at the edge of the vast sea of solitude with a little splash and crowed, "I'm so totally alone!"

I can't tolerate isolation.

I have to do whatever it takes to get out of here.

I unsteadily got to my feet. And continued traversing the four-and-a-half-mat tatami rooms.

• • •

There's no one.

I haven't exchanged a word with anyone.

When was the last time I spoke to Ozu?

With each passing day, it got harder to have hope as I walked. Climbing over windowsills became too much trouble. I no longer talked to myself. I didn't sing. I didn't wipe myself down. I didn't feel like eating fish burgers.

No matter what, I'll just come out in the same four-and-a-half-mat tatami room.

It'll be the same no matter what.

It'll be the same no matter what.

It's the same scenery going on forever.

All I did was murmur those things in my head.

• • •

What happened the previous autumn, while I lurked in Higuchi's four-and-a-half-mat tatami room absorbed in Battleship?

Ozu engaged in yokai-esque secret maneuvers like a yokai.

First, he took advantage of the vice head of the Printing Office attending a conference in Hokkaido to use his deputy authority to halt operations. That was the first time that had ever happened, so Aijima gave up on me and rushed to deal with the Printing Office.

Ozu appeared before Aijima with the avaricious face of an unscrupulous salesman.

"I have questions about Lucky Cat Chinese Food's leadership. Someone appears to be plotting an insurrection. So I want you to hold a meeting."

Aijima must never have suspected that Ozu wanted to take over the whole thing. While negotiating with Aijima, Ozu was also laying groundwork with the other organizations.

He was good friends with a former member of the religious Mellow softball club, and that alum could exert latent power in other clubs, so that sped things up. The director of the School Festival Office was also Ozu's friend, and every last shady research association knew Ozu. In order to persuade them, he promised to divert a huge chunk of the Library Police's take of the Printing Office's revenue to the other clubs and associations. Using his connections from his Library Police days, he drew as many people over to his side as he could. As for the people he couldn't get on his side, he sent the Happy Bicycle Disposal Corps around and got them shut up in their houses on the day of the meeting.

It could only be called an extraordinary display of diverse prowesses.

The conspiracy invited Aijima in, surrounding him on all sides.

The meeting was over the moment it began.

The ignominious fact that Aijima had mobilized the Library Police to abduct Jogasaki's beloved over a personal grudge was exposed; after he was thrown out by the Happy Bicycle Disposal Corps, the meeting quietly continued.

"Ozu, why don't you do it?" The representative from the Mellow softball club nominated Ozu.

"It's too much for me to handle." Ozu did pretend to beg off.

In the end, it was decided that Ozu would be Chief of Library Police *and* vice head of the Printing Office.

• • •

The night Ozu was crowned Chief of Library Police . . .

I left my safe house for the first time in a week and cautiously set foot on campus. During the week I'd been hiding out, it had gotten a notch colder, and it seemed as though all the autumn leaves had fallen. I stole through the vicinity of the law faculty under cover of night and slipped into the basement lecture hall where the meeting was to take place. I saw Ozu's coup succeed, and how easily Aijima was thrown out.

After the meeting concluded and the students dispersed, Ozu was sitting alone on the platform. I stayed where I was, sitting in the corner, and looked at his face. The lecture hall, with just the two of us in it, was cold and silent; our breath froze white with each exhalation. I sensed none of the dignity befitting his imposing dual title; he still just had a weird Nurarihyon face.

"You're a force to be reckoned with," I said sentimentally, but Ozu just yawned.

"This is just a game," he said. "But either way, you're off the hook now."

We ducked out of the lecture hall and went to eat Neko Ramen.

It was my treat, of course.

So it was that I washed my hands of Lucky Cat Chinese Food and embarked on a voyage to a new world—or I should have, anyway; it wasn't so easy to make up for the wasteful way I had spent the previous two years. I started spending more and more time holed up in Shimogamo Yusuiso.

I thought I should cut ties with this force to be reckoned with, but that didn't go very well, either—because while I was shut up in my four-and-a-half-mat tatami room, Ozu was the only one who came to visit me.

• • •

Ozu was in the same year as me. Despite being registered in the Department of Electrical and Electronic Engineering, he hated electricity, electronics, and engineering. At the end of freshman year he had received so few credits, and with such low grades, that it made you wonder whether there was any point to him being there, but Ozu himself didn't give a damn.

Because he hated vegetables and ate only instant foods, his face was such a creepy color it looked like he'd been living on the far side of the moon. Eight out of ten people who met him walking down the street at night would take him for a yokai goblin. The other two would be shapeshifted yokai themselves. Ozu kicked those who were down and buttered up anyone stronger than him. He was selfish and arrogant, lazy and contrary. He never studied, had not a crumb of pride, and fueled himself on other people's misfortunes. There was not a single praiseworthy bone in his body.

But he was my only friend.

• • •

I continued my pitiful march.

One day, the four-and-a-half-mat tatami room I was staying in had film stuff on the bookshelves. Weird videocassettes I didn't own were stacked between the desk and the bookcase. Sipping coffee and smoking, I was digging through those videos when I found a tape that had "The Clash at Kamo Ohashi" written on it in a violent scribble. The label said "Ablutions." I found myself feeling interested, so I popped it into the VCR.

It was an extremely bizarre movie.

The only two actors were Ozu and me; it was a two-man show. It was about two men who inherited a prank battle with roots in the pre–Pacific War period, as they obliterated each other's pride with all the wit and strength they could muster, and it featured a bizarre performance by Ozu, his expression as unchanging as that of a Noh mask; overly energetic theatrics from me; plus all sorts of merciless pranks. During the finale, in which Ozu, his entire body dyed pink, and I, with half my head shaved, clashed on Kamo Ohashi, I couldn't help but hold my breath, but afterward, that made me feel pathetic; that's the kind of film it was.

Seeing Ozu's face for the first time in seventy days or so was actually moving.

I missed him terribly.

At the end of the movie, there was a "making of" segment. Well, it was called that, but it was clearly staged. Ozu and I were having a meeting about the script on camera, building the drab set, and so on. There was also a lame segment called "How'd You Like It?" and it seemed like pretty much no one would tell us their impressions. Just one girl said, "You made another dumb movie, huh?"

But no, I'd seen this girl somewhere before.

"It's Akashi," I murmured.

• • •

Used book fair. Akashi. Mochiguma. *Twenty Thousand Leagues Under the Sea.*

During the summer of my sophomore year, I suddenly had the urge to get a part-time job. There was a bookstore called Gabi Shobo in Kawaramachi that happened to be seeking part-timers for the used book fair, so I applied. The owner, with a face reminiscent of simmered octopus, gruffly told me, "Just so you know, it pays practically nothing."

My co-worker at that job was Akashi. The owner was always gruff with me, but whenever he was talking to Akashi he looked like the old bamboo cutter must have when he found Princess Kaguya. The gap between simmered octopus and old bamboo cutter was intense.

The riding grounds stretching north to south alongside the approach to the shrine were crammed full of sellers' tents, and tons of people were strolling around on the hunt for books. No matter where I looked, I saw wooden shelves packed with books; it made me a little dizzy. On the cloth-covered benches set up in rows, people who must have gotten book fair sick like me hung their heads. It was muggy, but the buzz of the cicadas provided a certain atmosphere. As I sat on the railing of the little bridge drinking ramune during my break with nothing particular on my mind, creeping around for that idiotic organization, the "Library Police," or whatever, started to feel really stupid.

I saw Akashi multiple days in a row. Her short haircut must have kept her cool, and she had an intellectual brow. Her sharp eyes seemed to always be staring at something. I got the impression this hawk wasn't hiding her talons. Her job was mainly to look out for shoplifters, but any thief glared at with those eyes wouldn't have been able to touch a thing.

In contrast to the brute strength she put into her stare, something awfully cute was dangling from her bag. It was a bear plushie made of spongy material. One evening after cleaning up, I saw her furiously kneading the bear with the serious look of a philosopher on her face.

"What is that?" I asked.

Her eyebrows instantly relaxed, and she smiled. "This is a mochiguma."

Apparently she had five in different colors that she lovingly called the Fluffy Mochigumen Rangers. "Mochiguma" was a hard name to forget, but the smile on her face when she said "This is a mochiguma" was even more unforgettable.

As you may have already guessed, this is all to say that I fell for her, right there and then.

The evening before the final day of the fair, I found a mochiguma next to the little bridge. Akashi had dropped it on her way home. I thought I would give it to her when I saw her the next day, so I took it with me, but on the last day, she didn't come. Something came up, so she had to cancel, the owner told me gruffly. I bought a copy of *Twenty Thousand Leagues Under the Sea* as a memento of the fair and left Shimogamo Shrine.

I'd been taking good care of the mochiguma for the six months since then, always thinking that I needed to get it back to Akashi. What a heavy blow it was when it disappeared at the laundromat.

"Ohh, how vaguely long ago that was . . ." I murmured as I watched Akashi on the TV.

• • •

Seeing Akashi's face gave me some get-up-and-go.

The next day I began destroying walls and traveling again, but as I silently swung the wrench, I was thinking about that videotape. I had never made movies with Ozu. But that movie was made by Ozu and me. Reflecting on myself, I felt I did indeed have the dark impulses that could result in my making such a film. The tape had an Ablutions label. I recalled memories from way back when I was a freshman standing in front of that fateful clock tower. Wasn't the name of one of the clubs I didn't join "Ablutions"?

The way the rooms were all slightly different.

Videotapes I hadn't made.

A bookcase lined with books I had failed to buy.

A scrub brush I had never bought.

Kaori, who never should have been living with me.

One day, I stopped traveling. I stood in the middle of the four-and-a-half-mat tatami room and looked up at the ceiling.

I finally understood the makeup of these rooms.

I was embarrassed that I hadn't noticed it sooner. The four-and-a-half-mat tatami rooms endlessly lined up in this world were definitely mine. But each one of them belonged to a me who had made a different decision. These past weeks, I had been on a trip through the homes of my twins in parallel worlds.

My whole body felt weak.

There was no way to know what sort of order they were arranged in. And I had no idea why this world had appeared. And I had no idea why I had found myself lost in it.

But I realized something.

Even the tiniest little decision changed my fate. Every day I made countless decisions, which created infinite fates. They created infinite mes. They created infinite four-and-a-half-mat tatami rooms.

So on principle, this tatami world had no end.

• • •

I was lying in bed listening intently.

The tatami world was ever so uninhabited and noiseless.

There was no one to talk to. There was no one for me to tell anything to. I had no one to tell that to, and that me had no past and no future. There was no one to see me like this. There was no one to mock me, respect me, ignore me, or fall in love with me. There was no chance of such a person ever appearing.

I was like dusty, stagnant air inside a four-and-a-half-mat tatami room.

No matter whether the world had gone missing or I had, from my perspective, I was the only one in existence. I had passed through hundreds of four-and-a-half-mat tatami rooms, and I didn't manage to meet a single person.

I had become the last person in the world.

Is there any reason for the last person in the world to go on living?

• • •

If I ever get out of here, there are so many things I want to do, I thought.

I want to eat tasty food and slurp Neko Ramen. I want to go to Shijo-Kawaramachi. I want to see movies. I want to argue with the simmered-octopus-faced owner of Gabi Shobo. I guess it might also be fun to go to school and attend lectures. I could perform a dance for the gods at Shimogamo Shrine. And I could go up to the second floor and indulge in smut talk with Higuchi. I could go for a checkup at Kubozuka Dental and lick Hanuki's delicate fingers. I should go console poor Aijima about his ousting from Lucky Cat. I wonder how everyone's doing. Are they having a good time in the world filled with life? Are they healthy? Is Jogasaki happy with Kaori? Is Ozu still fueling himself on other people's misfortunes? Is Akashi looking at her Fluffy Mochigumen Rangers minus one bear wondering whatever to do, or has she picked one up somewhere she never would have expected? I want to find out.

But none of those wishes would ever come true again.

• • •

I felt something hard on my back. When I felt around for it, I realized it was the wisdom tooth I'd had pulled at Kubozuka Dental. "Meh-heh-heh," I laughed, a dangerous laugh, even for me. I put the cavity-ridden tooth on my palm and rolled it around. *Why is this thing here?*

This was FHMTR0. It was my starting point.

I don't know where I went wrong, but somehow after weeks and weeks, I had ended up back in the room where I started. I must have been making a desperate little circle in one tiny corner of this infinite world.

The four-and-a-half-mat tatami rooms in this world weren't all identical. They reflected across doors and windows. So when proceeding, it was probably possible to mistake your direction and go the opposite way. My intention had been to choose my directions carefully, but my execution was imperfect.

What an utterly fruitless runaround that was, I thought.

But I was already in the pit of despair, so I didn't feel much. I quietly accepted the situation.

I lay in bed stroking my long beard. *I should just resign myself to settling down in this world. I need to forget my beautiful memories of the outside. I'll stop breaking down walls like a barbarian and lead a gentleman's life, keeping regular hours; I'll read good books, weaving in some erotica when appropriate, and put all my energy into cultivating my mind. If I can never leave this boundlessly vast zashiki prison, then I'll wait with dignity to die upon the tatami.*

That's what I was thinking as I fell asleep.

It was the seventy-ninth day.

• • •

I woke up.

The clock said six, but it wasn't clear whether it was six in the morning or six in the evening. I thought about it as I lay there, but I wasn't sure how long I had slept.

Squirming like an insect on top of my futon, I sluggishly got up.

It was quiet.

After a cup of coffee and a cigarette, I still didn't feel like getting the day started, so I flopped back onto my futon and sunk into thought. I picked up the holey wisdom tooth lying near my pillow. Holding the sinister cavity up to the light, I thought about what the fortune-teller in Kiyamachi had said.

I had concluded that my incomprehensible circumstances were entirely her fault. She sweet-talked me with lines like "You seem to be extremely hard-working and talented," and my desire to escape into the life I could've and should've had pushed me toward her. She put a four-and-a-half-tatami-mat curse on me.

Colosseo.

Ridiculous.

I no longer even had any need for that rose-colored, meaningful campus life; such a supremely great treasure should be locked up in Shosoin.

Still, what a tremendous cavity. I can't believe I put up with it for so long. The top of the tooth looked like it had been gouged out; the way you could see the inside made it feel like a science-class model. As I stared at it, it stopped looking like a tooth and seemed more like a giant building from ancient Rome . . .

"Colosseo," I murmured.

I heard a sound like something bumping against the half-open window.

In the next moment, something like a squirming black wind came pouring through the gap, flooding the four-and-a-half-mat tatami room.

Apparently the giant swarm of moths traveling this tatami world happened to be passing through FHMTR0. A multitude of moths coated the ceiling. Still, they continued to stream in.

Panicking, I decided to make a hasty escape into FHMTR1.

When I opened the door, I got a faceful of chilly hallway air.

The sticky, dusty hallway stretched darkly out. There were lightbulbs at intervals along the ceiling, flickering. Way over by the entrance, a fluorescent light was cheerlessly shining white.

• • •

I set off for the entrance. I paid no mind to the moths streaming out of my open door. Something was making a little puffing noise in one corner of the hallway. Someone must have been using the outlet in the corridor to cook their rice. The lure of freshly cooked rice nearly pinned me to the spot, but I made a point of not stopping. When I opened the shoe cubby, my shoes were inside as they should have been.

I left Shimogamo Yusuiso and wandered into the twilight of Shimogamo Izumikawacho.

Indigo dusk hung over the neighborhood. The cool breeze

blowing through the alleys caressed my cheeks. The smell was incomparably good. It wasn't just a single scent. It was the smell of outside. It was the smell of the world. It wasn't just scents; I could hear the world's sounds. The rustling of Tadasu no Mori, the burbling of the brook. The sound of a motorbike racing through the twilight.

I passed through Izumikawacho on unsteady feet. The hard asphalt went on forever. I could see streetlights, house lights, warm glows shining through windows. I passed Shimogamo Saryo, casting its light on everyone coming and going. Then I walked the approach to Shimogamo Shrine quietly lined with houses. Eventually I heard the sound of passing cars and students making a racket on the Kamo River Delta. I could see the delta's dark pine grove. I could see college kids having a party in the twilight.

I crossed the road and went onto the delta.

I passed through the pine trees on the embankment. I could hardly contain my emotions and fairly ran. I knocked on the trunks of the trees as I raced by. I shoved ecstatic college kids out of the way. They looked at me with what-the-fuck faces, but when they saw me with my long hair and beard, they pretended not to notice me.

When I made it through the trees, the clear, indigo sky opened up beautifully overhead.

I practically tumbled down the embankment and ran to the tip of the delta. The sound of the water swelled. Like the captain of a ship standing at the bow, I planted my feet on the delta's tip. The Takano River from the east and the Kamo River from the west mingled before my eyes to become one Kamo River and flow south.

In the lights reflecting here and there, the surface of the water looked like a sheet of metallic paper being waved like a stage prop. Before my eyes lay Kamo Ohashi. The lamps in a well-mannered row along its railing cast an orangey glow, and shining cars crisscrossed without end. All sorts of people walked over the bridge, all sorts of people were hanging around the Kamo River Delta; no matter where I looked, there were crowds of people. The lamps on the railing, Keihan Demachi-yanagi Station gleaming bright white, the rows of streetlights, the lights of the Shijo neighborhood down the river, the headlights of the cars going over the bridge—everything sparkled like jewels, so beautiful, and then blurred.

What in the world?

There's so much life.

It was as busy as Gion Matsuri.

I filled my lungs with the fragrant air, looked up at the sky going from pink to indigo, and grimaced.

Then I let out a roar—but I'm not sure what that was about.

• • •

Bathed in the fearful and disgusted gazes of the other people milling about on the delta, I was rapturous with the joy of being alive in this place.

I don't know how long I was in that trance, but eventually there was a disturbance on Kamo Ohashi. Looking up from the tip of the delta, I saw a ton of students closing in from either end of the bridge cheering and clamoring. *What's this fuss about?* I wondered.

As I watched, a man stood up on the bridge's thick railing.

He seemed to be arguing with the students closing in on him. When I looked at his face, illuminated in the railing's lamps, I saw it was Ozu. He was standing on the railing, making like he was about to jump, smirking, striking vulgar poses, and so on. Even after eighty days, he still had that impudent yokai face of his. Even while I was gone, he seemed to have continued charging down his cursed path.

The wave of nostalgia was so strong that I called out to him, "Ozuuuuuu!" but he didn't seem to notice.

What kind of idiotic nonsense is he up to, standing on the railing like that? Is it some kind of festival? As I was wondering what was going on, a shriek shot up behind me.

I turned around to find the area of the pine grove on the embankment submerged in a black fog. And within that black fog was a muddle of young people. They were half mad, flailing their arms and ripping out their hair. The black fog spread eerily and seemed to be heading straight for the tip of the delta where I was.

Black fog poured continuously from out of the pine grove. This was nothing to sniff at. With a trembling, fluttering, rustling, and flapping, the wriggling black fog flowed over the embankment like a carpet and swept over the delta's tip.

It was a swarm of moths.

• • •

A news item appeared in the next day's *Kyoto Shimbun*, but no one knew exactly why the extraordinary number of moths had appeared. Retracing their flight path, they seemed to come from Tadasu no Mori—that is, Shimogamo Shrine—but this wasn't clear. Even if every moth that lived in Tadasu no Mori had decided to migrate all at once, there wasn't a good reason for it. Apart from the official explanation, there were rumors that the moths had come, not from Shimogamo Shrine, but the neighborhood next to it, Shimogamo Izumikawacho; but that only made the story even stranger. Apparently, it was the area right around my apartment that had been flooded with moths and thrown into an uproar.

When I returned to my room that night, there were dead moths strewn throughout the hallway. My door was half open, as I had forgotten to lock it, so there were moth corpses all over my room, too. I gave them a respectful burial.

For those of you who have read this far, the mystery is probably no mystery at all.

This is what I think:

In the tatami world I traveled for eighty days, swarms of moths seemed to gather here and there. One of those swarms must have poured from the tatami world into this world through my four-and-a-half-mat tatami room.

• • •

Buffeted by the swarm of moths as they flapped into my face, sprinkling their scales around, sometimes trying to force their way into my mouth, I bravely stood my ground on the delta's tip.

That huge swarm of moths, though, was beyond the realm of common sense. The awful sound of their beating wings cut us off from the outside world; it was less like moths and more like little winged yokai passing by. I couldn't see much of anything. Through the slits of my barely open eyes, I could make out the gleaming water of the Kamo River, the railing of Kamo Ohashi, and someone falling off the railing into the Kamo River.

When the swarm had finally gone, the Kamo River Delta was filled with voices chattering about what a frightful experience that had been, but I stared at the river in silence. There was something like dark, dirty seaweed clumped around one of Kamo Ohashi's feet. *Isn't that Ozu?*

Students crowded around the railing, yelling:

"He really fell."

"Holy shit, holy shit!"

"Save him!"

"He can die, for all I care."

"This guy won't die even if you kill him!"

The river was running high, but I waded into the flow. Nearly losing my footing a number of times, I rushed to where Ozu was. I hadn't bathed in so long, I think it actually cleaned me up.

When I finally reached the foot of the bridge, I asked, "Are you okay?"

Ozu stared me in the face and said, "Hm? Sorry, who are you, again?"

"It's me, it's me."

He squinted for a few moments, but then finally seemed to get it. "But what's with the Robinson Crusoe beard?"

"I had a rough time."

"Mm. You're not the only one."

"Can you move?" I asked.

"Ah, owowowow. I guess not. This is definitely broken."

"C'mon, let's at least get to the bank."

"Ow, it hurts! Don't move it!"

Part of the restless crowd on the bridge came down to help.

"We'll carry him."

"You get that end."

"I'll take this end."

They seemed to know what they were doing and were very efficient.

"Ow, ow, ow—be more gentle, please!" Ozu made extravagant demands as he was carried to dry land.

There were a ton of people milling around from Kamo Ohashi to the west bank of the Kamo River. It was a total uproar. I freaked out when I thought I spotted Aijima in the crowd, but there was nothing to be afraid of anymore.

The group that formed crowded around Ozu, who was being rolled like a log along the riverbed.

Higuchi made a leisurely appearance and asked, "What about an ambulance?" to no one in particular.

Jogasaki told him, "Akashi called one. It'll be here soon."

Hanuki was there next to Higuchi looking down at Ozu as he groaned. "You really do reap what you sow," she said.

Lying on the dark riverbed, Ozu moaned, "It hurts, it hurts. It really hurts. Do something!"

Higuchi knelt next to Ozu.

"I've failed," Ozu said in a small voice.

"You're quite the promising disciple, Ozu," said Higuchi.

"Thank you, Master."

"But there was no need to go breaking bones. You're an incorrigible idiot."

Ozu cried softly.

Some haughty faces came out of the group of people encircling Ozu at a distance and began talking among themselves.

"Ozu won't escape, rest assured."

Higuchi snapped, "You can hold me accountable!"

It took about five minutes for the ambulance to arrive at the end of Kamo Ohashi.

Jogasaki ran up the bank and came down with the medical techs. The techs wrapped Ozu in a blanket and loaded him onto a stretcher with skills pros could be proud of. It would have been hilarious if they had just thrown him into the river like that, but emergency workers are admirable individuals who sympathize with all injured people equally. Ozu was packed onto the ambulance with a gravity disproportionate to his nasty ways.

"I'll go with Ozu," said Higuchi, and he and Hanuki both boarded the ambulance.

• • •

So what happened where I couldn't see it?

The events that led to Ozu being cornered on the bridge are exceedingly complex, and the details would be an entire story in themselves. So I'm going to keep this brief.

Higuchi and Jogasaki had been prolonging a mysterious fight called the Masochistic Proxy-Proxy War for some time. That May, when Higuchi got his yukata dyed pink, he ordered his henchman Ozu to take revenge. To get back at Jogasaki, Ozu stole Kaori, copying what Aijima had done the previous fall. He had been planning to leave Kaori with me, but since I was out, he gave her to Executive A from the Library Police. But A all too easily gave in to the temptation of improper conduct with Kaori and attempted to flee Kyoto, which is when things started to get out of hand. Ozu tapped his Library Police subordinates in a personal capacity, went after A in a rental car to stop him, and took back Kaori for a while. But as soon as it came out that Ozu had mobilized the organization for personal reasons, the clubs, research associations, and so on who were dissatisfied with the vice head of the Printing Office and Chief of Library Police dominating Lucky Cat Chinese Food leapt at this chance; in their pay, the Happy Bicycle Disposal Squad occupied the Printing Office and Library Police headquarters. During all of this, it had come to light that Ozu had been diverting Printing Office revenue to buy food and drink for Higuchi, so they were plotting to capture Ozu and recover the stolen amount. When Aijima, who had been waiting for a chance to get revenge on Ozu, sensed that his downfall was nigh, he apparently attempted to exchange custody of Ozu for his position in Lucky Cat Chinese back. He ran the underclassmen in the film club Ablutions around to root him out. The night of the incident, Ozu was on his way home when he most sensitively detected danger, so instead of going back to his apartment, he hid beneath the eaves of a house in Jodoji, contacted Hanuki from his cell phone, and requested a rescue from Higuchi through her. So it was that Akashi, with orders to save Ozu, slipped into the Jodoji area. The area around Ozu's building in Jodoji all the way to Kinkaku-ji had an encirclement ten to twenty layers deep, but Akashi came up with the idea to go through the Lake Biwa Canal, so Ozu was able to slip by. Evading the surveillance crisscrossing the area east of the Kamo River and north of Marutamachi-dori like infrared sensors, Ozu, having been cross-dressed by Akashi, went over the Tadekurabashi Bridge and reached Shimogamo Yusuiso. He was lying low in Higuchi's room when Jogasaki, furious over the theft of Kaori, inconveniently barged in; after being kicked into the street, Ozu was discovered by some associates of Lucky Cat Chinese Food patrolling the area. Though he was fortunate to be able to escape from clusters of associates time after time using his inborn speediness, he was finally cornered on Kamo Ohashi and, having nowhere else to run, jumped onto the railing.

He stood firm with the arrogant face of a tengu. "Keep threatening me and I'll jump! If you don't guarantee my safety, I'm not coming down there."

After that, he fell off the bridge into the Kamo River and broke his leg.

• • •

Once Ozu had been taken away, everyone left the riverbed like a tide going out. I went from eighty days of being completely alone to getting tangled up in this hubbub, so I just stroked my beard in a daze for a while.

While I was looking around the riverbed absentmindedly, I spotted a girl sitting on a bench. Her brow was furrowed, and she had her hands covering her pale cheeks. I went over to her.

"Hey, are you okay?" I asked, and she put on a wan smile.

"I really can't handle moths."

Ahh, I see, I thought. "There were a whole lot of people making a racket. What was that about?"

"Ozu . . . ugh, it's so complicated I can't even really explain it."

"You know Ozu?" I asked.

"Yes. I take it you do, too?"

"Yeah. We go back."

I introduced myself. I told her how I lived on the first floor of Shimogamo Yusuiso and had been hanging around with Ozu since freshman year.

"Were you by any chance in the Library Police?" she said. "You're the Seahorse Incident guy, aren't you?"

"Seahorse Incident?"

"Master Higuchi said he wanted a pet seahorse, so Ozu got him an aquarium. But the moment he filled it, it broke."

"Ohhhh, I know what you're talking about. Yeah, that really screwed me over."

"But apparently Master Higuchi never got his seahorse."

"Why not?" I asked.

"It was taking so long that he decided he wanted a giant squid instead."

"Don't think you could fit that inside an aquarium."

"Right, so even Ozu couldn't help him. I heard that instead, he bought a Ferrari flag to distract him."

She rubbed her pale cheeks.

"Why don't we get some tea or something to calm down?" I suggested.

It's not as if I was thinking anything so rude as stooping to using her weakness against moths to my advantage. Seeing her so pale, I was offering out of concern.

I walked to the nearest vending machine and bought two hot coffees, which we drank together.

"By the way, are the Mochigumen doing well?" I asked.

"Yes, but I lost one . . ." she said, and then pursed her lips.

She looked into my eyes, and then she looked as if she understood. "You worked at Gabi Shobo during the used book fair, right? Sorry I didn't recognize you."

"You remember?"

"Yes. I remember you, but that's one magnificent beard you've got," she said, staring at my face.

There's really no reason to speak at length about the feelings I had at that moment; suffice to say, after a fierce struggle to connect those feelings to action, I managed to spit out the following line: "Akashi, wanna go get some Neko Ramen?"

• • •

As we ate our ramen, I cried a river that overwhelmed even the owner. It was my first Neko Ramen in eighty days.

"It's that good?" Akashi asked.

"Mm, uh-huh," I moaned.

"That's wonderful." She nodded softly and slurped her noodles.

• • •

So that's my "Around the Tatami Galaxy in Eighty Days" story.

I wasn't about to sleep in a four-and-a-half-mat tatami room ever again, so for a while, starting that night, I slept in the hall. Then I found a new room in Mototanaka and promptly moved there. This time I chose a six-mat room, with its own bathroom and everything. That said, I sometimes catch myself going to pee in a beer bottle, and I recall those horrible eighty days.

The strange thing was that I wandered the tatami world for

so long, and yet in reality no time had passed at all. It was less like being spirited away and more like a dream of prosperity. But it wasn't a dream. The swarm of moths, the unruly beard, and the backpack full of thousand-yen notes were proof of that. That backpack paid my moving expenses.

• • •

How my relationship with Akashi developed after that is a deviation from the point of this manuscript. Therefore, I shall refrain from writing the charming, bashfully giddy details. You probably don't want to pour your time down the drain reading such detestable drivel, anyhow.

There's nothing so worthless to speak of as a love mature.

• • •

It's not fair for you to assume that I'd naively approve of my past just because there have been some new developments in my student life lately. I'm not the kind of man who would so readily affirm his past mistakes. Certainly I considered giving myself a big, loving embrace, but regardless of how it would go with a black-haired maiden of a tender age, who would have any interest in hugging a mess of a twenty-something guy? Driven by that inescapable anger, I firmly refused to give my past self salvation.

I can't shake the feeling that I never should have chosen the secret organization Lucky Cat Chinese at the foot of that fateful clock tower. If I had taken a different path, I would have had a very different couple of years.

But actually, given the impression I got wandering the tatami world for eighty days, perhaps they wouldn't have been so different after all. Above all—a terrifying thought—it seems that no matter which path I chose, I would have met Ozu. I guess it's just as Ozu says; we really are connected by the black thread of fate.

So I'm not going to give my past self a big hug, and I'm not going to validate my past mistakes, but I'm not opposed to overlooking them.

● ● ●

Ozu stayed in the hospital next to the school for a little while.

I have to say, it felt pretty great to see him strapped into a crisp white bed. He always had such a horrible complexion that he looked like a patient with an untreatable illness, but it was just a broken bone. I suppose it's lucky that he got away with just a broken bone. He grumbled that he wasn't able to perpetrate any of the misdeeds he preferred over three square meals a day, but I just thought, *That's what you get.* When his grumbles got to be too much, I crammed the castella I brought him into his mouth to shut him up.

Higuchi, Jogasaki, Hanuki, plus his friends and the underclassmen from the film club, his friends from the softball club, the director of the School Festival Office, izakaya managers, the owner of Neko Ramen, and tons of people affiliated with Lucky Cat Chinese Food formed an unending stream of visitors. I was surprised to see that even Aijima showed up. There were Lucky Cat Chinese Food members guarding his room every day to make sure he didn't try to escape.

One day, while Akashi and I were there with Ozu chatting, a neat, clean woman came bearing homemade lunch. Ozu got strangely flustered and told us to leave. Outside his room, Akashi laughed impishly, "Meh-heh-heh."

"Who was that?" I asked.

"Kohinata. She quit the film club Ozu and I are in, but she's been going out with Ozu since freshman year."

"Wait a minute, Ozu has a girlfriend?"

"He's so busy causing trouble, it's a wonder he has time to date," Akashi joked. "He hates introducing Kohinata to other people—I think because he's on his best behavior when she's around."

I glanced down the hospital's hallway.

There was a guy at the pay phone holding the receiver, pointlessly inserting a ten-yen coin, and taking it out again. I recognized his profile. I was sure he was one of the executives who had gone to abduct Kaori with me back during my Library Police days. When he noticed I was staring at him, he hurriedly hung up the receiver and disappeared into the shadows.

I sighed.

"Akashi, I think Ozu has too many enemies. He needs to lie low for a while."

"Yeah." She grinned. "I can help with that. Leave it to me."

• • •

Ozu had been my sole friend for the past two years, so I offered unsparing assistance, given his difficult situation.

"Even once you're out of the hospital, you're going to be in a world of trouble."

"That's as plain as the nose on my face."

"So until things calm down, run away somewhere. I'll cover the costs."

Ozu looked at me suspiciously. "What's your real motive? You can't fool me."

"You should learn to trust people once in a while. I'm not the only generous person out there. Plus, do you even have any money?"

"Like you're one to talk."

"Whatever, just let me pay."

"Why do you wanna pay so badly?"

• • •

I grinned.

"It's my love language."

"Gross—you can spare me," he replied.

A Note from the Translator

People often ask me if there is anything specific I pay attention to when I'm translating. I never really know how to answer that question, because it's just . . . everything. I pay attention to everything—at least, everything I'm able to perceive (and hopefully my powers of perception will sharpen over time). Most translators will agree we're trying to capture the "voice," and in Tomihiko Morimi's case, that voice feels very specific, so there's a lot to pay attention to.

But before I ever translated a novel, I was a Morimi geek. In the winter of early 2013 I was on my way to tai chi practice when I realized I didn't have a book to read on the train. I went to the bookstore inside the JR gate at Shinjuku Station for a quick fix. Swayed by the cute cover and the fact that it won a science fiction prize, I picked up Morimi's *Penguin Highway* (now available in English translation by Andrew Cunningham). After I finished it, I went straight to another bookstore and bought every single title by Morimi they had.

I started going to signing events, which is how I learned that I sometimes stutter in Japanese when I'm nervous. But I knew I would be nervous, so I wrote letters to hand to him, too—at least seven between 2013 and 2018. The early ones are . . . pretty embarrassing. I was stretching my Japanese to its limits while trying to have a sense of humor and make every ounce of my passion register (which included making references to his extremely entertaining blog to make sure he knew I was serious about him and his work). Even if he thought I was nuts at first, he allowed me to submit an excerpt of his debut, *Tower of the Sun* (forthcoming in English as of this note), to a translation contest. I didn't win, but I wasn't about to let that stop me. Looking back, it's entirely possibly I reminded him of his borderline-stalker protagonists (whom I firmly believe all have hearts of gold).

By the time I was hired to translate *The Night Is Short, Walk on Girl* for publication in 2018, I had done so much practice translating Morimi texts in workshops and on my own that I had no trouble returning to his "rotten" university student voice—that guy just barely muddling through his academics, pretentious and often cringey, fixated on a girl in some awkward way that would resolve itself if he would just relax and grow up a bit. Arriving back there to translate *The Tatami Galaxy* felt like coming home again.

Morimi has written (in *Sōtokushū Morimi Tomihiko: Sakka wa kijō de bōken suru!* [A Comprehensive Guide to Tomihiko Morimi: Authors Go on Adventures from Their Desks!]) that after the success of *Tower of the Sun*, his editor told him to write more university student stories to make sure they got through to people. To distinguish *The Tatami Galaxy*, his sophomore novel, from his debut, he added the idea of parallel worlds. While still in grad school, Morimi wrote all four chapters simultaneously, going back and forth when he felt stuck. The way he writes Kyoto University, and Kyoto itself, is what he is most famous for. To fall in love with

Morimi's work is to fall in love with Kyoto, which I definitely did. Not unsurprisingly, though, university students in the US and elsewhere also get up to some shenanigans, so in that sense, no matter how Japanese Morimi's retro vibes might seem, we can all wince nostalgic.

—Emily Balistrieri

Glossary

Aoi Matsuri: One of the three major three festivals in Kyoto, held every year on May 15 (pandemic permitting).

Bakumatsu: The final years of the Edo period (1853–1868) during which Japan ended its isolationist foreign policy and transitioned from a feudal shogunate to a modern empire.

Binbogami: A Japanese god who brings misery and financial troubles to whoever or whatever it inhabits.

Bon: Also known as *Obon*, it is a period in late summer to remember one's ancestors, who are thought to visit their families' household altars in spirit form during this time. The holiday lasts for three days, and people traditionally spend the time with family.

Castella: A popular Japanese sponge cake first introduced by Portuguese merchants in the sixteenth century.

Chirimen-zansho: A Japanese condiment made of dried young sardines and Japanese peppercorn berries. Usually sprinkled on rice.

Dori: The Japanese word for "street."

Enma: The king of hell and judge of dead souls in Japanese-Buddhist mythology.

Geta: A form of traditional Japanese footwear. They are usually made from wood and closely resemble flip-flops.

Gion Matsuri: Kyoto's largest and most representative annual festival, and arguably the most famous festival across Japan. Held during the month of July, the festival is famed for its elaborate float processions and nightly celebrations.

Gyudon: A Japanese beef bowl, composed of thinly sliced beef and green onions simmered in sweet soy sauce over rice.

Hentai: In Japanese, "hentai" often refers to someone or something that is perverted and/or abnormal. In English, "hentai" refers to a pornographic subgenre of anime and manga.

Izakaya: A Japanese-style pub that serves small dishes and plenty of alcohol.

Kamen Rider: Japan's beloved motorcycle-riding, grasshopper-esque cyborg superhero created by the manga artist Shotaro Ishinomori.

Kamenoko Tawashi: A famous brand of Japanese scrub brush. Small and handleless, its bristles are made with stiff palm fibers. *Kamenoko* means "baby turtle," and its name is in reference to its unique shape.

Kanji: Chinese characters used for writing Japanese.

Karaage: Classic Japanese fried chicken. Thigh meat is coated in potato or wheat starch before being deep-fried until crisp.

Keroyon: A cute, cheerful frog character who debuted on Japanese TV in 1964 as the main character of *Kaeru no bouken* ("Frog's Adventure") and became a popular mascot in the late '60s and '70s.

Kibi dango: Sweet dumplings made of millet.

Kitsune: The Japanese word for "fox." In Japanese folklore, kitsune are known to be intelligent tricksters with supernatural powers.

Mame mochi: A simple confection of rice cake with soybeans inside.

Maneki-neko: Beckoning cat figurines thought to attract luck (especially financial) and customers.

Mentaiko spaghetti: Spaghetti tossed with spicy cod roe sauce.

Miso katsu: Breaded meat cutlets topped with sweet miso sauce.

Momotaro: A classic Japanese folk tale in which an elderly couple discover a baby boy inside a giant peach. Bestowed upon them by the gods, the couple names him Momotarô (momo meaning "peach" and Tarô being a common name for firstborn sons in Japan).

Month with No Gods: During the tenth month of the year, the gods gather in Izumo, leaving mortals to endure *Kannazuki* ("a month with no gods"). Conversely, in Izumo, this period is called *Kamiarizuki* ("a month with gods").

Naginata: A pole weapon with a curved blade on the end.

Nasu no Yoichi: A samurai who, in a famous passage in the classic Japanese novel *The Tale of the Heike*, shoots an enemy clan's fan, mounted on top of a rocking boat, with one shot of his bow and arrow.

Nukazuke: Japanese rice bran pickles.

Nurarihyon: A mysterious and supremely powerful yokai with a gourd-shaped head and elderly appearance.

Ohitashi: A dish of vegetables steeped in savory broth.

Okuribi: Short for *Gozan no Okuribi*, a festival held at the end of Obon to bid farewell to the ancestral spirits as they travel back to the spirit world. Five bonfires are lit on mountains surrounding Kyoto.

Onigiri: Japanese rice balls.

Princess Kaguya: In the classic Japanese folktale *The Tale of* *the Bamboo Cutter*, an elderly bamboo cutter is delighted to find a little girl inside a glowing bamboo stem because he and his wife had no children.

Ramune: A popular soft drink sold in glass bottles sealed with a marble.

Sengoku era: Also known as the "Warring States Period" (1467–1615); a turbulent time of social upheaval, political intrigue, and civil war in Japan.

Shichimi: A spice blend with seven ingredients, including chili pepper.

Shingon: Esoteric Buddhist teachings transmitted to Japan from China by the monk Kukai during the ninth century.

Shining Prince Genji: The nickname of the protagonist of Murasaki Shikibu's *The Tale of Genji*, which is sometimes referred to as the world's first novel.

Shinsengumi: Active during the Bakumatsu period, a special police force commissioned by the shogunate. They are brought up here in reference to the famous Ikedaya Incident, during which the shinsengumi cracked down on pro-emperor forces at the Ikedaya Inn. Later, a pachinko parlor was built on the site.

Shochu: A distilled liquor made from grains or vegetables such as rice and sweet potatoes.

Shosoin: An eighth-century storehouse located on the grounds of the Todai-ji temple in Nara. Famous for housing cultural artifacts of the distant past.

Shūji Terayama: One of the most influential and towering figures of post-WWII Japan's avant-garde arts movement. His provocative, psychedelic 1971 film *Throw Away Your Books, Rally in the Streets*—an adaption of his eponymous play—follows a socioeconomically marginalized youth as he rages against the system.

Takeda of Kai: Takeda Shingen (see also: below). "Swift as the wind" (*fūrinkazan*) is a portion of the motto he borrowed from Sun Tzu and used on his war banner.

Takeda Shingen: Leader of the Takeda clan during the Sengoku period famed for his military and tactical expertise as well as his love of toilets.

Tanuki: A species of raccoon dog native to Japan. Tanuki are known in Japanese folklore as mischievous shape-shifters.

Tengu: A supernatural spirit in Japanese folklore. Often depicted as humanlike creatures with red faces and long noses, though some appear more birdlike. Geta associated with tengu can be thought of as single-toothed platform sandals.

Tokugawa shogunate: The military government active during the Edo period.

Urashima Taro: When Urashima Taro, the protagonist of the folktale that bears his name, rescues a turtle, he is rewarded with a trip to the underwater Dragon Palace. He enjoys some days there with the princess, Otohime, but when he returns to his village, it turns out decades and decades have passed and everyone he knows is gone.

Yakiniku: "Grilled meat" in Japanese.

Yakko-san: Origami folded in the shape of a man. A *yakko* was a servant to a samurai.

Yokai: A class of supernatural monsters, creatures, and spirits from Japanese folklore, some of which are believed to sometimes disguise themselves as humans.

Yukata: A light cotton kimono worn in summer.

Zashiki: A Japanese-style sitting room with tatami flooring.

Here ends Tomihiko Morimi's
The Tatami Galaxy.

The first edition of the book was printed and
bound at LSC Communications
Harrisonburg, Virginia, November 2022.

A NOTE ON THE TYPE

The text of this novel was set in Sabon, an old-style
serif typeface created by Jan Tschichold between 1964
and 1967. Drawing inspiration from the elegant and
highly legible designs of the famed sixteenth-century
Parisian typographer and publisher Claude Garamond, the font's name honors Jacques Sabon, one of
Garamond's close collaborators. Sabon has remained
a popular typeface in print, and it is admired for its
smooth and tidy appearance.

HARPERVIA

An imprint dedicated to publishing international voices,
offering readers a chance to encounter other lives and other
points of view via the language of the imagination.